The World is Empty

With Best Wishes

Rutley

ALSO BY R W KAY:

A Nastia Game
Bin Laden's Nemesis
Iraq's Retribution

The World is Empty

R.W. Kay

Matador
9 Priory Business Park,
Wistow Road, Kibworth Beauchamp,
Leicestershire. LE8 0RX
Tel: 0116 279 2299
Email: books@troubador.co.uk
Web: www.troubador.co.uk/matador
Twitter: @matadorbooks

ISBN 978 1785890 703

British Library Cataloguing in Publication Data.
A catalogue record for this book is available from the British Library.

Printed and bound in the UK by TJ International, Padstow, Cornwall
Typeset in 11pt Minion Pro by Troubador Publishing Ltd, Leicester, UK

Matador is an imprint of Troubador Publishing Ltd

THANKS:

My thanks go to the many friends who helped with comments on early drafts, but especially Julia Hamilton.

TO:

Hopeless romantics everywhere!

Author's Note

A romantic novel is about the relationship between two people, so there are two stories: hers and his. Similarly, a coin of the realm has two sides and during its time in circulation, typically forty years according to the Royal Mint, each face sees things from a different angle.

Mia and Mike were engaged when Mia was a twenty-six-year-old air hostess and Mike was a twenty-two-year-old maths graduate training to be a teacher. Their engagement lasted a year before circumstances conspired to ensure that they parted.

They never saw each other until they met by accident exactly forty years after their engagement, during which time they had married and brought up families. They rapidly realised the warmth of their bond had never cooled. As they recollect their year of courtship, their memories vary considerably. On their first Sunday alone in 1963, Mia had forgotten she had taken Mike to morning Mass. It was Mike's first time inside a Roman Catholic church, so he remembered the occasion vividly. However, when Mia reminded him that afterwards they sat holding hands watching Reginald Dixon playing the organ in Blackpool's Tower Ballroom, Mike could not recall the impromptu concert at all.

As their love reignites, responsibilities, passion and morality begin to dominate their lives. Mia tells her story in the first person, while Mike's version is related in the third person. This dual approach to relating their romance is unusual and, quite possibly, unique.

R. W. Kay

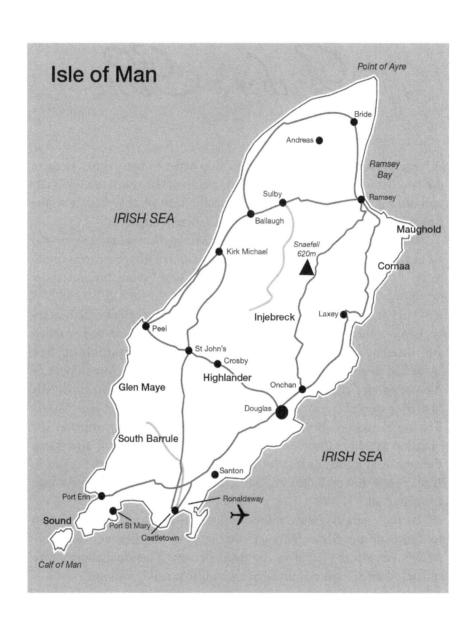

Isle of Man

Point of Ayre

Bride

Andreas

Ramsey Bay

Sulby

Ramsey

IRISH SEA

Ballaugh

Maughold

Kirk Michael

Snaefell 620m

Cornaa

Injebreck

Laxey

Peel

St John's

Crosby

Highlander

Glen Maye

Onchan

Douglas

South Barrule

IRISH SEA

Santon

Port Erin

Ronaldsway

Sound

Port St Mary

Castletown

Calf of Man

Chapter 1

Tuesday, 9ᵗʰ April 1963

'Fancy a game of golf?' Terry asked over their first pint.

A simple question, but hardly life-changing.

'A good idea. Where?' replied Mike.

An innocent reply, but for Mike it would be life-changing.

'Port Erin; we could go down on your scooter and hire clubs at the pro's shop.'

It had been a terrible winter in Britain. The average temperature in January had been the coldest on record for over two hundred years. Despite frozen pipes in his student accommodation and snow lying on the ground for months, Mike's Postgraduate Certificate of Education course at Leicester University had gone well, apart from his lack of success with the girls. He found teacher training enjoyable, as he was a natural in the classroom. Whilst on teaching practice, his pupils took to his charismatic, somewhat eccentric style. Although many of his one hundred fellow graduates on the PGCE course had degrees as good as his own, his tutor had hinted that Mike would be in the top ten when the course finished at the end of the summer term.

He had come back to his hometown, Douglas in the Isle of Man, for the Easter break and made contact with several of his old school buddies. Many of his pals were also home from different universities while others were now in jobs or nearing completion of their five-year apprenticeships. He would regularly meet them around lunchtime in the downtown students' pub, The Dog's Home. Always clean and cheerful, it was run strictly according to the local licensing laws by a retired policeman.

1

Beer was 3d a pint cheaper than elsewhere and the licensee's wife made wonderful, cheese-and-onion 'sand-wedges'.

The Tuesday before Easter was a beautiful, warm day. Spring had finally arrived. The sky was an azure blue. There wasn't a breath of wind.

The Rowany Golf Club was fifteen miles away. Dressed casually, they boarded Mike's BSA Sunbeam and roared away without a care in the world: no crash helmets or protective gear; no thought that the weather could change.

Halfway, as they were passing Ronaldsway Airport, Mike shouted over his shoulder, 'Fancy a coffee?'

Terry nodded.

They parked and entered the terminal building that had been opened ten years earlier to replace the original Royal Naval Air Station, HMS Urley. The café upstairs overlooked the main concourse. From there you could see the movement of airline staff and passengers below.

Casually leaning on the balcony, Mike turned to Terry behind him.

'Come and look at her.'

'Who?'

'Her.'

He nodded at an air hostess walking away from them across the hall below.

'She's a bit-of-all-right.'

She looked petite and had an hourglass figure that was enhanced by her close-fitting, navy-blue uniform. She appeared to have thick, honey-coloured hair under her pillar box hat and a walk that made him gawp at her legs: slim, fine ankles in court shoes; their colour matched her uniform. There was something about the way she walked that was different. Her slim thighs swung easily from her hips as she progressed across the concourse. The walk had its own signature.

It oozed self-confidence. Unforgettable, Mike thought.

While staring at her, Mike remembered the story of Lord Baden-Powell, the founder of the Boy Scouts, and how he'd found his future wife from the way she was walking in front of him. Baden-Powell had not even seen her face. The serendipity of the coincidence would remain wasted on Mike for some time. Her upright posture gave her a bearing that demanded attention. Her deportment suggested elegance and sophistication.

'What's she look like from the front though?' asked his mate.

But Mike had disappeared. Dashing down the stairs into the airport's main hall, he manoeuvred quickly, but discreetly, around the edge to get ahead of the striking air hostess who had stopped to talk to a colleague. He looked at her face. Five features hit him: big, emerald-green eyes, impossibly high cheekbones, a large forehead, kissable lips, and a perfect chin. She hardly wore any make-up. She didn't need to.

Weirdly, a nursery rhyme went through his head: *'My face is my fortune, sir,' she said.*

He was smitten by the young lady, who was probably his own age, in her Britair uniform.

Terry was at his shoulder. 'I think we should be going, don't you?' he hinted.

She hadn't noticed Mike observing her. Disappointed, he reluctantly turned and left.

I guess I'll never see her again.

The rest of the day was a blur. His heartbeat remained twice its usual rate and his golf, particularly his putting, suffered as he plotted how he might see her again. He decided he would get a copy of the Britair timetable on the way home, analyse the flights that had landed at Ronaldsway, and establish what her home base could be.

However, that evening his theoretical approach to tracking down the most beautiful girl he had ever seen hit a dead end. There had been three flights arriving at the airport: from Blackpool, Leeds and Gatwick. She could have been on any of one of them. Undeterred, he returned the following morning, approached the Britair desk and was told that the crews' bases bore no relationship to their flight schedule.

'Our crews are based as far apart as Edinburgh and Jersey,' he was told by the disinterested receptionist. 'The crews here yesterday could have been from anywhere.'

He was crestfallen. He'd had high hopes for a romance with an air hostess; in his eyes, easily the classiest, best-looking, female profession. He decided that he would return to the airport the following week at the same time and hope he would strike lucky. However, kismet was to intervene.

Traditionally, Saturday night was for hitting the town. The well-practised, but generally unsuccessful formula was to have a few beers with your chums, and then descend on a local dance to find a 'bird'.

The Palace Ballroom had opened for the summer season. Built late in the 19th century, its rectangular parquet dance floor was the largest in Europe. Halfway down the length of one side, a substantial, elevated stage could house a large dance band. Around the floor, six rows of tiered seats were arranged to accommodate onlookers. On the first floor, on three sides, a surrounding balcony, supported by decorated pillars, further allowed spectators to view the floor and stage. Used to present prizes at the motorcycle TT races in June, it was common for the ballroom to hold an audience as large as five thousand people. Its Victorian style of architecture could best be summarised as opulent. The lavish use of plaster figurines, lit by subdued lighting, and the coloured glass of its arched windows created a romantic atmosphere that, despite its size, felt warm and intimate. Its resident band was the nationally famous Ronnie Aldrich and the Squadronaires.

Various English hockey teams, both male and female, were playing in the Easter sports festival over the long weekend. That Saturday evening, the ballroom was crowded with a mix of locals and visitors. Mike and his pals arrived in his father's car around nine o'clock and began to eye up the talent.

He couldn't believe what he saw. There she was: his Helen of Troy, his Miss Britair. Sitting at a table with three girlfriends in a recess; they were busy in conversation and seemingly uninterested in the dancing. She was wearing a tight-fitting, blue dress and a short, matching jacket, not dissimilar to her uniform. She radiated refinement: immaculate hair, minimal make-up, matching patent leather court shoes with two-inch-heels. Even the way she sat was classy: erect posture, legs crossed and her skirt a fraction above her knee. She sipped white wine from her glass in a worldly-wise, confident manner.

His heart began to race; he could feel his blood pressure rising, his knees going weak. The fear of failure was gripping him as he wrestled to determine whether he should approach and ask her for a dance.

What if she says, 'No'? I'll look a right idiot in front of my pals, he thought.

'The next dance is a quickstep,' the compère announced.

Oh, bugger it; in for a penny, in for a pound.

He sucked in a lungful of air, pulled in his stomach, expanded his chest, approached her, looked into her Irish green, bottomless eyes and asked, 'Would you like a dance?'

She smiled, stood up and nodded.

He couldn't believe it, *She's accepted me!*

His heart was pounding against his ribs as he ushered her carefully towards the dance floor. He noticed, yet again, her signature walk: her toes, ever so slightly, pointing outwards, like a ballerina's.

She stood in front of him, looking him squarely in the face, hypnotising him. She hadn't spoken a word. He put his right arm around her slim waist; it seemed to fit perfectly, as if it was meant to be there. Bizarrely, two pieces of a jigsaw clicking together sprung to mind.

They began to move. To his relief, they found a joint rhythm as they smoothly manoeuvred around the other couples on the floor. He wanted to ask, 'Do you come here often?' However, he thought it was too trite and instead blurted, 'I saw you at the airport last Tuesday and never expected to see you again.'

'Why not?'

'I assumed you lived across the water.'

'No, I live in Douglas.'

'That's incredible, so do I.'

She accepted his offer of a drink on the balcony, away from her friends.

He spoke quietly, so as not to intimidate her. 'My name is Mike.'

'Mia,' she replied.

It was a small, neat, pretty name, like her really. When she had said her name, her lips had puckered, inviting him to kiss them. A tingle had entered his groin and he wondered if there was something wrong with his bodily fluids. He was trying his best to be suave and appear self-confident. He desperately wanted to impress her.

'Please excuse my dancing; I was born with two left feet.' It was a feeble attempt at humour, but it was all he could come up with. Mike, like most of his friends, had always thought he was pretty good at chatting up the women. He wasn't of course, for although his approach had been based on a compliment, a joke and getting them to laugh, his sum experience boiled down to one 'steady' and three or four 'swingers' at university parties with whom he had ended up fumbling behind a settee. He knew instinctively that Mia was someone different. *This could be for the long term*, he thought.

'An unusual name; I've never heard it before.'

She glared; her powerful, shining eyes frightened him. He realised he was looking into the face of someone with a strong, controlling character that more than made up for her slim, almost fragile figure.

'Mia is Swedish for Mary. My grandmother was Swedish,' she replied in a manner that suggested she had explained it many times before.

There was a pause as he wondered whether he should ask what the Swedish connection was.

She began laughing. 'You're wondering if I'm Swedish, aren't you?'

It was a relief for him not to ask. He didn't wish to spoil his chances by being too nosy before he had even begun to know her. He nodded. He had never met anyone from Sweden. He only knew of two Swedish women, both film stars. Ingrid Bergman, whom he thought was pretty, but too tall to be feminine, and Anita Ekberg, who had given him weeks of imaginative enjoyment in bed after seeing her in *La Dolce Vita*.

'Well I'm not a Swedish nymphomaniac, if that's what you're thinking.'

He agreed. She was more Ingrid than Anita.

Her face was lit up with a warm smile and her eyes radiated light.

'My grandmother met my grandfather in World War One when he was in the British merchant navy. His ship was sunk by a German U-boat in the Baltic on the way to Russia and his lifeboat was washed ashore in Sweden. Sweden was a neutral country. He and the other survivors were detained and had to remain there for the duration of the war.'

There was a pause as Mike wondered whether he should ask if she could speak Swedish.

Languages, French and Latin, had been his worst subjects at school.

She began laughing. 'You're wondering if I can speak Swedish.'

He nodded.

'My grandmother died before I was born, so the answer is "No."'

Her face had a cheeky grin that hinted at fun. When she laughed her cheeks blushed slightly. She was ahead of him – setting the pace.

This confused him. He felt uncomfortable. He was puzzled that she seemed to be able to read his mind. He knew he was not in control. She'd captured him. The white queen had snatched the black king. He was mated. She was frolicking with him, a cat playing with a mouse before the kill. He felt like a country bumpkin. He suspected Mia had more experience of life in her little toe than he had in his entire body. The sum total of his life was to have gone to school, and study mathematics at Manchester University.

He intuitively knew his 'find 'em, feel 'em and forget 'em' approach wasn't going to work with Mia. She would see him coming a mile off. He was going to have to work hard to capture her, and was unsure what to do next.

Totally enthralled, he imagined she'd had many boyfriends. Oddly, she was in no hurry to return to her friends. He wondered why.

What can she see in me?

She could have anyone in the ballroom.

Maybe she fancies me because she knows I'm green and wants to teach me a trick or two.

His mind was in overdrive. He'd heard of older women who went after inexperienced boys.

Perhaps she'll educate me in the back of Dad's car on the way home.

They continued to chat amicably about her job as an air hostess. He learned that she had left her job in an advocate's office 'to do something different' the previous Christmas. She had trained at Gatwick Airport for several months, but her job would end in October when the airline reverted to its winter timetable.

'What will you do then?' he asked.

'I might work my passage to Australia and visit Liz, my sister.'

He gasped. In 1963, Australia was as far away as the moon. A single trip to France with school was the extent of his foreign travel, but here was a beautiful young woman who saw nothing unusual in giving up her job and travelling to the other side of the world.

'How will you do that?'

'My experience as an air hostess should allow me to get a job as a stewardess on a liner. I'll jump ship when it docks in Sydney.' She laughed at the idea.

He had been brought up to believe that having a steady job was all-important; nothing else mattered. 'Work before play,' had been drilled into him by his father, a senior executive in the Isle of Man Bank.

'Get a job with a pension,' he used to say.

Mia's outlook on life seemed to be the antithesis of Mike's. This flummoxed him. On the one hand he hoped there could be a long-term future with such a classy prize, but conversely, if she was to be a one-night stand it was going to be an exciting evening.

They had several more dances before he asked to see her again before he went back to university.

She agreed.

'Can you come to the cinema with me next week?'

'I'll be free on Thursday.'

'*Come Fly With Me* will be on at The Regal.'

'Appropriate in the circumstances, don't you think?' she giggled. Her green eyes, bizarrely, reminded him of traffic lights.

He felt he was the luckiest man in the world. Her ebullience was tipping the balance of the scales toward a long-term relationship. The feeling was new to him. He had never felt this way before. He wondered if he was in love for the first time in his life.

'Can I take you home?' He asked the question hesitatingly, hoping she wouldn't think him too presumptive.

'I live in Stanley Square,' she said.

His heart sank.

The scales instantly swung back.

Stanley Square was one of the poorest parts of Douglas. The dull, dark stone, Victorian terraced houses surrounded the four sides of an unkempt, square park, each side measuring perhaps a hundred yards. Most of the three-storey houses had been converted into flats to accommodate the neediest families in Douglas who were not entitled to council houses. The houses had rear yards that backed onto narrow lanes that were littered with refuse, discarded furniture and broken glass. He had hardly ever set foot in the area, having been told by his mother that it was 'somewhere you are not to go'. He knew the dismal houses were badly in need of refurbishment. He'd been told they had outside toilets, and that their occupants had to share washing facilities. Although the town council was theoretically responsible for the upkeep of the public garden, it resembled a jungle. Consequently, families from Stanley Square were locally nicknamed 'the Weissmullers' as it was rumoured Tarzan lived in the square with Cheetah.

Heaven knows what my mother will think when I tell her I've been out with a Weissmuller from Stanley Square.

'That's OK,' he replied, trying hard not to show his qualms. 'I've got my dad's car. It will not be out of my way.' He was looking at her beautiful face and thinking, *Unforgettable.*

You're the classiest, most elegant woman I've ever met.

He wanted to ask, 'How on earth do you live there?' Although not the most tactful of individuals, he knew better than to ask. The enigma of her background vis-à-vis her sophistication could remain a mystery that he wasn't in a hurry to investigate.

They walked to his father's car. He opened the passenger door and noticed her slim thighs as she made herself comfortable. A shiver ran down his spine and his loins stiffened as he smelt her perfume during the ten-minute journey to her house. He parked outside. Instinct was telling him not to make a premature move.

'Will I call for you on Thursday, or shall we meet outside the cinema?'

'Call for me, if you like. We live in the downstairs apartment.'

'I may not have the car.'

'That's OK. There's a bus every ten minutes.'

He got out of the car, went around to the near-side door and opened it.

'I've loved meeting you. I can't wait for next week,' he said.

'Same here,' she replied, with a beam that suggested she meant it. She walked up the short path to her front door, turned and waved to him as he drove away.

As he exited the square, the drabness of the houses struck him. He couldn't comprehend how Mia could live in one of the poorest, most run-down neighbourhoods on the island. She was far too chic, too stylish and too cultured.

Chapter 2

Thursday, 18th April 1963

He wanted to tell his mother about his 'find': the most beautiful girl he'd ever met. However, he knew she wouldn't approve of him having a girlfriend from Stanley Square. It would need delicate handling. He decided, after much thought, that the answer might lie in bringing Mia home at some future date and letting his parents see for themselves what a delightful girl she was. They could discover her background later and he pondered on how he could best engineer their meeting.

When he called for her on Thursday evening, he was invited in by her mother while Mia finished getting ready. They shook hands. He introduced himself as Mike.

She smiled, and said quietly, 'Nice to meet you, Mike.'

He felt he was getting the 'once-over'. He hoped he would pass Mrs Mylrea's tests. A small woman with a warm smile, she appeared to be suffering badly from osteoarthritis. She excused her daughter for not being ready by explaining that Mia had only recently arrived home. 'Her flight from Birmingham was delayed. She won't be long. Would you like a cup of tea while you wait?'

Not wishing to offend by refusing her kind offer, he accepted, even though he was not particularly fond of tea. She went into the kitchen. She returned within a minute, but it was long enough for him to look around the lounge, presumably the original house's front room. With a high ceiling, the room was tidy and cosy. The furniture was lived-in and friendly. A rug in front of the fireplace covered the linoleum floor. Although it was not a particularly cold evening, a coal fire smouldered in the hearth keeping the chill from the north-facing room. His attention was drawn to a framed picture above the mantelpiece: a picture of Jesus with an open heart. He had seen the picture before in his next door neighbours' house when Mike and his parents lived at a previous address. He knew its significance.

The Sacred Heart – they're Roman Catholics.

How the hell am I going to explain this to my parents?

Stanley Square is bad enough, but Catholics too?

The scales were swinging against Mia being acceptable as a steady, long-term girlfriend.

'What are you going to see?' Mrs Mylrea asked.

'*Come Fly With Me*, a film about air hostesses.'

'Most appropriate, I'm sure Mia will enjoy it.' She disappeared for a few seconds and brought back a china cup and saucer. 'Do you take sugar?' she asked.

'No, I'm sweet enough.'

She smiled and Mike could see the family resemblance. She shouted down the hall corridor, 'Mia, are you ready? Mike is waiting.'

'It's OK,' he explained. 'There's no hurry, the film doesn't start until eight o'clock.'

There followed a brief silence as neither knew what to say while Mike swallowed his tea. When he had finished she asked him to invert the cup and twirl it over the saucer.

He had no time to ask why before Mia appeared. She looked a million dollars in a figure-hugging, black dress. She held out her coat, turned her back to him and indicated for him to help put it on. Her poise suggested she expected her boyfriends to do this automatically. He obliged obediently. She was already in charge. He didn't care.

She turned to her mother. 'I'll see you later, Mum. We won't be late.' Mia kissed her mother farewell.

'Enjoy yourselves.'

She let him hold her hand as they walked to the bus stop fifty yards away even though there were some locals waiting at the halt.

They're giving me the 'once-over' as well, he thought.

He wanted to ask whether Mia's family were practising Catholics, but he resisted.

In the cinema, they sat upstairs near the back. She didn't object when he put his arm around her shoulder, but she turned her head away when he tried to kiss her. This puzzled him.

After all, she's happy to sit near the back.

Is there something wrong with me?

Did I remember to splash some Old Spice under my arms?

He settled for her head resting on his shoulder for most of the second half of the film. Her perfume was thrilling. He had never been with a girl who used scent before. She had beautiful, smooth skin and, later, he was to discover that she rubbed some of her lipstick on her cheeks to match the colour of her lips. Such refinement was new to him. Mia was a cosmopolitan young woman who seemed to know her way around. The realisation worried him. He wanted to succeed with Mia where he had failed so often with girls before.

Not letting me kiss her; is this how she teases men?

Is she testing me?

He was realising he had a lot of catching up to do if he was to avoid being seen as a naïve yokel. He wondered if he could meet the task.

When they came out of the cinema, he asked, 'Would you like a drink?'

'Great!' she replied and nodded towards the Villiers Hotel across Victoria Street.

It was one of the few couth places in Douglas where you could take a girl for a drink. Again, he was out of his comfort zone. He had never ventured into the Villiers before, but Mia appeared to be familiar with its layout. The lounge bar was typical of so many Victorian hotels. The fittings were a mix of dark oak and polished brass. Comfortable club chairs in brown leather, some with wings, were arranged unobtrusively around small coffee tables so customers had a degree of privacy. Framed prints of old Douglas, lit by picture lights, gave the room a cosy, welcoming feeling. They sat facing each other. She had chosen a white wine, he – a pint of Castletown Bitter. He noticed, yet again, her lovely, slim legs. He imagined what might lie at the top and wondered how long it would be, if ever, before his hand reached its target.

Their conversation centred on their respective families. Mike learnt that Mia had two older sisters: the eldest, Liz, living in Australia, and Jenny, married to George, the owner of the best delicatessen in Douglas. Her younger brother, David, completed the family.

'What does your father do?' he asked in all innocence.

Her eyes flared; the daggers-drawn glare frightened him. He knew he had asked the wrong question. 'He lives in London. The bastard left Mum when I was eight.'

'I'm sorry, I shouldn't have asked.'

'It's OK, but it hasn't made life easy. It was why I had to leave school at fifteen to bring in money. I even had an evening job when I was only fourteen.'

'What did you do?'

'I sold ice creams in the Picture House.'

'I would have bought one from you.'

'So did a lot of boys. I sold more than anyone else. They used to queue up hoping I would sit next to them in the second showing of the "A" film. One night a boy bought four ice creams.'

'And did you sit with them?'

She laughed. 'Wouldn't you like to know?!'

He was intrigued by her secretive, but light-hearted response. Her approach to life was something new to him. Previous girlfriends had tended to allow him make the play, but Mia's approach appeared to be saying, *Come on, this is a game – try harder if you want me.*

Her flirtatious, outgoing nature was disturbing him.

How many boys have been out with her?

He grasped that she might be teasing him, and he conjectured how she could be so sophisticated. She was intriguing. He was a fly caught in her web.

She must be quite a bit older than me.

He posed his question carefully. 'When was that?' he asked.

She was no fool, and realised the question was loaded. 'Are you trying to find out how old I am?' She was grinning from ear to ear. Her face was registering the message: *I'm ahead of you.*

He nodded, trying not to show his embarrassment. He was out of his depth. His confidence was rapidly draining away.

She's in a different league to me.

'I'm twenty-six.'

God, she lives in Stanley Square, is a Catholic, hasn't got a father, and is four years older than me.

What else is there that can be stacked against her?

'You realise I'm a student?' It was an apology for his lack of worldly experience while hoping he could impress her with his academic achievements.

'Yes, what are you studying?'

'I graduated last year with a degree in maths at Manchester, and am currently on a teachers' training course at Leicester. I have to go back next week for the summer term.'

'Where do you want to teach when you've finished?'

'I thought I might go to Cornwall.'

'Cornwall? That's a hell of a long way from here.'

'I like open spaces.'

'So do I, but there are places a lot nearer than Cornwall.'

'I could always try and get a job in Blackpool,' he joked.

To his delight, she replied, 'Well, that would allow us to see each other more easily than if you were in Cornwall. However, my job terminates at the end of September. When the summer timetable finishes, the crews get laid off for the winter, including the junior pilots. I took the job as a break to get away from my office work that had begun to get me down.'

'You said you used to work in an advocates office. What exactly did you do?'

She looked at her watch. Rather than answering his question, she replied, 'We'd better get a move on or we'll miss the last bus. We've got five minutes to get round to the bus station.'

They ran to catch the 11.05 pm bus, but it was full. Mia got a seat, but Mike had to stand for the short journey.

Outside her garden gate, they stood looking at each other. Mike was unsure what to do.

Should I try and kiss her goodnight?

After several moments of embarrassing silence, he asked, 'I've enjoyed this evening. Will you come out with me again before I go back to university?' He was sure she had sussed his lack of worldly wisdom.

'We could go for a meal, perhaps?' she replied, smiling.

His heart missed a beat. He had never taken a girl out for a meal before. Hesitatingly he asked, 'What about Saturday?'

'Yes, I should be home soon after six. I'm on the Blackpool runs.'

'What does that mean?'

'I do four return flights to Blackpool with the Manx crew starting at 9.30 am.'

'We could go for a meal at The Highlander.'

He'd never been, but he'd heard his parents singing its praises and wondered what he was letting himself in for.

'Shall I pick you up around 7.30 pm?'

'Super! I've heard good reports from friends who've been there.'

He groaned inwardly. *God, she's used to eating out.*

The Highlander was a pub with a small restaurant five miles west of Douglas on the TT Course.

He was worrying that Mia would work out how inexperienced he was. *I'll have to hope for the best and pray I can get the old man's car*, he thought.

'I'll pick you up on Saturday,' were his last words as she walked up the path. He then had a twenty-minute trudge home. It gave him time to think how he was going to introduce Mia to his parents.

The scales were evenly balanced. On one hand he was confused by her family circumstances while, on the other, she was so cheerful, flirtatious, polished and elegant.

He would have to find out more about her. He looked around him as he exited the square. The sombre, dark houses with paint peeling from their window frames depressed him.

She's a Catholic and my old man's a lay Methodist preacher.

Her parents' marriage is broken.

She's four years older and has probably been around a bit.

Mum and Dad will never accept her.

In the past, although he had lied and cheated with girls, he had always had a soft spot for the underdog. He convinced himself he must give Mia a chance despite her Catholicism, Stanley Square, her age and class background. He resolved that for once in his life he must be honest. He would find out if she felt the same way as him. He was becoming convinced that he must be in love. If so, then he would tell her how he felt, and that he wanted a permanent relationship. He would give her one hundred per cent.

However, little did he appreciate the deep-rooted prejudice against Roman Catholics among the island's upper classes. He would soon find out, and it would change him for ever.

He picked her up punctually. She was waiting for him. She looked better than ever sitting next to him in his father's car. Her clothes, her poise, her hair – all were perfect.

He found it difficult not to stare at her shapely legs that had first attracted him the previous week at the airport. Yet again, part of him was imagining his hand on her thigh.

The Highlander was a one-storey, thatched cottage with a subtly lit bar at one end that could seat about two dozen drinkers. An archway led to a small annex that was laid out with tables for a similar number of diners. The restaurant was lit mostly by candles. Its pastel coloured tablecloths and burnt sienna walls hinted at an intimate dining experience. Managed by two male friends, it had gained a five-star reputation for the quality of its cuisine.

Over their leisurely meal of sautéed Manx queenies followed by vanilla panna cotta with a Chardonnay wine, he discovered more of her background. His attitude towards Mia began to firm up. He discovered she had recently qualified as a solicitor's clerk. After leaving school at fifteen, against her headmistress's wishes, she had taken work as a clerical assistant in a solicitors' office in Athol Street.

'I made the coffee, put the files away, even dusted the offices and swept the floors. "Clerical assistant" was a posh way of saying "office skivvy". After a couple of years, I knew their filing system better than the advocates and old-man Kermode, the senior partner, suggested I should get some qualifications.'

'Excuse me for interrupting, but is that Martin Kermode?'

'Yes, why?'

'He's the Isle of Man Bank's solicitor, where my dad works, and handles their legal work. He goes to our Methodist church at Rosemount. He's a church steward and has his own pew in the back row. I think he was once the Mayor of Douglas.'

She shrugged her shoulders and continued, 'He gave me an afternoon off every week to do some "O" Levels. He has been like a surrogate father and has known me since I was very young. My mother is a dressmaker and makes dresses for Mrs Kermode. I often accompanied Mum when she went to their house in Devonshire Road for fittings. I found English and geography easy. History was a bit harder, but I needed help with maths and economics from Mr Kermode.'

Again Mike interrupted. 'He gave you private coaching?'

'Yes, when Mum was altering the dresses, usually on a Saturday morning. He would set homework afterwards and I would hand it to him on Monday at work.

If Mr Kermode thinks so highly of her as to give her individual tuition, then she must be all right.

Perhaps my worries about her have been unfounded.

'By the time I was nineteen, I had five "O"s. Two years later, I had two

"A"s in commerce and English. By then, I had reorganised their files with a numeric index that made finding things much easier. Mr Kermode was so delighted he paid for me to do a correspondence course to become a solicitor's clerk. It took three years, but I made it.'

'To do all that in your spare time couldn't have been easy.'

'It wasn't. Initially, I managed to keep my job in the Picture House for two or three nights a week. It's where I learned how to dress smartly. Watching stars like Grace Kelly and Audrey Hepburn taught me how to use make-up and have my hair styled.'

'Well, all I can say is, it worked.'

'Thank you. The problem is I'm seen as something of a social climber because I work in Athol Street and have tried to improve myself while coming from Stanley Square. Since leaving school, for the past seven or eight years I've had to work hard in the evenings to get my qualifications. It has restricted my social life.'

'You make me feel a right sloth. I just drifted through my degree, doing the minimum, sitting the easier options such as statistics to pass the exams. I guess I've always found maths easy and I spent far too much time drinking, smoking, skipping lectures, playing bridge and going to parties.' He could have added that the purpose of going to the parties was to chase women, but thought better of it as he had hardly ever got any into bed. The admission momentarily took him back to the physics laboratory, a subsidiary subject in his first year, where he and his lab partner regularly fiddled the results by working backwards to get better marks.

God, I even cheated at university.

I mustn't cheat Mia.

She asked, 'Why do you want to be a teacher?'

'I've never really wanted to be anything else. I guess I was lucky having some wonderful teachers at school and I just wanted to emulate them. I'm not bragging when I say I'm good at it. And more importantly, I enjoy it.'

He was gaining the impression that Mia was interested in his career and was enjoying his company. She listened intently to him telling her of his limited background. He was not boring her, which had been his fear. He was feeling comfortable with her, and he began to relax. He sensed his affection was being reciprocated. They were not alone in the dining room, but their mutual cordiality and warmth blocked out their surroundings. Neither noticed other diners departing. It wasn't until the senior waiter coughed and asked, 'Will there be anything else?' that they realised the restaurant was empty.

He drove her home thinking that she really could be the gold medal he was looking for. Despite her background and her playful nature, she was a genuine, hardworking girl whose spirited personality was her way of coping with her upbringing.

Mia, you're the girl for me.

There was just a touch of concern.

Are you too good to be true?

Chapter 3

Mia's story to April 1963

I was born in my parents' ground-floor apartment in Stanley Square on Tuesday, 7th March 1937. It was a small three-bedroom flat with a communal toilet in the back yard. I was the third daughter: Liz was ten years older, and Jenny four. My mother had been through hell. I was conceived as a twin, but there were complications that I was never to fathom. I only learnt about this from Liz when I was in my late twenties. It may account for my birth weight being only five pounds ten ounces. I remained small for the rest of my life and, although now in my sixties, I still wear a size eight dress and weigh less than seven stone.

My brother, David, was born in 1940 and we were to become the best of pals. I have sometimes wondered if our exceptional closeness had something to do with the possible loss of a twin brother. Maybe there was a genetic link that modern science would claim as impossible, but needed satisfying in my psyche. By then my father was in the army and he would never return. Not because he was killed, but because he met a WREN in London on VJ Day. I only ever met him once after the war when I was in my thirties and living in Berkshire. All my life I hated him for what he did to my mother.

With no father in the home, Mum became more important than ever. Consequently, my relationship with her was closer than might be expected. We were like sisters. I would tell her everything in detail. She would listen and give advice. She trusted me totally to tell the truth.

We were brought up strict Roman Catholics. We attended weekly Mass and the Saints' days without fail. I started at St Mary's RC Primary School when only four and a half years old.

On the first morning, Sister Mary, the nun in charge of our reception class, asked, 'Can anyone write their name?'

I enthusiastically shot my hand up. 'I can, Sister.'

I was told to come to the blackboard. She handed me a piece of chalk. I wrote *MIA*.

The nun looked at me and asked, 'What else?'

I replied sheepishly, 'I can't spell my other name. It's Mylrea.'

She wore a nun's habit and, from under her rosary beads, she withdrew a leather strap. She snapped, 'Hold your hand out!'

She hit me on the palm. 'Never say you can do something, if you can't do it properly' she shrieked.

I bit my lip, determined not to let the others see me cry.

From that day on, I never trusted anyone in authority, whether directly or indirectly, who tried to control or dominate me. I didn't dare tell my mum what had happened for fear of getting hit again.

By the age of seven I had to make my first confession and take communion. I had nothing to confess.

I asked Jenny, 'What shall I confess?'

'Tell the priest you once told a boy to "Bugger off" when he was being nasty to you,' she said.

My penance was to say five Hail Marys.

Being small, I was often a target for bullies. They never won. My determination more than made up for my lack of physical presence. I remember vividly defending our bonfire in the middle of the square on one occasion when some bullies from Palmerston Park, a nearby, similar square to ours, wanted to prematurely set alight the fruit of our gang's labours. Wearing Jenny's cast-off dress, smothered and stained with dirt, and my knees scabbed from scrambling over the pyre, I laid into our foes, my eyes fuelled with anger, my fists flying. They retreated and left us alone. Thereafter, my friends knew when I was het-up. I had what they called a 'bonfire look'.

Although it would be fair to say that everyone who lived around the square was poor; as children we were happy. We could play outside all day without fear or hindrance. There may have been rogue families who were frequently in trouble with the police, but they never interfered with us. In Stanley Square everyone knew everyone. Jenny, David and I could wander for miles, perhaps along the shore to Port Jack two miles away. We'd be away all day catching small crabs in jam jars or pinching flowers from the gardens on the promenade to bring home to Mum. No one worried about our safety.

However, by the time I was in my early teens, I realised I was expected to bring money into the home. My first job was selling ice creams at one of the local cinemas, the Picture House. I lied about my age to get the job. Considering how small I was, it is surprising that the manager fell for my story. Maybe he took pity on me, as Jenny also sold ice creams at the same cinema and I suspected he fancied my eighteen-year-old sister. Perhaps he thought that giving me the job would improve his chances with her.

I rapidly learnt that my best customers were boys, usually a year or two older than myself. Their ulterior motive was to ask me to sit with them through the second showing of the 'A' movie. If I liked them, I would agree, but tell them I had to catch the 9.20 pm bus home so I could only be with them for the first half of the film. Consequently, two things happened. Firstly, I would see much of the main film twice and learn from the female stars how to look glamorous and chic. I would study their hairstyles, their use of make-up, the fashion of their clothes and their elegant deportment. Secondly, but not so positive, I was, unknowingly, gaining a name for having many boyfriends. In a small town, an early reputation of being a flirt, no matter how innocent, became a character flaw that would one day come home to roost.

I left school at fifteen despite being in one of the classes where everyone was expected to take "O" Levels. My mother was a gifted seamstress and not only did alterations, but made dresses according to her clients' designs. Mrs Kermode's husband was the senior partner in a firm of advocates in Athol Street, Corlett and Kermode. Their friendship helped me get my first job. I left school as soon as I could after my fifteenth birthday and joined as the office girl on a weekly wage of £2 per week. I would give Mum £1 10s and keep 10s for myself. I was rich, but still kept my cinema job for a further two years. I remember saving up for my first outfit – a black two-piece suit similar in style to one worn by Grace Kelly in *Rear Window*. It cost £2 10s 0d and I remember Mum asking incredulously, 'How much?!' when I showed it to her. 'I could have made it for half that,' she added.

To be fair, she never queried how I spent my money. 'You've earned it,' she would say. 'Just keep yourself looking nice, and I will always be proud of you.' I would go to the hairdresser every month and have it styled like Grace Kelly. Several people remarked about our similarity: we both had large foreheads and thick, fair hair; although my eyes were green and hers were blue.

I always enjoyed dancing and light entertainment and joined the local choral union that put on a show each year at the Gaiety Theatre. The society gave me an opportunity to meet local drama enthusiasts like myself. The first show I appeared in was *Merrie England* in 1955. I subsequently never missed a show until 1964.

David had shown an exceptional talent for golf, and had left school as soon as he could to become the assistant pro at the local course. His wages were only 25s per week, plus whatever he could accrue through giving lessons. He practised his teaching on me and I became quite proficient, joining the ladies section of the club on my eighteenth birthday. My entry to the club allowed me to mix with boys three or four years older. Two were to become Island Champions. I was beginning to learn that older boys were more hip than those of my own age, and they treated me accordingly. They liked to be seen with me because I was always dressed in the latest fashions. Mr Kermode was a former captain of the club and kept an eye on me at the formal functions, protecting me whenever he saw attempts being made to overdo the flattery and top up my wineglass. My other chaperone was Jenny. She could recognise who could be trusted and who could not.

'If they say they love you and put their hand on your breast, then push them away, and have nothing more to do with them,' she said many times. Consequently, by my twenty-first birthday, I was still relatively naïve and sexually inexperienced. I was studying most evenings to become a qualified solicitor's clerk so there was little time for socialising.

Mum would frequently ask, 'Why don't you go out more often?'

With my head in a book, I would explain, 'I want to get qualified first.'

Occasionally I would be invited to social events by trainee solicitors and accountants from the golf club. Most of them had been vetted by Jenny. At no time did any of the relationships become serious. Whereas girls I had known at school were marrying and having families, my mother was beginning to worry if I had been left on the shelf.

Two things were subconsciously mapping my life. Firstly, the determination, laid down on my first day at St Mary's to have no one in authority over me, and secondly, the resolve never to be dependent on anyone for money.

Nonetheless, by the time I was twenty-five, and about to become fully qualified, I was beginning to think I needed a dramatic change to my lifestyle.

I had finished my final exams in December 1962 and felt mentally worn out. In the national exams, out of over five hundred students, I was given a distinction that put me in the top fifty.

During the Christmas holidays an advert appeared in the local press for a Manx-based air hostess:

> *Wanted: a presentable, single, young lady to join the Manx-based crew of Britair. Based at Ronaldsway Airport, the applicant must be articulate, be educated to "O" Level in English and maths (or equivalent), be able to swim one hundred yards, be prepared to be flexible with working hours and to stay overnight away from base as required.*
> *Full training will be given.*
> *Applications by letter to–*

It was a heaven-sent opportunity to do something different and break the mould of the relatively narrow life I had been leading. I applied, was interviewed and was successful. I undertook ten weeks' training at Britair's HQ at Gatwick before starting on Monday, 1st April 1963. My first flight was the 0830 hours trip from Ronaldsway to Blackpool, a town that would become especially significant in my life. The change of job was dramatic. From an office with a handful of employees, I was meeting hundreds of passengers every day. One of the first celebrities I met was Adam Faith on the Leeds flight. Later that summer Billy Fury was to fly with me to the island from Blackpool.

I'd been in my new job less than a fortnight when on Easter Saturday evening, after a busy day, I arranged to meet three former school friends. We had a drink in the Central Hotel at the bottom of Broadway and then agreed to go to the Palace Ballroom, the largest in Europe. The hall was packed, mostly with sports teams, both male and female, as the Easter Hockey Festival was in full swing. There were over fifty teams staying in Douglas and several had flown with me during the week from as far away as Birmingham and Glasgow. My friends and I had been sitting in a quiet alcove for about half an hour when a young man, whom I had never seen before, somewhat shyly asked me for a dance. He was above average height, athletically built, and dressed smartly in a navy-blue suit. With brown, Brylcreemed hair and dark blue eyes, he stood before me, rather hesitatingly gauche; as if he was expecting me to say, 'No'. He had a nice smile on an innocent face that I found intriguing. I know it's a cliché: love at first sight, but he was the most handsome man I had ever met. He reminded me vaguely of Gregory Peck. I stood up and smiled back. He gestured me towards the dance floor. He stood about six inches above me when he held my hand and put his other arm around my back. We moved slowly together and I noticed he was steering me, watching carefully not to bump into other couples on the busy floor. I could tell he wasn't a natural dancer as I felt he was driving me like a car.

Bizarrely, I was reminded of my driving instructor. 'Always try to keep a bubble of air around your vehicle,' he used to say. 'If someone comes inside your bubble, treat them as an idiot and be on guard.'

However, the quickstep went well, if somewhat mechanically, and when the music stopped we were nowhere near where we had started. He smiled and asked, 'Will you stay on the floor with me, or have you had enough?'

I laughed and nodded appreciatively. 'I'd like another.'

It was peculiar being with a boy I had never known, but who made me feel warm inside. My heart was throbbing. It occurred to me that I had let him enter my bubble. Previously over the years, I had built a shell around myself and never let anyone inside. In front of me stood a dishy stranger, who I guessed was younger than me. His lack of confidence gave him away and I was finding the experience exciting: my toes were tingling, my stomach fluttering and my throat had gone dry. Strangely, I wondered if we were twin yolks in an egg.

Sub-consciously, I may have been waiting for Mr Right and he'd never appeared. Perhaps I'd been too particular, or maybe as a young teenager enjoying playing the field in the cinema I'd gained a bad name. My reticence to get seriously involved with boys had undoubtedly been determined by seeing what my father had done to my mother. She had worked her fingers to the bone, scrimping and making do, and I'd decided it was not going to happen to me.

Yet that evening, a seemingly innocent, callow youth had entered my life who I wanted to be my first lover – yes, I was still a virgin at twenty-six. However, my Catholic upbringing demanded marriage or abstinence. I had to win him, but how?

How could I have fallen in love so quickly with him? I didn't know it, but that evening something changed in my life. Nothing would ever be the same again. In front of me was a young man with whom I wanted to make love.

After turning twenty, I'd seen a decline in the number of suitable bachelors as they'd settled down, married, and disappeared from the social scene. I wasn't aloof, but Douglas was a town where you were 'expected to know your place'. Nowadays it is hard to believe, but being a practising Catholic in the 1950s and 60s, plus living in one of the poorest areas, was second only to having leprosy. My protective mechanism against this stigma – dressing and grooming smartly – had probably given many people the impression that I was 'stuck-up': someone who thinks she is something she isn't.

We danced much of the night away and got to know a little about each other. I always remember him admitting, 'It's as well I saw you at the airport last Tuesday.'

'Why?'

'My usual chat-up line is to claim I'm an airline pilot on an overnight stop. Had I spun that line with you, then you would have seen through me.'

We had a job to stop laughing. Being with him was wonderful. Here was a boy who took me for what he saw, not what he had heard. By the time I had agreed he could see me home, I knew he was training at university to become a teacher and lived in upper Douglas. I also knew he was completely different from any boy I'd met before.

That night, before getting into bed, I prayed that Mike would be my first lover, that we would marry and live happily ever after.

He called to take me to the cinema the following Thursday. I'd arrived home late from work. Mum had invited him in while I got ready and made him a cup of tea. I remember she was impressed by his manners, but unsure whether he was the right boy for me, as when she read his tea leaves, she told me later they were a mess. That she could take the leaves seriously had always been a mystery to me, especially as she was such a devout Catholic. Whenever she and her friends met socially in each other's homes, they would 'read the leaves' and I had always assumed they did it for fun. However, that evening when I returned home, she looked grave. 'There's something not right about him. I can't put my finger on it, but there is a split in his life-line.' I asked her to amplify her doubts, but she wouldn't elaborate.

I told her we had gone to the Villiers Hotel after the cinema for a drink. I had found out about his background, including the fact that his dad was big in the Isle of Man Bank and that they lived in Cronkbourne Drive.

'Oh, very posh!' she instantly remarked.

I said Mike would be returning to university in a week's time. 'I like him Mum, he makes me laugh and feel good in a way that no one has ever done before. He wants to take me out for a meal on Saturday before he goes back.'

'Then I hope it will work out for you. It would be nice having him as a son-in-law. School teachers get long holidays and are not badly paid. Take no notice of what I said about his leaves.'

'Mum, we are a long way from getting married.'

'I know, darling, but I'm a hopeless romantic.'

Our evening at The Highlander, a restaurant halfway to Peel, was a great success. We never stopped talking as we explored each other's background and interests. We discovered we both enjoyed playing golf, swimming, going to the cinema and walking through the island's many glens. We were the last to leave the restaurant. On the way home, we turned left at Union Mills and went down the quiet road to Tromode. It wasn't the most direct way back to my home, so his choice of route surprised me. However, out of the blue, he slowed down and asked whether I would mind if we stopped for a few moments. Thinking he wanted to continue with our animated conversation, I nodded. He switched off the engine and leaned across the seat. He put his left hand around my shoulder. We kissed. I could feel his right arm around my waist. It seemed to fit perfectly as he gently pulled me toward him. I didn't resist. It all seemed so natural.

'I love you Mia. I've never felt like this before,' he said.

I was excited and overjoyed.

My hopes were being raised that I had, at long last, found my one and only true love and yet all I could think of to say in reply was, 'Same here.' It was such an inadequate response that it now embarrasses me to think that it was all I could think of saying. I was so excited, he'd left me speechless.

We stayed there for almost an hour, talking and kissing. Although he held me closer each time we hugged, and despite my pushing as close to him as I could, he never did anything untoward. I wanted him to feel my firm breasts, but his right arm remained around my waist. It was locked between my hip and ribs like two pieces of Lego. I had never felt so warm before. It wasn't the warmth you get from sitting in front of a coal fire where you can feel the heat hitting you. This was radioactive. Its effect was to make me glow. My pulse raced, my heart throbbed, and my cheeks flushed. I wanted it to go on for ever and would cheerfully have stayed in his arms all night.

'It's almost midnight,' he said suddenly.

'God, is it that time? Mum will be wondering where I've got to.' I began straightening myself.

We met once more before he went back to Leicester. It was a sober date as both of us realised we might not see each other until he returned at the end of the summer term. The thought left me with an empty feeling. I knew that I was going to miss him even though we had spent so little time together. Already he had become a part of my life. There was hardly a moment in the day when I wasn't thinking of him. The least little thing would trigger my thoughts and I would dream we were together. We promised to write to each other every other day – a promise we both kept. His letters were wonderful; full of lovely ideas and his wishes for our future. Although he never proposed marriage, I could read between the lines that this was in the back of his mind and I began to romanticise with thoughts of a white wedding when I went to bed. However, I would come back to earth the next morning with a thud. Mike's parents were strong Methodists. His father was a lay preacher. It was not going to be easy and, although Mike knew my family was Catholic, he and I had never discussed religion. I still had not met his folks. I guessed they would not see an older girl and a Catholic from Stanley Square as a suitable catch for their only son.

April 1963

Mike returned to Leicester a different man from the one who'd left for the Easter break three weeks earlier. From being a twenty-two-year-old graduate with few female successes to his credit, he'd suddenly hit the jackpot: a girl who was beautiful, elegant, witty and had fallen in love with him. He couldn't believe his luck, nor understand why. Suddenly life was rosier. Their two worlds had collided and they'd become one. He couldn't get her out of his mind, thinking about her all the time. If he was playing bridge in the students' union while skipping lectures, she was sitting opposite him. If he was on the squash court, she was in the balcony watching him. He imagined a grand future with Mia. He wanted her more than anything. If a Catholic marriage was what it would take to win her, then so be it. He would risk losing his parents to wed Mia.

Getting a job in 1963 as a junior maths teacher would be easy. There was a national shortage of science graduates. He knew he could virtually pick and choose anywhere in the country. Mia had hinted Cornwall was too distant, but possibly Westmorland? Rural areas appealed to him. They would be happy together wherever they lived. He pictured them sitting together on a settee in front of a log fire making love. *We'll have ten children*, he thought, and began giving them names: Matthew, Mark…

The *Times Educational Supplement* on Friday, 3rd May advertised three jobs in Blackpool. He applied for all three, hoping he would be successful and wrote excitedly to Mia.

He was the proud possessor of a photo of her that he showed to his fellow students. She won their approval, but they thought he was crazy for already dreaming of getting married.

'You hardly know her,' Monty, his flat mate, said. 'She looks a cracker, but that's not the point. Has she got a sense of humour? That's the key requirement for a wife.' He'd a lot of time for Monty who had taken a short-service commission in the army prior to going to university. Consequently, he was three years older and world-savvy. His sage advice was worth listening to. However, caution was not in Mike's character. 'Fools rush in...' described his approach to courting. He didn't realise it, but it accounted for his lack of success. With Mia he was sufficiently canny to slow down, but he was diving into the deep end. He'd never done that before.

He'd been back at Leicester a little over two weeks when Mia's letter told him she would be overnighting the following weekend in Blackpool and she would be free all day on Sunday. Could he come up and they would be able to spend the day together?

He instantly replied, *Where do we meet and when?*

Her answer read, *I'll be staying in the Red Court Hotel, just off the south shore, near the airport. I will wait until you arrive.*

He went to Leicester's railway station to enquire about trains. The earliest he could arrive would be eleven o'clock.

No good, he thought. *Half the day will be gone.*

He'd passed a small second-hand car lot each day on his way to university for eight months and remembered it advertised: *Cars for hire, competitive daily rates.*

A deal was struck. He could pick up the Ford Popular as early as he liked on Sunday, but had to drop the keys through the letter box before midnight. Otherwise, he would be charged for Monday as well.

'I was thinking of leaving at about five o'clock in the morning. Would that be all right?' he asked.

'Where the hell are you going?'

'Blackpool, to see my fiancée.'

The proprietor seemed impressed that he was engaged. He wasn't, of course, it was just wishful thinking. Perhaps the dealer was sympathetic when he was shown Mia's photo. He agreed Mike could pick up the keys on Saturday evening, but not the car.

Mike was so excited at the thought of driving to Blackpool and having the car for the day that he never asked himself how the owner could check on the time of his arrival back in Leicester. He began planning his route for what would be the longest, most continuous drive of his life: the A6 through the centre of Derby, then Matlock, Manchester and Preston, from where he would take the road through Lytham to Blackpool, a total distance of approximately 140 miles.

It could take me between three and four hours, although at that time on a Sunday the traffic should be minimal.

It was barely daylight when he left his flat at 5.00 am and walked rapidly to the waiting car about a mile away. He'd shaved and had a bath the previous evening. He'd polished his shoes, pressed his trousers and generally made himself as smart possible to meet Mia. His heart was aflutter as he started up the engine and prayed he wouldn't get a puncture. He desperately didn't want his hands to get dirty, or to be late for the only girl in his life.

The roads were deserted and progress was unhindered as he swept north through the Derbyshire Peak District. The car, with three forward gears, struggled to reach its top speed of sixty-eight miles per hour. After Stockport, there was no alternative but to go through the middle of Manchester, but at eight o'clock in the morning traffic was light.

By 9.15 am he was parking outside her hotel. He nervously entered the foyer to be met by a middle-aged woman, whom he later discovered was the proprietor.

She asked, 'Can I help you?'

'I've come to see Mia.'

A frown appeared on her face. 'Who?' she asked.

'The young lady from Britair, my girlfriend. She is overnighting with you.'

She put two and two together quickly. 'Ah, yes; she told me she was expecting you. She hasn't come down for breakfast. Why don't you go up and see her. She's in room five.' There was a mischievous grin on her face.

He climbed the stairs and knocked on the door. There was no answer.

'Hello?' he shouted through the door. Still no reply.

He opened the door a tad, just enough to peer through. 'Can I come in?'

Mia sat up in the bed, a broad smile covering her face that said she was delighted to see him again. Her pale, lime green nylon nightie revealed sufficient of her shoulders for his imagination to go into overdrive. He noticed a small mole near the top of her left breast. He imagined it winked at him. He began to tremble. He hoped she wouldn't notice and think he was an incompetent, inexperienced idiot – which he knew he was. She listened intently to him describing his car journey and how he had left Leicester at the unearthly hour. If he was boring her, she didn't show it. He wanted to ravish her there and then. Something was telling him he would never get a better chance. But he was clueless; he wouldn't have recognised a 'come hither' look if had hit him in the face.

'Blackpool Education Authority has acknowledged receipt of my job applications,' he said.

'Marvellous,' she replied enthusiastically. 'I know you'll be successful.'

'There are three vacancies, so I should be lucky.'

'I'll keep my fingers crossed.'

They chatted about what they could do for the rest of the day. He wasn't really listening as her mole distracted him from paying attention.

'I'd like to get dressed now,' she said and he left to wait downstairs in the lounge.

When she came – what an entrance. She was wearing the airline uniform that hugged her figure like a glove. His pulse raced, his heart pounded and his hands felt cold.

He was reminded of Ursula Andress coming out of the sea in *Dr No*.

As they breakfasted together, she said she wished to go to church at 10.30 am.

'You know I'm a Catholic and must go.'

It was the first time Catholicism had been mentioned.

The announcement was not a shock, as he remembered seeing the Sacred Heart above her mother's fireplace. However, he had hoped she paid lip-service to church like himself. Although he had been brought up in a Methodist church with its Sunday school, junior guild and badminton club, he had not been to church since going to university. Away from parental pressure he'd lost the habit. It wasn't that he didn't believe in God; it was pure laziness. Sunday morning was for recovering from Saturday night's hangover. And anyway, *When one or two are gathered together in my name...* was his 'get out of jail' card. He was an agnostic, a doubting Thomas.

He wondered if Mia would want him to convert to Catholicism and what his parents would think. Would they shun him? Could he convince them that Mia was so exceptional that she was the only woman he could happily spend the rest of his life with? If he came to a crossroads, he'd decided he would take the road signposted *Mia*, but suspected he could be in for a bumpy ride. He knew what he had to do – go to church for the first time in many years.

'Of course, can I come with you?'

'I'd love you to come,' she replied, pleasure registering on her face.

'I've never been to a Catholic service before,' he added apologetically.

Goodness knows what my parents will think when I tell them I've been inside a Catholic church. My mother will go mad.

As the church was over a mile from the hotel, they drove to St Cuthbert's. On entering, the interior was so different from any church he'd experienced previously. The atmosphere was cold and dark, but the first thing he noticed was Mia dipping her finger in holy water and making the sign of the cross. He'd never seen this done before and wondered if he should follow suit.

When in Rome, do as the Romans do, he thought.

The irony of the double entendre went amiss.

She led him to a row in the middle of the church. She genuflected, entered the pew, knelt, crossed herself again, and began to pray. Embarrassed by his ignorance of Catholic rituals, he moved into the pew and sat beside her. He thought he had better show willing, closed his eyes, put his hands together and thought, *What the hell have I let myself in for?*

For Mike, the Catholic Mass turned out to be about as far removed from a Methodist service as was imaginable. A Methodist service was always five hymns, two Bible readings – one each from the two testaments – a twenty-minute sermon and a few prayers, not in that order. By contrast, he found himself in a dreamlike state and went through the hour-long service feeling distinctly uncomfortable. He was convinced everyone was looking at him, whereas they were probably eyeballing Mia in her smart uniform.

When are they going to start singing hymns? he wondered.

However, as he tried to follow the Mass in the prayer book, in Latin with an English translation, Mia would occasionally smile at him encouragingly. But bells ringing and incense swinging were novel. He didn't have a clue what to make of it and wondered if he'd been transported back to the 15th century.

If I become a Catholic, I'll never get used to this nonsense, he thought.

When Mia went to the altar for communion, she placed her hand on his knee and gestured for him to remain sitting.

'It's OK, you're doing fine,' she whispered. Her smile was reassuring. He relaxed and his heart rate slowed to normal.

It was a relief to exit into the warm sunshine although his mind was racing with questions.

Can we have a successful future together as a mixed marriage?

Will she expect our children to be brought up as Catholics?

Will she demand I convert to Catholicism?

Will she be happy to have a civilian marriage?

And so it went on…

She sensed his distant manner, held his hand and asked, 'Are you all right?'

'I'm fine, just a little bewildered by the service,' was his tactful reply.

Perhaps understanding his baffled incomprehension of the ritual, she changed the subject. 'What are we going to do now?'

'I thought we might go for a walk,' he replied. 'Shall we drive towards Fleetwood?'

'Let's first of all go to the Tower Ballroom. Someone in the hotel last night mentioned that Reginald Dixon practises on Sunday mornings and the public can watch for free.'

An hour passed as the pair, holding hands, watched the maestro make the Wurlitzer do everything except fly. Captivated by the organist's expertise, Mike suspected that the impromptu concert could be the highlight of their day. When the presentation was over, it was lunchtime. They found a swanky restaurant fronting the North Pier. With her uniform displaying her figure at its best, a young waiter showed them to a table overlooking the sea. Mike noticed other diners staring unobtrusively at Mia. He felt a million dollars.

She loves me, not you, he wanted to shout.

With their meal, honey-glazed roast lamb with Dauphinoise potatoes followed by rhubarb and orange compote, they had a bottle of Moët & Chandon. Mike had never sipped champagne before. This, he thought, was the height of refinement. By contrast, Mia seemed at home in the surroundings and probably didn't notice the admiring glances that she was receiving from the male clientele.

He was revelling in being her companion. His chest had swollen giving him a feeling of self-importance that he had never felt before. Mia was truly an exceptional looker. He briefly worried whether this was all he saw in her: someone to show off.

He wondered, *Is this the definition of love – someone with whom you want to be seen.*

They discussed plans for the future. They agreed that if he was successful getting a job in Blackpool, she would go back to working at Corlett and Kermode's for the winter months. They would be able to see each other regularly as flights between Blackpool and Ronaldsway were frequent, even in the off-season. Marriage was never mentioned, but he was getting the vibes that she was thinking along the same lines as himself. They had a long-term future together.

Afterwards, they drove north. Leaving the car at Anchorsholme Park, they wandered towards Rossall School. Being alone with her was bliss. With his arm around her waist, she became part of him. As they strolled slowly, her hip rubbed against his thigh; this excited him. In the warm sunshine they found a bench facing the sea. She placed her head on his shoulder. They never said a word, but when he moved closer, she raised her face toward him and their public kiss was charged with emotion.

'I've got a summer job,' he whispered. 'I'm conducting on the buses. I've got to start before the end of June, so I'll be skipping the last week of my course. My tutor has said it will be OK as I'll only be missing the awards' ceremony. I'll be coming home on the afternoon boat on the Wednesday, 26th June. Any chance you can meet me?'

She beamed. 'If I'm not working, I'll be there. I promise.'

He left her at seven o'clock in high spirits. He had the drive to Leicester ahead of him, but his mind was not on the road. Instead, the thought of them someday living together in Blackpool was all that was whirling through his mind.

May 1963

The following week, Mike received a letter inviting him to an interview on Tuesday, 28th May in Blackpool. He saw this as an opportunity to have a weekend on the island and see Mia. He wrote excitedly to her that he would catch a bus from Leicester to Birmingham Airport and fly over on the Friday evening's Britair flight to Ronaldsway. He would then take the early Tuesday flight to Blackpool for the interview, afterwards returning to Leicester by train. He also outlined this plan to his parents, asking his father to meet him from the plane when it landed at 7.00 pm.

To his delight, Mia replied that she was the scheduled air hostess on his flight. Furthermore, she added, Sunday was her day off. They could spend the whole day together.

This was the chance he had wanted. His parents could meet Mia at Ronaldsway in her uniform.

After collecting his baggage, Mike eagerly asked them to wait and 'meet someone special'. They waited for fifteen minutes while Mia completed her post-flight administration. The introductions seemed cordial, but the journey back to Douglas became cool when Mike told his father Mia's address. Nevertheless, before Mia had got out of the car, Mike managed to get his parents to agree that Mia could come to lunch the next day before she began her late shift.

The following day Mike called for Mia and brought her to his parents' home. In her uniform, he could see his father giving her admiring looks and warming to her as they chatted, while waiting for lunch. With Mia sitting next to his father at table, her impeccable manners, wit and wide-ranging conversation secured their relationship. She won his father over despite him asking probing questions about her family background. His mother sat passively listening to her answers. Mike could see that a Catholic girl with no father was not to her liking. His mother said little. She had made her mind up.

Listening to his father and Mia getting along like a house on fire, Mike was impressed by her honest answers: the defence of her faith when asked about Catholicism and schooling, her track record of education and self-improvement, and her knowledge of the law that had clearly been gleaned from working at Corlett and Kermode's.

Afterwards, Mike drove Mia to the airport.

'How will you get home tonight?' he asked.

'I'll catch the special airport bus that brings passengers into Douglas. Don't worry, I'll be all right.'

Mike's mother said nothing when he returned from the airport. Her silence was deafening. Her body language was unmistakeable. It was obvious she disliked Mia. His father had gone to play bowls that afternoon and wouldn't be home until early evening. Mike decided his best ploy was not to confront his mother, but to get out of the house. He made an excuse to go and see Henry, one of his old school pals with whom he occasionally played tennis. 'I'll probably go to the pictures afterwards,' he said as he disappeared through the door.

On Sunday morning Mia picked Mike up in her brother's car. They travelled to Glen Maye, had lunch at the Waterfall Hotel and spent the rest of the afternoon at a conveniently quiet spot off the road towards Port Erin. With his arm around her shoulder, she would look at him from under her eyelids. When looking into his face, it was as if she was peering from her soul. He had never experienced anything like it. Her magnetism was overpowering. Her lustrous eyes hinted at humour. They had a smile of their own. Her aura of authority left him breathless. He wondered if she knew he was captured in her web.

Their infatuation with each other intensified that afternoon. He sensed Mia was torn between her desire to release her passion and the strict laws of her church. The way she struggled with his advances made him believe she could be sexually less experienced than him. It seemed unbelievable considering her degree of sophistication and their age difference, but it made him love her all the more. He resolved not to hurt her and, possibly lose her. Without thinking too deeply about how far their love-making should go, he decided that nature should take its course. If their love could only be truly satisfied when they were married, so be it. He had decided he wanted their future to be permanent.

He vowed to himself that he would make damned sure he would be successful in getting a job at Blackpool. Then he would propose to her. Then he would marry her when his probationary year was complete. Then they would live happily ever after.

May 1963

My flying schedule was becoming ever more hectic as the summer season built-up, with trips as far afield as Amsterdam, Edinburgh and Jersey.

After our wonderful day in Blackpool, I knew Mike was the man with whom I wanted to spend the rest of my life. I wanted him to make love to me and make me a woman, but my strict Catholic upbringing was holding me back whenever I was in his arms. Birth control would have been a sin that I couldn't come to grips with. I wanted him to break my fear of the unknown and although I could sense he was yearning for me as much as I was for him, he somehow always managed to be 'the gentleman'. I could feel, when in his arms, that he was frustrated and struggling within himself. Somehow we always managed to stop short.

I could remember the nuns at school telling us that we must go to the altar on our wedding day as virgins. When someone in the class had innocently asked what this meant and how was it done, the nun told us we must always keep our legs tightly crossed 'with boys in the long grass'. Reluctantly, I realised that unless we married we would not fulfil both our sensual needs. The problem was could I overcome the three major hurdles in my path?

I worried that if Mike would not convert to Catholicism, then we would have to marry in a register office. I knew this would hurt my mother deeply. I wouldn't be happy either, but if shove came to push then I knew I would go through with it and hope Mum would eventually come around.

Secondly, I realised that his mother didn't like the idea of her son marrying someone whom she considered to be from an inferior social class. Mike didn't appear to notice this, or, if he did, he chose to ignore it. How was I to win her over?

Finally, there was money, or rather the lack of it. How could we cope? Two-bedroom apartments in Blackpool were typically selling for about £2,000. If we were to survive, then we would have to postpone having a family and I would have to keep working indefinitely. It worried me that finding a job as a solicitor's clerk on the Fylde might not be straightforward. Mike would be earning more than me, but his teacher's salary would be less than £700 per year.

A week or so after Blackpool, his letter told me he had an interview for a job. He planned to fly to the island from Birmingham on the Friday evening prior to the interview the following Tuesday.

It gave us an opportunity to see each other over the weekend. By chance he was to be on my flight – the last of a long day that had seen me flying as far as Leeds and Exeter. I remember spending an inordinate amount of time on the flight talking to him, even though the plane was full. We were planning the weekend around my schedules. The plane arrived punctually at seven o'clock and his parents were there to greet him. Having already said farewell to Mike on the plane, I had gone into Britair's office to complete my flight report. When I came out into the concourse, however, there he was with his mum and dad. He had persuaded them to wait and give me a lift home.

The introductions were made and I knew instantly that I had the seal of approval of his father, but not his mother. Her smile, when shaking hands, was false. A barrier had gone up. No matter how hard I was to try over the following months, it never came down. Subsequently, I have often wondered whether this is true of all boys' mothers – no girls are ever good enough for their sons. With Mike and me sitting in the back of his father's car holding hands, conversation was stilted all the way to Douglas. When they dropped me off at home, there was no spontaneous, 'We look forward to seeing you again soon.'

However, Mike had asked, 'Can Mia come to lunch tomorrow?' His mother appeared to agree reluctantly. I could feel Mike was embarrassed and he squeezed my hand as he promised to pick me up.

As I entered our front door, I could feel a welling in my eyes. I wondered if I had somehow failed. I gritted my teeth and remembered the nuns at school.

His mother is not going to beat me.

I will marry her son.

The next day we had a roast chicken lunch before Mike took me to work in his father's car. I thought the conversation at table went down well, especially with his father, but Mrs Moore remained frosty. I formed the opinion that she hadn't much to say and, possibly, wasn't too bright. It's an unkind idea, but it's one that has festered in my mind ever since, as her range of conversation never seemed very extensive.

On Sunday, I had the day off, and my brother let me have his car. I picked Mike up after morning Mass. I never saw his parents and assumed they were still at church. We drove to Glen Maye. At the Waterfall Hotel we had lunch and afterwards walked down the glen to the stony beach. We sat in the warm sun for ages, talking about nothing in particular. We were just happy being together.

There were other people around. Wanting to be alone, we walked the mile back to the car and I drove south towards Port Erin. At Mike's suggestion we turned off the road onto a narrow track leading to Eary Cushlin. Safe from prying eyes, we kissed more passionately than I could have imagined. His hands wandered inside my blouse and I was experiencing something new – the earthiness of sensualism as my juices began to flow. As our fondling grew ever more vigorous, full-blooded lust was beginning to win over years of Catholic morality. My libido was beating my conscience. In the struggle between hormones and reason, I learnt for the first time that hormones win every time.

I lost my nerve, however, when he put his hand on my knee and tried to prise my legs apart. I knew we had to stop otherwise I would surrender everything.

'No,' I warned. 'That's far enough.'

He looked sheepish and apologised. 'I was carried away. I do love you, Mia.'

We managed to be together on the Monday evening when we had a quiet drink in a pub on the Laxey road. We stopped near Onchan Head on the way home and managed to keep our wallowing under control. On Tuesday morning he caught the early flight to Blackpool for his interview at eleven o'clock. I was not on duty that day until after lunch, so I never saw him off. His letter three days later proudly announced that he had been successful. I would not see him until the end of term, but I felt things were looking rosy for us, except for the one possible cloud on the horizon – his mother.

Chapter 7

Wednesday, 26ᵗʰ June 1963

Mike came off the boat at three o'clock. Mia was waiting for him. It was a perfect summer's day. He'd sent his trunk and suitcases ahead – passengers' luggage in advance (cost 5s 0d). Consequently, he was only carrying a small holdall.

'Mia, you look beautiful. You're wearing the same outfit you had on when we met at the Palace.'

A radiant smile lit up her face. She was clearly delighted to see him. They hugged each other on the Victoria Pier in front of the terminal building. With his arms wrapped around her slim body, he lifted her into the air.

'Will you marry me, Mia?'

Her eyes opened ever larger. 'Of course I will,' she replied quietly.

He kissed her with her feet still off the ground, squeezing her so tight she was gasping for air.

She congratulated him on getting the job at Blackpool that would start in September.

'Where is it exactly?' she asked. 'You never said in your letter.'

'It's a secondary modern school in Cleveleys, beyond the Norbreck Hotel.'

They were already walking up Victoria Street. 'Come on,' he said 'We've got to find an engagement ring.'

At the first jeweller's shop in Strand Street they saw what they wanted: an eighteen-carat gold ring with a solitaire diamond.

'Can you afford it?' Mia asked, frowning.

'I'll earn plenty of overtime on the buses during the summer. Don't worry.'

'What now?' she queried.

'Douglas Head,' he replied.

'Why?'

'With the day as beautiful as this, where else is there to put the ring on your finger? It's got to be against the backdrop of the loveliest bay in the world. Come on.'

He grasped her hand and they skipped down Duke Street with Mia almost having to run to keep up with him. When they crossed the swing bridge over the quay, both were gasping with the thrill of becoming each other's life partner. Ahead of them lay the one hundred steps to reach Fort Anne Road.

'I'll race you to the top,' she said and began running. He gave chase, but by the resting place, where a bench had been thoughtfully provided by the town council, she stopped, turned and admitted the pace had been too great.

'I'm ready for a rest too. Can we get our breath back?'

They sat close together, with her on his left side. There was no one else on the steps. He put his right hand under her knees and lifted her legs over his left thigh. 'I love you so much,' he whispered. He took her left hand and slipped the ring on her fourth finger.

She laughed. 'It's not the most romantic spot in the world, is it?'

There was a faint whiff of urine; human or canine, he couldn't tell. Maybe the drunken revellers coming back from the Douglas Head Hotel had stopped there? However, it didn't prevent them kissing intensely. They remained as close together as possible for some time, talking about their future and making plans. They agreed they should get married the following autumn, after his probationary year in Blackpool.

'Suppose you don't pass?' she asked, alarm written on her face.

'I've just come ninth on my course. I won't fail, I promise you.'

They wandered back into town and decided to visit The Dog's Home for a celebratory drink. To his surprise, she asked for a pint of Guinness.

'Getting engaged is thirsty work.' She grinned.

Marvellous, he thought, *having a wife who can appreciate a pint.*

They then went to the office of the local newspaper, *The Isle of Man Times*, in Athol Street. Excitedly, they placed an announcement in Friday's weekly paper:

The engagement is announced of Mia Yvonne Mylrea, youngest daughter of Mrs E. Mylrea of Stanley Square, Douglas and Michael John Moore, only son of Mr and Mrs Thomas Moore of Cronkbourne Avenue, Douglas.

It was past six o'clock by the time he arrived home to be greeted aggressively by his mother. 'Where have you been? It doesn't take three hours to walk up from the pier.'

'I've asked Mia to marry me and we've become engaged.'

'You've done what?' she yelled.

'I'm going to marry Mia.'

She showed her feelings by snarling, 'What is your father going to say when he comes in?'

Mike went upstairs to unpack his things with a heavy heart. He realised a divide was opening up between himself and his parents. His father would be caught between a rock and a hard place. It wasn't as if they hadn't met Mia. After all, he thought, she had visited them for lunch that weekend before he'd gone for the interview. He remembered Mia had charmed the socks off his old man.

He suspected his mother had been getting some of her cronies to do some rooting. 'Find out whatever you can about her.'

He heard his father arrive home from work and went down to meet him. His mother had already announced the news. His father played a straight bat. 'Did you have to act so quickly?' were his first words. Not 'Congratulations' or 'I hope you'll be happy.'

'I thought you liked her, Dad.'

'I do, but you hardly know her.'

'I know what I want, and it's to live the rest of my life with Mia.'

'Then I hope you won't regret it.'

He knew then that his father, for whom he had the greatest respect, had sided with his mother, for the time being at least.

'Can I have the car tonight? I'd like to take Mia out to celebrate.'

'As long as you're sensible and don't drink too much.'

'I'll be careful, don't worry.'

When he went to collect Mia, the reaction of Mrs Mylrea was the exact opposite of his own mother. She opened the door and welcomed him as if he was already her son-in-law. She insisted he had a cup of tea. She wanted to read his tea leaves – again!

With Mia watching, Mike had to go through the ritual of swilling what little tea was left in the cup in a circular motion and then turning the cup upside down in the saucer. Mrs Mylrea waited for the tea to drain and then looked at the pattern left inside the cup by the leaves.

'You will marry someone who wears a uniform,' she said.

'Mia is an air hostess.'

But Mrs Mylrea looked serious.

'There are many troubles ahead.' She looked solemn and thoughtful, as if she didn't like what she was seeing.

'Come on, Mike. Don't take any notice. Mum's just having a bit of fun.'

He rose from the chair and smiled at his future mother-in-law. 'Mia and I are going for a celebratory drink. You can come, if you like.'

'No, goodness me, no. This is your party and you'll want to be alone. Enjoy yourselves. The leaves say you are both going to be very happy.'

She didn't add her proviso, *But not with each other.*

'He's not in yet. What do you think he's up to?' Mike's mother was asking his father.

'How the hell do I know? He's twenty-two.'

'That's another thing. She's four years older than him and, from what I've heard, far more experienced. She's not our type.'

'What do you mean by that?'

'Her last boyfriend was a man old enough to be her father.'

'Rubbish!'

'And she's a Roman Catholic.'

'So what? Many of our friends are Catholics.'

'But we're not married to them. She'll want a wedding at St Mary's.'

'Look Hilda, we've had this before. I've told you I like her. Martin Kermode came to see me today on business. He mentioned that he'd heard Mike was going out with Mia and casually remarked, "I think Mike is a lucky lad."

'I asked him, "Why?"

'He told me he was sorry when she left his practice to be an air hostess and was hoping she would come back when the summer season is over. His exact words were, "I'd have her back any day. She's a lovely girl who was always smart and polite with our clients." He's known her since she was a little girl and added, "I'd be proud to have her as my own daughter."

'I asked him why was she was still single at twenty-six and do you know what he said?'

'What?'

'He said, "She has ambition. Some would say she doesn't know her station, but that's not true. All the eligible boys of her age can't see beyond the fact that she's a Catholic from Stanley Square. She's far too good to be married to an Irish navvy and end up with six kids."

'Your problem, Hilda, is you take too much notice of tittle-tattle. Most of your cronies' gossip is based on hypocrisy and jealousy. And, anyway, I'd rather have a daughter-in-law who is a practising Catholic than one who doesn't go to church at all.'

'That's the point; she'll want their children brought up Catholics.'

Mike thought it was time to call a stop to their argument. They hadn't heard him come into the house and ascend the stairs. He knocked loudly on their bedroom door, opened it slightly, coughed, stuck his head through it and said, 'I'm home.'

'What have you been doing to this hour?' his mother asked.

'Mum, we've been talking, that's all.'

Her face was flushed with fury. He knew she didn't believe him. She looked at her husband expecting him to reprimand their son.

His father smiled. 'Your mum's upset. Don't worry. We'll see you in the morning.'

Mike went to bed wondering who Mia's 'old enough to be her father' could be, and whether there was any truth in his mother's allegation. A seed of doubt had been sown that was causing the scales to begin wavering.

The following week he began working as a bus conductor; a job he had done for the previous three years during the long summer vacations while at Manchester University. He knew his driver well, and he tried to synchronise his days off with those of Mia. When there was a clash, one of his fellow student conductors would usually switch duties. As the word got around that he was engaged to Mia, however, an undercurrent of hints, some subtle, some not, began. People, some of whom he hardly knew, would intimate that he had made an error. There seemed to be considerable prejudice against Mia. The implications were that she was too old, too worldly wise, from the wrong social background, had had dozens of boyfriends and 'been around'.

The phrase, 'She's an RC' was used frequently, as if she was a Martian.

It was the overt bias against Catholics that perplexed him most of all. It was becoming clear there was considerable social prejudice in the island against Roman Catholics. They were seen as third-class citizens.

He had never encountered such blatant bigotry before. His Catholic pals, when living in Westbourne Drive, had been equal members of the gang – all were in the 1st Douglas Cubs. True, they'd disappeared by the time they were sixteen as they'd left the island to find work. It had never occurred to him that they'd gone to get away from the religious unfairness that prevented them from attaining the better jobs in the civil service, the banks or the post office. As he thought more about the conundrum, he calculated the scale of the odds that were stacked against Catholics. He mentally began counting the number of churches in Douglas. Without checking his sums, he ran out at twenty-one, only one of which was Catholic.

No wonder there is such narrow-mindedness, he thought.

He tried to ignore remarks such as, 'You don't need to jump in the river to get a drink of water.'

He bitterly resented any criticism of Mia. Innuendoes, however, can gnaw away. Like a weevil in the gut, it is difficult to kill, and despite telling people it was none of their business, the seed of a doubt remained.

Can I have made a mistake?

Is she as perfect as she appears?

Why isn't she married already?

There were no answers to his questions. He had to trust his own judgement. His problem was cowardice. He hadn't the courage to ask Mia about who her former 'old enough to be her father' boyfriend was. He was afraid to ask who her previous suitors were. He didn't want to know in case there were grounds to doubt her sincerity when she claimed she loved him. He hoped his qualms would go away. He hoped that once away from the parochial atmosphere of the Isle of Man, they could live together in England, free from the narrow-minded, opinionated scandalmongers.

June 1963

I will forever remember Wednesday, 26th June 1963, but not for the same reason as the rest of the world. That day in Germany, President Kennedy made his famous *Ich bin ein Berliner* speech. In Douglas, however, I met Mike off the boat. On Victoria Pier he picked me up like a trophy and asked me to marry him. We hurried into Strand Street and bought an engagement ring that fitted perfectly. He insisted he had to put it formally on my finger overlooking the bay and we rushed across the old swing bridge and up the steps towards Fort Anne Road. Halfway up, we stopped to catch our breath. It wasn't the most romantic place, but Mike couldn't wait any longer. He proposed for the second time in less than an hour and slipped the ring on my finger. I was the happiest girl in the world. We stayed there for some time before walking to the office of *The Isle of Man Times* by way of The Dog's Home. Mike couldn't believe it when I asked for my celebratory drink to be a pint of Guinness. The announcement of our engagement would appear two days later in the weekly newspaper. We walked to my home up Bucks Road with his arm around my waist. We were so happy together, totally ignorant of events in Berlin.

That evening we went out to celebrate, but I felt things had not gone down too well at home for Mike. He was subdued and would not elaborate, although he tried hard not to show his feelings.

However, we made the most of having his father's car. We drove to The Highlander and after a lovely meal, returned to Douglas via Abbeylands. There we found a quiet spot. In the pitch darkness we climbed into the back seat. Our love-making went further than it had ever done previously. We were both so close that I have often wondered what stopped us from consummating our union that evening. We were so exhausted when we had finished that we spent some considerable time holding each other with our eyes closed in a dreamlike state. I've often pondered whether we were actually asleep in each other's arms.

It was late when Mike took me home. I sneaked in quietly so as not to disturb Mum and David. I lay in bed for ages thinking of our future, now that we had become engaged. Instinct was warning me that I would have my work cut out to win over his mother, but I had always overcome bullies at school. I was determined Mrs Moore was not going to browbeat me. A new phase in my life was beginning.

That summer was busy and enjoyable. My flying duties were largely ferrying holidaymakers to the island from Glasgow, Edinburgh, Leeds, and Birmingham. The customers on the Blackpool flights were frequently in the entertainment business: Ken Dodd, Kenny Ball and his jazzmen, Kathy Kirby, Gerry and the Pacemakers – to name but a few. They typically came to the island to give one-night performances or stay for a short, one-week show. Meanwhile, Mike was bus-conducting and earning as much overtime as he could, presumably to pay for my engagement ring which I proudly wore every day. Dating was, therefore, erratic, but being able to borrow his father's car or David's helped.

Jenny and George, her husband, had bought a small cottage in Andreas, a small village in the north of the island, as a long-term investment. On my free days, Mike would swap his schedule with a fellow student conductor and we would spirit away to the cottage to be on our own. I would take ingredients for a meal and prepare lunch. We would sit in the private garden in the sunshine and be happy together. Our courtship always stopped short of intimacy, but somehow we were always left satisfied. I have often marvelled at our innocent contentment. Today, liberal free-thinkers would consider our inexperienced love-making strange. Maybe we were both wet behind the ears. We were supremely at ease with each other's company, as if there was a conduit that linked our personalities. We instinctively knew what the other was thinking. We sometimes played golf at Port Erin, went bowling at Ramsey, or went for walks to places like Spanish Head. As long as we were together, nothing else mattered. Most memorable was a hot, sunny day when we walked to the summit of South Barrule. We lay on the soft turf, miles from anyone. After cuddling amorously for some time, by which time we were stripped to the waist, we fell asleep and woke up sunburnt.

Returning to Douglas we came across hedgerows full of multi-coloured foxgloves in full bloom. Mike stopped and picked a dozen.

'They're for your mother,' he said. I loved him all the more for thinking about my mum before his own. His warm feelings for my mother were sincere. I suspected they were based on our hardship of making ends meet in our fatherless family and seeing Mum struggle with arthritis. The contrast with his mother, living in a swanky part of town and being relatively well-off, must have been enormous. He apologised to my mum when he gave her the flowers, expressing his reserve that picking wild flowers might be unlucky. 'Flowers can never be unlucky,' she replied. I have never forgotten her words and can still remember her smile and moist eyes as she thanked him.

When side by side, we tingled – a feeling that was indescribable and which, I have to say, I'd never felt before and would have to wait a long, long time until I felt it again. We were impregnable inside our own cocoon. That summer was the happiest of my life: work was good; being with Mike was even better.

I tried to meet Mike's parents whenever it was possible within the constraints of my flying programme. I always made an effort to dress as smartly as I could, mind my Ps and Qs, and help his mother in the kitchen if food was being prepared. Slowly the ice began to melt. I'd always called her Mrs Moore. One day I was instructed, 'Call me Hilda.' I hoped a corner had been turned.

His parents were fond of picnicking and, if flying allowed, Mike and I would accompany them. Usually they chose remote beaches such as Port Cornaa or Ballaugh. There, Mike and I would go swimming, often with his father, before we would gather flotsam and make a fire on which to cook sausages or burgers. On one occasion on that long, hot, dry summer we picnicked at Injebreck, above the reservoir. I remember we could clearly see the remains of buildings that had been covered for generations as the water level in the reservoir was so low. I was seeing parts of the island I had never been to before. It all added to the euphoria of that wonderful summer.

Unfortunately, the day approached when Mike had to leave the island and begin teaching. As my job didn't finish until the end of September, we knew there might be some chances of our meeting in Blackpool. I had been promised my old job back with Corlett and Kermode, but seeing each other before Christmas would have to be confined to Mike's half-term weekend. When the time came for Mike to leave, it was Hilda who suggested that I could come for tea on Friday evenings so that Mike could ring me and we could chat. My mother didn't have a phone. This became a regular feature that winter and his father would drive me home afterwards before he went to his bridge club. I began to hope I had won over my future mother-in-law, although there was always an underlying unease that I now believe never went away. In the event, I saw Mike once during my final days of working for Britair.

September 1963

Mike started his teaching appointment at the beginning of September and moved into his digs two days earlier. His lodgings were ideally situated, being only a ten-minute walk from school. His landlady, Kit, worked in Blackpool Education Authority's offices in the town centre and was in her late forties. Divorced with no children, she had welcomed her tenant and given him the freedom of her home: a pre-war, three-bedroomed, semi-detached house in North Drive, on the edge of Cleveleys. She lived on her own, but had a male friend, Adrian, who worked as a senior administrator in the education offices.

When introduced to him, Mike explained he was engaged and was saving to get married. Adrian replied he was looking for someone to teach maths on Wednesday evenings at a local night school to a class of civil servants who wished to pass a promotion exam to the executive grade. The extra money would boost Mike's monthly salary by ten per cent. Mike jumped at the opportunity, but unintentionally this would lead him into temptation.

At Mike's first evening lesson, sitting in the front row was a pretty woman about his own age. She sat with her shapely legs crossed, her skirt seductively above her knees. She had a nice smile and throughout the two-hour lesson, including a short coffee break, he found it difficult not to stare at her legs. When he left the night school, situated in the south of Blackpool, she was waiting at the bus stop. They sat together going into town. He discovered that Wendy lived in Cleveleys. At Talbot Square, where they had to change buses, he invited her for a quick drink in Yates' wine bar. She accepted. Two years younger than him, she revealed that she was already divorced, her ex had custody of their daughter and she was back living with her parents.

A savvier operator would have seen red lights – a warning signal. Mike, however, saw her as an opportunity to increase his experience with women.

No one will ever know.

After a second glass of an indefinite wine, they caught the tram along North Shore. Throughout their fifteen minute journey she made it obvious she fancied him. Even Mike's inexperienced antennae were picking up the signals. When they alighted he accompanied her to her parents' house, less than half a mile from his digs. With her parents already in bed and presumably asleep, they made love on the lounge floor in front of the dying embers of a fire. Assuring him she was on the pill, she was the first woman with whom he had completed copulation. It was the beginning of an affair that would remain secret from Mia. His libido would in future be satisfied with a woman he knew he could never love. To his twisted mind this was perfectly acceptable. Two-timing his fiancée was part of 'the great game of life'. As a cheat and liar, Mike was experienced; now he had added licentiousness and perfidiousness to his list of attributes. Ironically, throughout his affair with Wendy, he would remain certain he loved Mia and no one else.

A chance remark made by Mia to one of the Blackpool pilots, Bill Niven, that her fiancé was a maths teacher in Cleveleys led to another money-earning opportunity. Bill's son, David, was to take the Eleven Plus later that academic year. Every Friday evening, Mike would take the bus into Blackpool town centre, change for St Anne's and tutor David to pass the verbal reasoning tests used for the Eleven Plus. The boy would be successful and gain entry to King Edward VII School in the September 1964 entry. It was an easy way to make £5 cash-in-hand and exactly paid Mike's weekly rent.

Mia had made it clear she wanted a white wedding at St Mary's. Consequently, Mike promised to undertake conversion lessons to the Roman faith so that they could have a nuptial Mass. He had calculated that they needed at least £500 to cover the wedding costs and buy a flat. It was an ambitious target, but both agreed to be as parsimonious as possible during the forthcoming winter months in order to get married the following autumn.

Mr Kermode had decided Mia could shadow the retiring chief clerk until the end of the year. She would then take over the reins and receive a pay rise. Everything was beginning to look favourable for their future.

Mike began scouting for a suitable apartment. Typical two-bedroom flats with sea views were being built at St Anne's, and would require a £200, ten per cent holding deposit. It was a large amount, but Mike thought such a sum should be within their joint budget by Easter and so he signed a document of intent.

Keeping in touch with Mia wasn't easy as they had no telephone at her home. Writing letters was the only method of communication as there wasn't a phone in his digs either. Each Friday evening, Mia had started having tea with his parents. It allowed Mike to ring home from a public phone box and speak with her. Mia assured Mike she felt his mother was attempting to overcome her prejudices. Mike wasn't so sure. He hoped it wasn't simply a case of wishful thinking. He wondered if a trap was being set. Was his mother hoping Mia would make a faux pas that could be used against her?

His teaching was going well. His classes, mostly eleven, twelve and thirteen-year-olds, were generally well-behaved. He was the junior maths teacher in a department of four. The head of maths, Mrs Ward, was an irrepressible fifty-year-old widow, friendliness personified. She saw Mike as a surrogate son and took him under her wing. Her advice was always sound when he asked for guidance on how certain topics should be taught. When she discovered he was engaged to Mia and was thinking of converting to Catholicism, she gave him every encouragement, arranging for him to meet the local priest at St Teresa's RC Church, less than a mile from his digs.

Towards the end of September, with Mia on her last week of flying, he had been back in his digs after school for less than an hour when the doorbell rang. He was unsure as to whether he should answer.

It must be someone wanting Kit.

However, when he opened the door there she was, with a wide smile on her face and a taxi waiting at the bottom of the path in case he hadn't been home.

'Mia, what are you doing here?'

'The Jersey flight has been cancelled because the plane has developed a fault and I am stuck in Blackpool. We can have the night together.'

'Marvellous. Let me pay the taxi driver.'

She had arrived with a small overnight bag, carried by all aircrew in case of such emergencies. As they kissed in the hallway, his lungs were filling with her delicate perfume. With his hands around her waist, warmth was being generated in his nethermost regions; an exothermic reaction that he'd noticed whenever he held her. He lifted her off her feet and held her aloft, looking into her smiling, mischievous face. He'd done it the day she had met him off the boat and they'd become engaged. She was so light that he felt he could hold her in the air indefinitely. She was the most beautiful girl he had ever seen and he knew he would never get tired of looking into her face.

He showed her his digs: the front room, the dining room, the kitchen and, finally, his bedroom. There, they stood looking into each other's eyes. He said he would sleep downstairs on the couch in the front room and she could have his bed.

She whispered, 'Kiss me,' and stretched up towards him, her lips gathered in expectation.

The devil inside him was saying, *Make the most of it before Kit comes home.* Despite their love-making gradually becoming ever more intense, it had always been starry-eyed and innocent. However, over the summer, his lust had become ever more difficult to control and he hoped Mia was feeling the same way. They fell slowly back onto his bed.

He found his hand undoing the buttons of her blouse. She began breathing deeply. She wasn't resisting as he fondled her. His hopes were rising. They remained embraced, kissing ever more passionately as he unhooked her bra and his tongue slid down her body. However, when he placed his hand on her thigh, she began to protest. Wriggling her legs this way and that, she tried to halt him, but he had become determined and, being much, much stronger, he forced her legs apart as his hand moved upwards.

Pleas of 'No' and 'We mustn't' were ignored.

'We agreed we would wait until we were married,' she gasped and continued to fight him, but his ardour was out of control.

'You bastard,' she suddenly yelled and struck him with her open hand across his face.

As if awakening from a nightmare, he stopped.

They collapsed in each other's arms and lay there, mutually feeling guilty. Neither was able to admit that they had just denied each other the experience they both wanted.

'I'm sorry, Mia. Please forgive me.'

'It's OK. Just hold me close and tell me you love me.'

What seemed like ages passed before Mike spoke. He looked into

Mia's sad eyes and knew he had hurt her. 'I am sorry,' he repeated. 'Will you forgive me?'

She said nothing as he gently kissed her forehead.

He knew he had let her down.

'I won't do it again, until we're married. I promise,' he said, but he knew he had put up a black mark that could have terrible consequences in the future. He tried to make amends by holding her as tenderly as he could. They lay together, saying nothing as he continued to kiss her eyes and cheeks. 'I swear it won't happen again; I love you and always will,' he promised, but in the back of his mind the devil was telling him, *Don't worry, tomorrow is Wednesday.*

She said nothing for ages, until, finally, she whispered, 'You will marry me, won't you?'

'You know I will. We'll get married next year at St Mary's and go to Ireland for our honeymoon.'

'Promise?'

'Promise.'

They straightened themselves and went downstairs to make something to eat in the kitchen. He apologised for his lack of culinary skills.

'I make good scrambled eggs with sausages, will that be all right?'

She smiled at him. 'Anything you do would be wonderful.'

Afterwards, they travelled into town along the promenade in an open-top tram admiring the Blackpool Illuminations. At the cinema, opposite the North Pier, they saw *Doctor in Distress*, a light hearted comedy with Samantha Eggar playing a lead role. The resemblance between the girl sitting next to him and the heroine did not go unnoticed.

They returned to his digs where Mia met Kit, who immediately fell for Mia. She insisted she wanted an invitation to next year's wedding. The three took a nightcap together, a whisky and soda, nattering about Mia's plans to find work in Blackpool after they were married. Kit showed surprise when Mike asked if it would be OK if he slept on the sofa in the lounge, but she made no comment.

The next day Kit made a remark that Mike would remember for the rest of his life. 'You both deeply love each other. It's so obvious that you must never let her go.' Quite why, she made the remark, he never knew.

However, by the following evening he found himself with Wendy. Their amoral relationship was taking off. Treachery had been added to his shameful record.

Nevertheless, it didn't prevent him beginning weekly lessons to convert to Catholicism. He was unsure what his motivation was. His twisted logic even believed his relationship with Wendy was assisting by strengthening his need for a permanent relationship with Mia. As the lessons proceeded, he realised so much was based on the articles of faith promulgated in the Catechism. Throughout he remained a doubting Thomas. He didn't do mysticism, but Mia was everything. Consequently, when he took his vows, he knew he was not only double-crossing Mia, but God himself.

He had fallen as far as it is possible to go: he'd cheated at school, cheated at university, cheated on Mia and now was cheating the Almighty.

Chapter 10

November 1963

I was back working at the advocates' office in Athol Street when Mike came home for half-term. That Friday was All Saints' Day and we went to evening Mass at St Mary's. Mike had started taking lessons for converting to Catholicism; something that he had kept secret from his parents. We held hands throughout the service, apart from when I went to receive the sacrament. That evening I felt the bond that linked the two of us was now permanent. Our love was absolute and nothing could tear us apart. I believed Mike must truly love me if he was prepared to convert to my faith. His half-term was little more than a long weekend and flew past all too quickly. We saw *The Great Escape*, went to the Highlander and had an evening with Jenny and George, at the Liverpool Arms.

I continued to visit his parents' house after work on Fridays so that Mike could ring me. His mother was slowly becoming friendlier, or so I thought. In mid-December, she asked if I would like to accompany them to the Isle of Man Bank's annual Christmas ball at the Grand Island Hotel in Ramsey. The invitation came out of the blue. The ball was about a week before Mike came home. I bought a ball gown: a black, full-length dress made of velvet with a pompom at the front where the straps gathered. I would keep it for many years. In future, I would buy many such dresses, but that tight-fitting gown, my first, remained my favourite for the rest of my life. I asked myself whether there was an ulterior motive for the unexpected invitation. Was it yet another check to see if I was a suitable daughter-in-law? Despite attending a ball where most people had a partner, I was made to feel welcome by the bank staff and enjoyed the experience as I knew several of them from the golf club and had seen others in Athol Street during my lunch breaks. I kept wishing Mike had been with me, but when his father dropped me off at home in the early hours I was sure I had passed their test.

At Christmas, Mike and I had three wonderful weeks of seeing each other as often as possible. We never tired of being on our own. God knows what we did, but our happiness and mutual contentment never seemed to stop. Whenever we met, I would tingle with warmth. We attended several balls and formal dinners, such as his old scholars' association dinner at the Derby Haven Hotel, now long converted into apartments. Whenever we danced together, the dancefloor seemed empty. Our enveloping cocoon had translucent, as opposed to transparent, walls. We went to Christmas Eve midnight Mass at St Mary's, and the following day had dinner with his parents. For a present, he gave me a KIGU musical powder compact. It had a stunning red enamel lid with a golden flower design on top. I still have it forty years later and its condition is as new, except the music, a Mozart minuet, no longer plays. As every day passed, our relationship intensified and it was a wrench when he had to return to Blackpool.

He managed a long weekend home at half-term during February. Fortunately, Easter was early in 1964, so I didn't have to wait too long for the Easter break. By then Mike had converted to Catholicism and I had decided our physical relationship should be fulfilled totally. I didn't have long to wait.

We took communion together for the first time on Easter Sunday at St Mary's. I vividly recall being proud, as we returned to our pew, that my future husband was by my side. I wanted to shout to the other communicants, 'This is my man. We're getting married and nothing will ever prise us apart.'

The next day we went to Jenny's cottage. It was a cold, damp day and we spent most of the time on the carpet in front of a roaring fire consummating our love for the first time. I lost count of my climaxes, never thinking for a minute of the possible consequences. Looking back now, I realise we should have taken precautions. What a difference it would have made to my life.

Mike will soon marry me, I thought.

We had decided a date in October for the wedding, coinciding with his half-term. We would be married on Saturday and fly to Dublin afterwards for five days of touring Ireland. Unknowingly, however, that day I surrendered something that, at the time, I didn't think mattered – my mystique. I sometimes look back now and wonder if this was all that Mike ever wanted from me.

Mike had chosen an apartment in St Anne's, a sufficient distance from the school to keep the kids away. His plan was to move out of his digs during the last two weeks of the summer term so he could begin preparing the flat as our new home.

However, by the time he came back to the island for the summer half-term, a long weekend in late May, he'd changed. Over that month I'd noticed his letters had gradually become less affectionate, but I'd chosen to ignore my suspicions.

It's only my imagination, I told myself.

When we met, he was remote, showed little warmth, had become monosyllabic, and I began to form the impression he didn't want to be with me. I tried to console myself that it was all in my head; that it was me who was feeling different. I'd missed a period and had begun worrying if I might be pregnant. My fears had begun to affect my body chemistry, reasoning and personality.

We'd been out for a drink in Port Erin the night before he was due to return to Blackpool on Tuesday 26th. Things had gone from bad to worse all evening. I'd dressed smartly for what would be our last time together until the end of term in mid-July. I tried my damnedest to lighten his mood. He didn't respond to anything. He'd become offhand, even rude. Eventually, I'd had enough and suggested we leave. We were sitting in his father's car outside my home trying to discuss our future when Mike began to drone on monotonously about our lack of savings. Inside me it understandably triggered a short fuse.

'How much have you saved?' he asked.

'About thirty quid,' I replied.

'Is that all?' he exclaimed.

'Don't forget, I don't earn anything like as much as you. Anyway, how much have you managed?'

'About £120.'

He stopped; staring at me as if I was a spendthrift. After a minute of deafening silence, he said coldly, 'There's no way we are going to be able to get married. The flat requires a £200 deposit. I'm going to have to borrow from the bank to make up the amount when I go back as I'm now legally committed to buying the apartment in St Anne's. I thought you'd be able to give me the £80 difference. God knows how we're going to cope. There'll be nothing for the wedding or the honeymoon, not to say furniture, etcetera.'

I felt terrible.

Is it my fault?

Have I let him down?

'Perhaps we could get married in a register office,' he mumbled.

'No, Mike; we know our marriage is only seen as valid by the Vatican if it is conducted in a Catholic church. We'll have to postpone it for a year.'

'You're bloody joking. I'm not waiting that long.'

'Aren't I worth waiting for?'

He didn't answer for a few seconds and then he may as well have stabbed me with a knife. 'You can bugger off to your bloody church for all I care. I should never have taken conversion lessons; it's all a load of crap. Here, you can keep this.' He tossed the signet ring that I had given him into my lap.

I said nothing, but my guts were not only feeling different; my mind was blowing-up. I could feel myself beginning to shake with rage, but I bit my lip. I wasn't going to let him see me cry. I remembered my first day at school.

'You can be a right bastard at times. I hope you rot in hell,' I yelled.

I got out of the car, slammed the door so hard I wouldn't have been surprised if it had fallen off its hinges, ran indoors and went straight to my bedroom, threw myself on the bed and wept uncontrollably. I cried all night as I tried to analyse what had gone wrong. I began to see that allowing Mike to make love to me on Easter Monday had satisfied his lust. Having had me, he no longer wanted me. I was not even worth waiting for. My enigma had gone. I was no longer his white queen. My blues deepened. I began to panic. I was unsure what to do. Our engagement was over and I was in the family way.

Who do I tell first?

Mike, Mum, my priest, or Dr Donaldson, our family doctor?

I'll go to Mike's house first thing in the morning, before he goes back to Blackpool, and tell him.

He'll stick with me and we can get married quietly.

And so my worries went on. The next day, after struggling to project normality with Mum at breakfast, I decided to see Dr Donaldson that evening.

With luck, I might not be pregnant.

A few tests and, two days later, my worst nightmare was confirmed. For the rest of the week I was too frightened to tell anyone that I was pregnant by a man who no longer loved me.

Eventually, I plucked up enough courage to tell Mum.

'Mum, I'm going to have to tell you sooner or later, but I think I may be pregnant.'

'What?'

Instinctively, her voice expressed shock and anger at the same time. I could read her like a book. I knew what was going through her mind.

How could my youngest daughter get herself into such a state?

I've tried to bring her up decent.

What will the neighbours think?

Mum looked at the picture, hanging on the wall over the fireplace. It had hung there ever since I could remember. She crossed herself.

'Oh Mia, what have you done? Have you slept with Mike?'

I nodded, avoiding eye contact.

I was ashamed and knew I had brought disgrace on our family. We were poor, we lived in one of the most deprived areas of Douglas and could not afford a telephone or a television, but Mum had her pride. Our apartment was always spotlessly clean and we didn't owe anyone any money.

The Head of Chambers, Martin Kermode, had encouraged me to train to be a legal secretary. 'Your daughter can do it,' he used to say to my mother whenever she went to his house to alter dresses for his wife. 'It might be the hard way, but Mia can do it.'

And I'd done it, too.

By studying in the evenings, I'd sacrificed a lot. Now I'd undone all my hard work for the sake of a boy who no longer loved me.

What a bloody fool I've been.

Mum was right, there was something not right about him.

The tea leaves were accurate after all.

Since our engagement, I'd worked flat-out for the only thing I really wanted in life – to be a good wife for Mike. Now everyone would discover I'd allowed myself to be seduced. My sisters and brother would shun me. I'd be the subject of gossip in the neighbourhood: *Mia has a bun in the oven.*

Half of Douglas would soon know about it.

'I'm certain Mike will marry me,' I said apologetically.

'It's not the way to begin a successful marriage. You will have to give up work and struggle to make ends meet. You should know better than anyone what it is like having no money. You always had to wear your sister's cast-offs when you were young. I've struggled to bring you up decent and this is how you reward me. Oh Mia, how could you?'

Mum began weeping, using the bottom of her apron to wipe away her tears.

She continued, 'His parents, you know what they're like, particularly his mother. She will blame you and will never accept you as her daughter-in-law. It would have been bad enough if you could have waited. I told you there was something not right about Mike.'

Perhaps realising she had been too harsh, she opened her arms wide and hugged me. We cried together for several minutes before she wiped our eyes and said, 'We must pray together for guidance.' She put on her best coat, and holding hands, we walked in silence to St Mary's, ten minutes away.

We knelt together in the empty church with our rosary beads and prayed silently. Many minutes had passed when there was a cough behind us. We looked up to see Father Johns standing in the central aisle.

He smiled and asked, 'Is everything all right, Mrs Mylrea?'

'Not really Father, Mia has got herself in the family way.'

He looked at me, but showed no reproachful reaction whatsoever. 'Would you like to come into the presbytery?' he asked kindly. 'It's my housekeeper's day off. We'll be alone.'

He made a pot of tea.

I explained how Mike and I had spent Easter Monday at Jenny's cottage in Andreas and had made love for the first time.

'It hasn't happened since, Father,' I promised. 'We both wanted a nuptial Mass wedding. Mike has converted to our faith after taking instructions in Cleveleys.'

'Do you love him, my child?'

'With all my heart, Father. There'll never be anyone else.'

'Does he know you're pregnant?'

'No, not yet.'

'Did you consent to have sexual intercourse with him?'

The phrase sounded cold and detached; as if it had been a physical transaction without any tenderness. I wanted to tell him that it had been an exciting, passionate day, loving and caring – an afternoon full of beauty and emotional intensity.

However, with my mother staring at me and hanging on my answer, I panicked.

'No, Father,' I wept. 'I tried to stop him, but couldn't.'

'Then, he doesn't love you,' Mum spat. 'A good man would have waited until he'd married you.'

The priest coughed to intervene. 'He doesn't respect you, my child,' he said. 'You know you shouldn't marry if you are carrying an illegitimate, unwanted baby?'

'But Father...'

'What is my daughter to do Father?' interrupted my mother.

'She must go away and have the baby adopted. I can arrange that through the Sisters of Mercy.'

I was crying uncontrollably.

I am ashamed now that I wasn't braver. I still believe Mike would have done the decent thing and we could have been married quietly in the register office in Blackpool. After all, I was twenty-seven and Mike twenty-three. We were hardly under-age. By not returning to the island for a year, or two, the whole thing would have been forgotten.

Instead, the priest continued to harangue me, accusing me of breaking the spirit of the Ten Commandments. The questioning seemed to last for hours. It was probably no more than ten minutes. Until I lied that Mike had raped me, Mum had been quiet – not supportive, but certainly not aggressive. She had immediately changed on hearing my lie. It would never occur to her that I was being dishonest, as all my life she had trusted me. Suddenly, she took the priest's view. I must go away, keep the birth secret and have the baby adopted. Father Johns promised to implement the plan straight away, but then Mum came up with a different idea.

'Mia can go to Australia, stay with her sister, Liz, and have the baby there.'

'Can you afford the flight?' the priest asked.

'I know who will lend me the money,' she replied confidently.

Mum had decided. Nothing would change her mind. I wasn't asked for my opinion. Her decision was final.

Three days later, exactly a week after my blow-up with Mike, I left the island. I flew to Manchester, and would not return for four years. Only then did I discover that Mrs Kermode had generously given Mum the money in exchange for making her some new dresses.

While waiting at Manchester Airport for the BEA connection to Heathrow, I bought a packet of five cigarettes. I chose the cheapest make, Woodbines. I carefully placed my engagement ring in the middle of the packet, surrounding it with the cigarettes to protect it, and scribbled a note to Mike. I decided to send it to his parents' address – to make him wait to get it. I was giving back a part of my life and tears were flooding down my face. My heart was to bleed for a long time. I now believe the scars never healed.

From Heathrow, the QANTAS Boeing 707 took thirty-four hours to reach Sydney, with eight stops: Rome, Cairo, Bahrain, Karachi, Calcutta, Bangkok, Singapore, and Darwin. I remembered every one. As each stop took me further away from Mike, my despair deepened.

How can I be happy having to bring up his child without his support?

I was knackered when I arrived, but no one would have guessed I was pregnant. Secretly, I had half-hoped the journey would kick off a miscarriage, so I could go home and marry Mike. Wishful thinking perhaps, but for better or for worse, it was not to be.

Chapter 11

Saturday 6th June 1964

The door opened.

In front of Mike stood Mrs Mylrea. Hovering behind her was David, Mia's brother.

'You bastard, you raped my daughter,' she yelled at him.

'Sorry?'

'Don't give me that, pretending you don't know what you've done.'

'I've just come off the plane. I've flown over for the day specially, and came here immediately to see if Mia is all right. She hasn't replied to my letters since I went back after half-term.'

'Fuck off, you bastard,' shouted David. 'Don't ever come back. Mia won't ever see you again. You deserve a thrashing for what you did.'

And with that the door was slammed shut in his face.

Mike stood frozen to the spot. He couldn't understand what he could have done to deserve such brutal treatment. He thought their disagreement ten days previously was no more than a spat that would have been forgotten. He'd written to Mia and apologised as soon as he'd arrived back in his digs. When he'd not received a reply, he'd rung his parents that Friday as usual to be told Mia hadn't turned up. Three further letters begging forgiveness had gone unheeded.

He turned and walked down the short path. He crossed the square and headed towards the bus stop.

What have I done?

What's gone wrong?

Where's Mia?

How do I make contact with her?

He decided the solution lay with asking George, Jenny's husband. He had his own business near the quay. Mike had always got on well with George;

they'd shared a few beers together on several occasions. He caught the bus into town and ten minutes later he was confronting the man whom he thought would one day become his brother-in-law.

'Mike, you know what the family is like. My wife, Jenny, is as fiercely Roman Catholic as Mia and her mother. They have strong moral principles. I remember Mia giving me a right bollocking for bring Jenny home the worse for wear on one occasion before we were married. We'd been to a party and been drinking heavily. Mia's a little dynamo; she has veins of steel. I know she confided in Jenny that you had slept with her and forced yourself on her so that she was no longer a virgin. When Mia told her mother, she was frogmarched down to the church and made to confess to the priest.'

'But George, it was all so natural. We spent last Easter Monday together in your cottage. We love each other, and it just went a bit further than usual.'

'But did Mia try and stop you?'

'Yes, of course she did, but I thought she was play-acting. I want to marry her. I can't do without her. Won't you tell me where she is hiding? Is she at your house with Jenny?'

'No, I can promise you I haven't seen her – not since she and her mother went to see the priest at St Mary's. I suspect she's left the island. I'm fond of you, Mike. I've always got on with you. The four of us – you, me, Jenny and Mia – have had some good times together. Last New Year's Eve, for example, we had a great time. I know Mia gave Jenny the impression that the two of you had argued over the wedding arrangements when you were over for half-term.'

'Yes, that's true, but it was little more than a minor falling-out. I had to fly back to Blackpool the next morning and so didn't get the chance to say sorry. But I wrote a grovelling letter as soon as I got back to my digs. I've not had a reply and now her mum won't speak to me.'

'If I knew where Mia had gone, I'd tell you because I was looking forward to having you as my brother-in-law. Jenny probably knows, but she won't tell me as she knows I'd tell you.'

Mike walked home in low spirits to find a letter waiting for him.

'It came a few days ago,' his mother proudly announced. Mike suspected she already knew of the bust-up. Her network of spies included several wives or their husbands who worked in Athol Street. Word would have spread like wildfire that Mia had left Corlett and Kermode's at short notice. She was gloating that their engagement was finished. He wasn't going to give her the pleasure of asking why she hadn't forwarded the letter to his digs.

He recognised the handwriting instantly – it was from Mia. He went to his room and sat on the bed. His depression lifted briefly as he tore open the envelope. However, the note, wrapped around a packet of Woodbines, simply read:

> *I'm sorry we can never marry and I will not see you again, but I won't ever forget you.*
>   *Mia xx*

Tears flooded into his eyes as he sat paralysed: his world shattered, his confidence smashed, his future finished. The small, delicate ring was parcelled inside the packet with the cigarettes to protect it. He remembered when he had so proudly put it on Mia's finger a year previously. He examined the envelope.

Where has the letter been posted?
Manchester.
What the hell is she doing in Manchester?
She has no relatives there.
I've got to find Jenny, who will tell me where Mia is, even if I have to twist her arm.

He went to Jenny's house. She opened the door, took one look at him and before Mike could usher a single word, she slammed the door shut. He rang the bell again and heard Jenny shouting, 'Bugger off.'

Knowing it to be hopeless, he trudged home, heartbroken.

He sat down in his bedroom; his eyes welled-up and he penned a letter:

> *My one and only Mia,*
>   *By the time you get this letter, you...*

He placed it in a sealed envelope, writing his signature over the seal. He walked into town, had a pint at The Dog's Home, and went to see George before he closed the shop for the weekend.

'George, I don't expect I'll ever see Mia again. Would you keep this letter somewhere safe and give it to her whenever you see her next?'

'I've no idea when that may be. It could be years.'

'Yes, but someday you will see her. I won't.'

'OK, I'll put it in my personal file where I keep birth certificates and things. When I see her, I'll give it to her.'

'What you seem to be saying is that you think she's gone to Australia to see Liz.'

'I don't know for certain, but it's my guess. When she comes home, as I'm sure she will someday then I promise I'll give her the letter.'

'Thanks, George. You've been a good mate. I'm sorry things have worked out the way they have. I really did love Mia, you know. You and I would have made good brothers-in-law.'

That evening, he caught the last flight back to Blackpool more depressed than he'd ever been. His reception at Stanley Square, the accusation of rape, George's suspicion that Mia had gone to Australia, the return of her engagement ring, notwithstanding that he had given her his signet ring, and how his blasphemy must have hurt Mia deeply – all weighed on his mind. It was all over, and solely his fault.

Chapter 12

June 1964

When Mike returned to Blackpool after his fleeting visit to the island, he tried to cancel his contract to buy the flat in St Anne's. He discovered he had a choice: pay the deposit and lose the apartment or pay the deposit and complete the purchase. He chose to go through with the acquisition, hoping Mia would miraculously reappear. They would then make up and marry quietly in the local register office. He made enquiries and discovered the licence fee was only 13s 6d – a sum that would save a huge chunk from their original planned expenditure. Furthermore, by not having a honeymoon, he recalculated their wedding costs and wrote to Mia:

> *Dearest Mia,*
> *We can afford to get married if we marry in a register office, don't have a honeymoon, and don't have a reception...*

He sent it to George at his shop asking him to send it on. There was no reply.

The remainder of the summer term was characterised by wonderful weather, interschool cricket matches and Kit going away to Spain with Adrian for the last two weeks before the schools broke up. This allowed Mike the free run of Kit's house. His weekly liaison with Wendy intensified. She began sleeping with Mike in Kit's double bed. His adulterous sex life compensated for the loss of Mia. When between the sheets with Wendy, he began to imagine fate had decreed that his calling was to become a serial philanderer – a modern-day Casanova, but he was puzzled. Why was his scorecard so low?

Wendy had begun to hint that she would move in with him. The empty St Anne's flat was now legally his. The suggestion totally confused him. He liked her in bed, but knew he didn't want her around twenty-four hours a day. He fobbed her off by telling her that she should wait until he could afford some furniture.

The problem was Mia. Even when bedding Wendy, Mia was on his mind. She wouldn't go away. He tried to excuse their breakup by telling himself that it served her right. But inside him, a niggling moral code, perhaps now a Catholic conscience, was telling him – *It is you that is wrong. Mia is your destiny. Go and find her.*

Trying his damnedest to forget Mia, Mike spent the six weeks of the school holidays at home with his parents. Playing two or three times daily at the Onchan golf club, his handicap tumbled down to single figures. He found playing was a temporary release from thinking of Mia. However, when not on the golf course, he watched Athol Street and Stanley Square inconspicuously to see if there were any signs of Mia returning to the island. There were none. On occasional trips to George's delicatessen, he was assured by George that Mia was in Australia and that he had given Mike's second letter to Jenny to forward to her. With old school pals, evenings were spent in dubious places such as the Texas Bar and the Mount Murray Hotel looking for female holiday makers seeking a quickie romance. His successes were very few. However, his drinking increased.

In late August, Wendy wrote saying she was getting back with her ex. The news meant Mike would be returning to an empty flat without a bit on the side. His state of mind deteriorated. The prospect of living alone in the St Anne's flat began to horrify him.

Even Wendy would have been better than nothing.

He questioned whether he could cope. Mia was still haunting him whenever he wasn't on the golf course.

Within days of returning to Blackpool, he'd come to terms with the fact that the mortgage on the apartment was financially crippling him. So, too, were the council rates, the heating and lighting bills, the building and contents insurance, the service charges associated with the block's upkeep, the transport costs and the groceries. By the end of the month he was penniless. He solved the travelling problem by buying a second-hand bicycle for £1 10s, but regretted choosing a flat eight miles away from the school. The forty-minute cycle ride along Blackpool's famous promenade, although level, could be particularly exhausting into a westerly wind. He would arrive hot and sweaty at school. By leaving home early, however, he could take a shower on arrival and, thereby, save on his hot water bill. He volunteered to take dinner duty each day, allowing him to have a free meal. He ate heartily so that he didn't have to eat in the evening. He couldn't afford to rent a TV or go to the cinema. Worse than the physical deprivations was the fact that the flat was empty. Mia would have been the interior designer; now it was bare. Not being able to afford a bed, he slept on a mattress on the floor. The idea of swimming into the sea with stones in his pockets occurred to him on more than one occasion.

His fellow teachers were sympathetic to his plight and several of his male colleagues organised boys' nights out playing snooker at the Norbreck Hotel. When it was his turn to buy a round of drinks, he had to swallow hard and count his pennies to see if he had enough money. He learnt to make half-a-pint of mild last as long as possible. His Eleven Plus tuition had stopped as his pupil had passed the exam and was now a first-former at King Edward's school. The evening classes had finished too. The only consolation was that the cycling and enforced diet ensured he was becoming fitter than ever.

Mrs Ward and one of the other female members of staff tried matchmaking by giving dinner parties at their homes. Nothing worked; he knew he was responsible for the breakup with Mia. The most beautiful, stunning girl he had ever known had left him and gone to Australia because of his immaturity and inability to handle the overt pressures from, among others, his mother. In the evenings, after he had marked homework books, he would sit looking at an empty wall. It gave him plenty of time to think.

He pondered why his mother had been so anti-Mia. Initially antagonistic toward Helen, his previous girlfriend, she had eventually accepted her. In the end they had got on quite well. What was the difference? He concluded it was their different backgrounds. Helen was the daughter of a wealthy farmer whose acreage included prime, south-facing land on the lower slopes of South Barrule, near Ballasalla. As the only child, she would, no doubt, have inherited the farm and become a wealthy young woman. Even his father had once commented to him that the farm was 'prime land'. He wondered if this observation had been intended to encourage his relationship with Helen, whose parents were also strong Methodists like his own. However, after Mia, there could be no going back. Whereas Helen had been acceptable to his parents, she had become predictable – boring, even. Mia had given him a taste of excitement associated with the unknown. She had flirted with him. He was never quite sure what she was thinking. Mia was mysterious. He found this exhilarating. Every time they were together it was new – he was forever entering unfamiliar territory.

A mood of hopelessness began to affect his teaching. He no longer had the enthusiasm to prepare his lessons properly. He knew they were not to the standard they should have been. He could see himself becoming one of those schoolmasters, characterised in comedies, who always wore the same tweed jacket, with leather patches on its elbows and cuffs. The thought horrified him and by half-term he had decided to leave at Christmas. His colleagues warned him that the system demanded a full term's notice, but he didn't care.

He badly needed to forget Mia whose spirit was now following him everywhere he went. She was in the apartment waiting for him when he arrived home from work. She was waiting for him to come down to breakfast. At school, she sat in the back row of his classes. When he faced the blackboard to write, he could feel her eyes in the back of his head. He couldn't get her out of his mind. Whenever he saw her, she was glaring at him, giving him one of her bonfire looks. The animosity in her eyes would momentarily stop his heart and he would plead, *I'm sorry, Mia; it was my fault.*

She wouldn't go away.

It was four months since their breakup, but he had finally accepted that the failure of their relationship was his and his alone. He no longer made excuses. It wasn't the deprivation of Stanley Square. It wasn't Catholicism. It wasn't money. It was him. He had been unable to cope with jealous, snide remarks from people he hardly knew, or handle the responsibility that comes with a long-term relationship. Almost every moment of the day he was apologising to Mia, hoping against hope that her ghost would materialise. It never did.

There was only one course of action. He decided to pursue the idea of going abroad and began scouring *The Times Educational Supplement* for jobs. Each week, the British Council advertised for teachers in Europe,

Africa and elsewhere. In mid-October a job appeared for a maths teacher in La Paz, Bolivia.

An experienced graduate required to teach mathematics to "O" Level. Spanish speaker preferred, but not essential as training will be given.

He applied, was called for an interview in London, and hit lucky. The excellent reputation of the maths department at Manchester University and his 2:1 degree won the day.

'Can you start in April, for what is effectively the school's autumn term?' asked the interviewer.

'I'm supposed to give a term's notice,' Mike replied, 'but I'll resign immediately if you wish.'

'That won't be necessary. The Department of Education allow us to forgo the usual rules. We would like you to undertake a three-month course in Spanish at a college we support in Alicante, starting in January. Believe it or not, it's cheaper for us to send you there for a residential course than to train you in England. By immersing yourself in Spanish for three months, you should be fairly fluent by April. You realise that by going to South America in April, the Bolivian winter will be approaching?'

'So you want me to do three years, plus an extra term?'

'Yes, are you happy with that?'

'Of course.'

'The consolation is that the climate in La Paz is temperate. There's not much difference between winter and summer. In fact, the winter is in some ways more pleasant, as it is drier.'

Mike accepted the challenge, not daring to admit that he had been hopeless in French and Latin at school. Languages were not his strong point. He immediately put his flat on the market, finished the term in Cleveleys, went home for Christmas and left the Isle of Man for Spain on 5th January 1965. He would not see his parents until Easter when he would return briefly before departing for South America.

The course began on day one with the teacher walking into the classroom and not speaking a word of English. Her hand gestures encouraged the class to repeat what she was saying. On day two she introduced a variety of common objects – a glass, a bottle, a knife, a fork and so on. Still not a word of English had been spoken. Mike began to wonder if she could speak

English at all. By the end of the week, the students could say a few simple sentences. Each evening they had to watch Spanish television and by the end of the first month they were answering questions about the TV programmes with a vocabulary of about two hundred words. There were five other students on his course, all teachers. Three were going to South America, but to different countries. The other two were going to teach in the Philippines. After successfully completing their training, they had to commit to signing the three-year contract. It would take Mike to the middle of 1968 by which time, although he didn't know it, his father would be a widower.

He spent the Easter weekend with his parents. His mother didn't want him to go to the other side of the world and couldn't understand why he needed to make such dramatic changes to his life.

'What's wrong with the Isle of Man? You could easily get a job here,' she said.

'It's your fault,' he said to her on Easter Monday, when, yet again, she was harping on about him going to Bolivia. It was a year since he had spent the day making love with Mia. The memory had triggered a resentful mood that made him short on patience. In front of his father he yelled at his mother, 'If you'd let me marry Mia, I would still be teaching in Blackpool and she'd be here with us now.'

His father turned on him. He hadn't seen his dad so angry since he was a little boy. 'If you'd loved Mia, you would have found out where she'd gone and followed her to the ends of the earth,' he scolded.

'Mum never liked her,' Mike replied.

His mother, who was in the early stages of Alzheimer's, had begun to weep. 'I only wanted what was best for you,' she replied, defending her position. 'You never did know your place.'

The remark was red rag to a bull. Mike's blood pressure shot through the roof.

'Mia was everything I ever wanted. We would have been happy,' he screamed at his mother.

Mike then turned on his father. He blurted, without thinking, 'I converted to Catholicism for her, so don't you tell me I didn't love her.'

'You did what?' gasped his father.

'Yes, you've a son who became a Catholic.'

His mother began to cry.

'Now look what you've done,' said his father.

'No. You look what she's done. She ruined my chance of happiness with Mia.'

There followed a stony silence.

There's no way I'll ever tell them it was my fault that Mia left me.

His mother left the room, presumably to calm down. Mike heard her shuffling up the stairs. The two men stood eyeball to eyeball, slowly calming down.

'You know, I once told your mother that I would prefer you to have a wife who went to a Catholic church, than one who didn't go to church at all. I admired Mia. She had a lot of guts; getting out of that hellhole of Stanley Square when you're a Catholic and without a father took some doing. Martin Kermode thought very highly of her.'

'I know, Dad. It's water under the bridge now. I've given it much thought since last summer. I suspect Mia went to her sister in Australia to get away from me. I think she realised she was breaking up our family because of her devout Catholicism. We'd had a row, a serious disagreement over money, or rather, the lack of it. We'd realised we couldn't afford to get married for another year and neither of us would admit we'd failed. I expect Mia will stay out there and, in time, will marry an Ausssie. Who knows? Perhaps I'll meet a nice girl in La Paz. One thing's for sure: I'll make more money as a teacher in Bolivia than in the UK. My 2:1 maths degree has come in useful after all.'

'Had you explained the money problem, I would have been able to help. I could have got you a mortgage on favourable terms from my bank.'

'We wanted to be independent in case Mum threw it back in our faces at some future date. One thing Mia and I had in common was an independent streak. We're both black sheep. It's probably what attracted us to each other. It's been nine months since Mia left and returned her engagement ring. I'll keep it safe just in case. In the distant future, who knows?' His voice tailed away at the possibility that perhaps one day he might meet the only girl who could have made him truly happy and return the ring to her.

The following day he left the island. His mother never came to see him off; he didn't care if he ever saw her again. He didn't know it, but he never would.

Chapter 13

April 1965

Mike was astounded by how quickly he settled into the boarding school lifestyle. However, he'd been surprised when the principal had told him he'd been made a housemaster. Typically, he hadn't read the small print in his contract.

Not so easy was acclimatising to the altitude. La Paz, at twelve thousand feet, was the highest capital city in the world. He'd noticed, when flying into the international airport, that the aeroplane was half-empty. It had been explained that this was necessary as the air was so thin.

With 240 girls and boys of all ages from four to sixteen, the school, St Andrew's, had been founded in 1950 predominantly for the children of diplomats, and was situated in the southern, residential part of the city, almost 2,200 feet lower in altitude than the most northerly areas of La Paz. Consequently, temperatures could vary considerably across the city. With the Bolivian winter approaching, Mike was surprised how sunny and warm it was during the day, but how cold it became in the evening.

Not only did children of diplomats to the Bolivian government attend, but children of diplomats to the Peruvian and Chilean governments boarded from the age of four. Furthermore, such was the international reputation of the British educational system that the diplomats' children came from all corners of the globe, not just English-speaking countries. The Overseas Oxford and Cambridge "O" Level syllabuses were taught in English. Mike taught maths to pupils from the age of ten to the sixteen-year-olds taking their GCEs. He wondered why he had been given the three-month Spanish course as, within the school grounds that extended to seven acres, he never spoke anything other than English. The locally recruited domestic staff, who wished to improve their English, insisted on speaking it all the time. Furthermore, the Bolivian teachers, about half of the staff, were fluent in English.

There were four houses, two for boys and two for girls, each with approximately thirty-five pupils. The children of the diplomats based in La Paz were usually day pupils. The other boys' housemaster, Walter, taught history.

He explained, 'It's because we're single and it's cheaper to give us free board and lodging.'

Living in the school as a housemaster kept Mike busy. He was, effectively, working seven days per week. The weekends were, if anything, busier than schooldays. Saturdays were taken up with lessons in the morning and organised sports in the afternoon. Sundays involved a non-denominational service in the school's church in the morning and extra-curricular activities in the afternoons, such as sailing on nearby Lake Titicaca, where the water temperature remains constant all year at 10° C, and was an hour away in the school's minibus, or skiing in the Cotapata Park on the edge of the Andes. He would have liked to have joined the La Paz golf club on the east side of town. He'd calculated that his drives would probably travel fifty yards further owing to the rarefied air, but it was not a practical option as finding half a day for a round of golf at weekends would be impossible. Every evening his duties included supervising meals, checking the boys' ablutions and ensuring lights out.

The only time Mike had to himself was after ten o'clock when he was too exhausted to do anything other than read a few chapters of a novel, knowing that in eight hours the next round of daily school life would begin.

His first monthly cheque had come as a bolt from the blue. He discovered he was being paid in Bolivian bolivianos, known as BOBs. As a result of inflation over a period of thirty-odd years, twelve months previously had seen the introduction of a new peso BOB at the rate of one to one thousand old BOBs. However, inflation continued and, having re-read his contract, he realised he had no alternative other than to accept the South American currency. Consequently, he began stashing away the equivalent of US $50 monthly in a deposit account with the La Paz branch of the Chase-Manhattan Bank. Each month the amount of BOBs required to make up the $50 increased. However, with no bills to pay, his balance slowly increased so that he would not need to dig into his savings to make the most of his school holidays. He hoped that by the end of his contract, he would have saved over $2,000 including interest – sufficient to put a substantial deposit on a property when he returned to England. Furthermore, with the pound sterling beginning to weaken against the US dollar, his financial future looked promising.

He had hoped that there would be opportunities to travel widely during his three years in Bolivia. Before leaving Britain, he had drawn up a list of places to visit. It included Tierra del Fuego, Manaus where Caruso had sung in the Opera House, Devil's Island to sit on the chair of Dreyfus, and sailing through the Panama Canal. However, he had totally underestimated the scale of his ambitions. To get to Manaus was a twenty-hour flight, involving changing aircraft twice. French Guiana was even further away. Determined to see something of the continent on a limited budget, he decided to purchase an off-road Honda and use a one-man tent to explore Chile, Peru and Ecuador. To travel further south than Chile's capital, Santiago 1,500 miles away, looked impossible. He therefore, of necessity, began to modify his plans. The sheer scale of the continent was unimaginable to a Manxman. Brought up with a map of the Isle of Man on every classroom wall at junior school, he knew that to travel from the top of a map to the bottom was a forty-five minute journey. This false sixth sense had carried over to all maps. Bolivia was twice the area of the UK, with relatively primitive communications by rail and road.

Furthermore, he was having doubts about the security situation. Chile was in turmoil. Allende's Marxists, perhaps inspired by Castro's success in Cuba, were rumoured to be gaining popularity. Among the school staff, some of whom had close contact with the consular officials, it was being suggested that the CIA was plotting a coup. Things were no better in Peru where the military was struggling to counter the communist guerrillas. By contrast the Bolivian military rulers, who had come to power shortly before Mike arrived, ensured that stability and the rule of law were the norm. Political repression it may have been, but life was safe on a day-to-day basis.

Before the school's winter holiday began, Mike accepted an offer from the headmaster to remain in the empty school for the six-week duration as the de facto caretaker. A generous remuneration was agreed. It gave Mike time to explore La Paz on most mornings. Furthermore, the head had contacted the secretary of the golf club, who agreed to allow Mike to become a temporary member for July and August. The weather was sunny and dry, but bitterly cold. On only five days was there snow on the course which usually had cleared by late afternoon. This allowed him to play fairly regularly in the afternoons. He discovered that the Bolivians played with the bigger 1.68 inch diameter American ball, as opposed to the British 1.62 inch ball. His drives, therefore, never went as far as he had calculated.

He also stayed in the school over the four-week Christmas and New Year holiday when temperatures were only five degrees warmer than in July, but the days were much wetter. He planned his trip to the north of the country for the next mid-year vacation. The Pando region is where the three major Bolivian rivers – the Mamore, the Beni and the Dios – become tributaries of the Amazon. The Bolivian jungle was known to contain sloths – the world's slowest animal, capybaras – the world's biggest rodent, and anacondas – one of the world's largest snakes. He wanted to see all three. It would take him over a week to get from La Paz to the Amazon.

Consequently, his holidays, he decided, would have to be confined to Bolivia. However, such a diverse geography – the Andes to the east, the Amazonian jungle, and the plains and warm valleys in the south near Argentina – would ensure the vacations would be varied and interesting.

Apart from Walter, the rest of the staff were typically ten years older and settled domestically. The two girls' house-mistresses were both middle-aged spinsters and locally recruited. Walter had few interests that Mike could share. Consequently, life, when not busy with the children, was lonely. He was occasionally invited to dinner parties hosted by one or two of the more sociable teaching staff or the minor UK diplomats – of whom there were only a handful in the small British Embassy. However, there were never any unattached females present. The absence of the opposite sex triggered thoughts about why he was in Bolivia. He'd gone to get away from Mia and yet, he gradually thought more and more about her, their year together, and wondered what she would be doing.

Does she think about me?

Where is she now?

How could I get in touch with her?
Would she have me back?

He found that reflecting about her gave him comfort, particularly at night when he was about to fall asleep. He would yearn for her warmth – that strange effect she had on him when they were close: the sheen on her face, the smoothness of her delicate skin, her puckered lips and longing eyes when they kissed. The thought would make him glow, keeping out the cold harshness of the real world. His last reflections, as he would fall asleep, were of the pair of them nestling together, safe from the outside world. It was ironic, but he was dreaming more about her than ever. He concluded they had been meant for each other. He'd had his chance and blown it. Falling in love with Mia had been a new experience for him. No other girl had made him feel the same way, so he had not recognised it until it was too late. It puzzled him that when they had been together, they were always on their own. They could have been anywhere – Timbuktu or Siberia, it would have made no difference. He speculated whether he should resign and chance going across the Pacific to try and find her in Australia. He was convinced she was with her sister in Sydney, but his mathematical brain was telling him the statistical chances of finding her were zero. He knew little or nothing of Liz, or even Liz's surname, assuming she was married.

After having returned from camping in the north of Bolivia with his trusty Honda, he realised that he was faced with either becoming a recluse for the rest of his time in La Paz or seeking friendship outside the school's small social circle. He made enquiries and found a bridge club, but discovered the members were at least twenty years older. He located a badminton club. It was thriving and, to his astonishment, he found the shuttlecocks were specially designed for the thin air. The females in the club, which was attached to a nearby church, St Columba's, tended to be aged anywhere between fifteen and thirty. All were extremely attractive in the Latin style – swarthy skin with jet black hair. For the first time, he was glad that his Spanish was reasonably proficient.

One girl in particular was friendly; she had a cheerful smile with gorgeous dimples. She was about his age and a junior doctor in the university hospital in the area of Achocalla in the south of La Paz. Maurina, however, wanted to improve her English. Yet again, whenever he talked with locals, he was frustrated at not being able to practise his Spanish. She accepted his invitation for a date, but surprised him by insisting they go to McDonald's before they went to the cinema to see the latest James Bond movie, *Thunderball*, with Spanish sub-titles. Their friendship blossomed, but not in a passionate way. Time together was mostly confined to the evenings if he could get Walter to cover for him. He played badminton with her weekly as well as going to the cinema and occasional concerts. As the Christmas period approached, she came to several school parties, dances and concerts. Afterwards the staff would comment favourably about her. They seemed keen that his relationship with her should flourish into something permanent. However, it was not to be. When he finally met her parents, they encouraged him to attend their RC church, St Diego's, and meet their local priest. When he explained he had to work on Sundays, they visibly cooled. Perhaps not believing him and thinking he wasn't serious about their daughter, the romance cooled too. He thought about telling them he was a Roman Catholic convert, but had second thoughts when he remembered his outburst to Mia, 'You can bugger off to your bloody church for all I care'. The words still haunted him and he wondered if he was, deep down, a religious bigot like so many he knew in the Isle of Man.

How could I have said such a thing?

I might as well have stabbed her in the back.

His friendship with Maurina from there on began to fade, and she was the nearest he came to a fruitful relationship with a woman in Bolivia.

The following year, he travelled south-east to the border with Argentina. There, he came across a hippie community who made him very welcome, possibly because he was travelling alone on a motorbike. Copious quantities of rough, red wine with barbequed steaks were consumed every evening. On several mornings Mike awoke in his tent to find a different woman sleeping next to him. He would later swear that he couldn't remember how they got there. When he returned to La Paz, a letter was waiting from his father to tell him his mother had died. The burial had long passed and there was nothing he could do except to send a condolence letter to his father by return. He knew, however, that even if he could have made the funeral in time, he wouldn't have bothered. His mother had lost him over Mia. Perhaps unfairly he would never forgive his mother to the day he died. Revengeful and spiteful were two more adjectives that could be used to describe Mike.

When the "O" Level exams finished in mid-June 1968, Mike packed his bags and flew back to Britain via Caracas, Madrid and London.

He was astounded by how badly his father had taken the loss of his wife. The fine, upright, smart man Mike had remembered from three years previously had faded to an old man living on his own. Although still only in his fifties and having taken early retirement from the bank, he appeared to have lost all his interests – no longer taking part in the bridge club or the bowling club. He would sit and stare at a blank TV screen and fall asleep. Mike tried to get him out of his rut while at the same time searching for a job.

Finding a suitable position proved easier than helping his father. Maths teachers were not two-a-penny. After a quick interview with the agents Gabbitas-Thring in London, he accepted the post of head of maths in a private school fifteen miles to the east of Kendal in Westmorland. Its geographical location would allow him to make easy, swift trips to the island via Blackpool Airport to see his father.

Chapter 14

June 1964

The 707 arrived at Sydney airport late in the afternoon. I was dazzled on stepping out of the plane by the bright sunlight and clear blue sky. Despite it being the Australian winter, it felt warm as I walked from the aircraft to the terminal. There, waiting for me, was my elder sister who, despite my not having seen her for nigh on a decade, I recognised immediately. The cordiality of our greeting, as we hugged, had us both in tears.

'Welcome to Australia. It's wonderful to see you after all these years. You're looking fantastic.'

'Mum's told you why I've come, hasn't she?' I asked hesitatingly.

'She rang me the day you left the island. Don't worry. Everything will work out fine, you'll see. To be honest, I'm excited at the idea of becoming an aunty.'

As we travelled into town, Liz explained she shared a house with her Thai partner, Darika, in a fashionable, older part of Sydney. Both in their mid-to-late thirties, they had met when working as caterers on a cruise ship and became good friends. An opportunity had arisen to buy a down-at-heel bistro in a row of terraced properties and they had taken it. An interior decorator – a friend of Darika – had changed the ambiance to reflect the menu of Darika's national dishes.

Darika greeted me warmly when we arrived. 'Welcome to our home,' she enthused. 'Liz has told me all about you.' Clearly excited, she wanted to show me the restaurant.

The brasserie was quite large, capable of seating fifty people. Liz looked after the front of house, while Darika was the chef with two Thai assistants. There were four further fulltime staff: two barmen and two waitresses, as well as some occasional weekend helpers. The successful business had been open about four years. It was closed on Mondays, but busy during the rest of the week.

Impatient, as always, Liz could hardly wait for Darika to finish. 'Come upstairs. See what I've done in the last two days.' She carried my suitcase and led the way to my bedroom on the second floor. Liz had worked hard to prepare it for me – decorating it as a nursery in bright colours.

'What do you think?'

'It's lovely, Liz, but you shouldn't have bothered.'

'I've enjoyed doing it. Now unpack and then come down-stairs. Our first customers don't arrive until 7.30 this evening, so I thought we could have our meal early, and then you can go to bed. You must be shattered after such a tiring flight.'

'I don't feel too bad, but I am ready for something other than airline food.'

Their welcome had been so friendly that, as I packed, I temporarily forgot my reasons for being there.

During our meal together, I confided my secrets to Liz and told her the whole truth – that I had not been raped and was still desperately in love with Mike.

'What happened at Jenny's cottage was as much my fault as Mike's,' I explained.

I hoped that by confessing to my eldest sister, it would, in some way, go towards relieving the pain of sin. She listened sympathetically and made no criticism of my behaviour.

'I think you should keep the baby and live here for as long as you like. Perhaps someday you and Mike can meet up and you will be able to present him with his child,' she said.

Heartened and uplifted by her attitude, I felt more upbeat than I had since telling Mum about my pregnancy. I knew Liz's support over the next year would strengthen my ability to cope with whatever the future might bring.

It was not until I went to bed that evening, however, that I felt homesick. Depression suddenly returned with a vengeance. As I knelt in prayer, I began talking to Mike as if he was in the room.

'How have we got ourselves into this mess, Mike?' I asked.

It was only in my imagination – some would say wishful thinking, but

I heard him reply, 'I will always love you, Mia. If we never meet again in this world, I will be waiting for you in the next.'

'Please come and take me home, Mike. I will do anything for you.'

'It's impossible now, Mia. Someday I will meet you and our baby. Just bring him up in your faith.'

'Are we to have a boy, then?'

But there was no reply. He'd gone.

I knew it was wrong that I was to have his baby on the other side of the world simply because I had lied to Father Johns and my mother about being raped. It was a cowardly, immoral act. I asked Mike for forgiveness and then prayed for absolution. However, deep inside I believed I had damned myself to serve in purgatory for ever. Despite feeling shattered, it took ages to get to sleep.

When finally I nodded off, I slept through to four o'clock the following afternoon. The journey had been exhausting and I needed a further two days to fully recover.

As I watched how the restaurant functioned during the following weeks, I saw what hard work it was. I observed the clientele, studied their behaviour and began to recognise awkward buggers before their grumbles began. It was similar to being an air hostess, where a problem foreseen was a problem avoided. I gradually began helping more and more, occasionally in the kitchen, but mostly as either a waitress or behind the bar. My depression slowly lifted as Liz took every opportunity to show me the sights of Sydney on her free days. What a wonderful city it is. My overriding memory was not its architecture or people, but the sky – it always seemed so blue.

As the weather began to get warmer, we would venture further afield despite 'Fred', my bump, getting bigger. As the time for my delivery drew near, I drifted into a state of limbo. Whenever Fred kicked, I would put my hand on my bump and say to myself, *Hello Mike, how are you today?* He would reply with one kick for *OK* and two kicks for *I'm missing you.* My heart was still bleeding for him. Every day I thought about Mike and our baby. Would it be a boy or a girl? Mike and I had often dreamed about the names we would give our family. We had joked we were going to have ten children. The first boys' names would be Matthew, Mark, Luke and John. The first girl was to be Christina, then Mary, and so on.

But my conscience kept pricking me. I was thinking more and more about the sin I had committed. I had attended Mass twice weekly since arriving and as I began to get bigger, other churchgoers were noticing Fred growing and were putting two and two together.

Where's the father?

She's having a bastard.

It's funny that in these circumstances you think the worst. Liz would try to keep my spirits high. 'You're supposed to get post-natal depression, not pre-natal depression,' she would say.

I would smile and hope that I would get through the trauma. Nonetheless, I became ever more desperate knowing there wasn't going to be a father for Fred. I used to pray every day that Mike would walk through the door, put his arms around me and say, 'I've come to marry you and take you home.' But he never did. God was not hearing my prayers and I began to become somewhat cynical about my deeply held faith in the Almighty.

Matt's birth, just before Christmas, on 16th December, was difficult. I was in labour for ten hours and forceps were required. However, within hours he was baptised by the hospital's priest and after we left hospital, everything changed. I was too busy to worry about Mike. Matt's arrival cured my unhappiness. I loved having him all to myself: feeding him, changing his terry towelling nappies, putting him to bed, and taking him for long walks. The first six months of his life were wonderful and as he began to grow and take his own form, his face grew ever more like Mike's. Mike had come to live with me in the shape of my own son. By the time of Matt's first birthday, I was hardly ever thinking of Mike. Matt was everything to me. Days, even weeks, could pass without my thinking how Mike might be coping back in Britain. Time was healing my wounds.

I was beginning to accept my position in life – that of a single mum. Without realising it, my steely backbone, so prevalent as a youngster when dealing with either intimidation from the nuns or the bullies from Palmerston Park, had returned. My confidence and self-belief had come back. My resolve to survive the future, whatever it might throw at Matt and me was remorseless. The thought that I could still fire-up a bonfire look made me smile and heartened my determination to come through on top.

As Matt's second birthday approached, he was big enough to accompany me when I went to Mass on Sunday mornings with Liz. Initially, we had left at the end of the service, but we gradually began to stay behind and talk, over a cup of coffee, to a small group of Liz's friends, often clientele. I had noticed a man on several occasions looking at me. He was tall, handsome, with a hint of grey hair around his temples. He reminded me of Stewart Granger. I guessed he was ten years older than me. When one week I returned his smile, he came across to us. He introduced himself as Phil Cookson. We chatted politely, but I found out very little about him. However, the following Wednesday he turned up in the restaurant with some friends. I was waitressing that evening. He admitted he had made enquiries about Liz and I after we had left church, discovered Liz had a restaurant and 'Hey presto' was the way he put it. When he left, he booked a table for the following Saturday.

I went to bed excited that a handsome man could show interest in a single mother. I told myself not to be silly.

Expect nothing and you will not be disappointed.

Nonetheless, my juices were flowing for the first time in several years and my heart fluttered for the next two days, hoping he would return.

He arrived with different friends. When leaving, he asked, 'Will I see you at church tomorrow?'

I nodded, embarrassed by my inability to make conversation.

Liz could see what was happening. 'He's going to ask you out,' she said when he'd gone. 'What are you going to do?'

'I don't know. What should I do?'

'Well, you can't become a nun and you can't stay single for ever. Especially not at your age,' she joked. 'So, agree.'

Sure enough, he asked me out and on Monday, he took me to a swanky bar at the opera house overlooking Sydney harbour. He told me he was an architect working for an international firm based in London. The company had offices in New York, Singapore, Johannesburg and Sydney. He was on a six-month detachment. I encouraged him to tell me as much about himself as possible to fill the time. I was worried that if I told him about Matt too soon, he might not wish to see me again. It was a silly ploy as he had seen Matt with me at church. Sure enough, he eventually asked the question I had been dreading.

'What is the little boy's name?'

I swallowed hard and bit the bullet. I blurted, 'His name is Matt. His father lives in England and doesn't know of his existence. It's a long story and I'm sure you don't want to know about my problems.'

He immediately apologised. 'I'm sorry. I didn't intend to be nosy.'

I replied that it was OK and, embarrassed, mumbled something about telling him what had happened another time.

To my delight, he replied, 'I would like that very much. When can we see each other again?'

We began courting, if that's the right word, twice weekly as well as seeing each other after Sunday Mass. We often went for long walks with Matt in the pushchair. Phil was not in the least embarrassed with Matt. He would pick him up, play with him and bring him presents. Three months had passed. We had started playing golf together. Phil was impressed that I had a brother who was an assistant pro. He congratulated me on my swing and the fact that I could break 90 gross regularly. He was a member of a golf club, known as The Berkshires, near Ascot and had a respectable handicap of eleven. It was one afternoon when I had just beaten him on the seventeenth green that he asked me to marry him. During our dating, he had always been cool. We hadn't even kissed passionately. I was somewhat flabbergasted, for although I liked him and enjoyed his company, this came as something of a bombshell.

I must have looked blank for he quickly continued, 'I have to return to London next month. Come back as my wife. We can have Matt's surname changed by deed poll. I will accept him as my own and have his birth certificate changed accordingly.' I remained dumbfounded. 'It will all be above board and legal,' he added.

I didn't know how to respond for several minutes and then asked, 'What will your parents say if you come home with a wife, and a son who cannot possibly be yours?'

'I'm forty next birthday. I have my own house in Sunningdale and I am not without a bob or two. When they see what a wonderful person you are, they will soon love you like I do. There's nothing to worry about.'

I wasn't convinced. For the first time in ages I remembered Mike's mother and the awkward relationship I'd had with her.

'Can I think about it?' I replied. I was thinking, *I'll need to discuss this with Liz.*

What will my mother think if I return to England with a husband?

I asked Liz for her reaction.

'Why do you think I'm still single?' she replied.

'I don't know. I've never thought about it.'

She continued, 'There's an old Persian proverb along the lines that you only have one true love in life, all the others are experiences. Face up to the fact that Mike has gone. You lost him and he'll almost certainly never come back. This is your opportunity to find happiness with Phil. Don't be a fool, go for it. Good men are hard to find. Back home only Mum and the priest knew you were pregnant when you left. Neither Jenny nor David knew?'

I nodded that they didn't know.

'You'll be able to convince everyone on the island that Matt is Phil's son.'

'Liz, you haven't explained why you are still single.'

'Do you remember Billy McNeil who lived in Derby Road, near us?'

'Vaguely.'

'We went out together for four years and fell out over nothing; money I think, or rather a lack of it. It's why I went to work on cruise liners and ended up in Australia. There have been several boyfriends since, but I couldn't shake Billy out of my system. Time has passed me by, Mia. Don't turn down your second chance.'

And so, on Monday, 5th June 1967, we married quietly. Phil adopted Matt as his own. His birth certificate was amended to show Phil as the father. He'd sworn an affidavit to that effect. A few weeks later we flew home together to England. My lifestyle as the wife of a wealthy architect was to raise my expectations and horizons dramatically.

There was just one problem. Mike was Matt's biological father. Could I now build a successful home with Phil as Matt's surrogate father? I remembered Liz's words about love and experiencing love. Was it Phil or Mike who was my true love? I wanted it to be Phil. I vowed to try hard for it to be Phil. However, something in my gut was telling me it would not be easy.

Chapter 15

July 1967

For the first weeks at Sunningdale, I could have been on the back of the moon. I knew nothing about Phil's family, his house or his work schedule: up at six o'clock, a rushed breakfast, and catch the 7.10 am train to Waterloo. I would then be on my own until he returned in the evening, usually around 6.30 pm. The day with Matt was usually spent shopping for essentials, or taking him for walks in his pushchair. However, Sunningdale was a million miles away from Stanley Square. The gentlemen you met in the street would smile, raise their hats and say, 'Good morning.' They saw me as a young, married mother with a beautiful son. All the houses had manicured gardens. There wasn't a scrap of refuse to be seen. However, not being able to talk to Liz, Darika or the other workers in the restaurant, meant I was lonely. Three years previously I had been homesick for the Isle of Man, now I was homesick for Sydney. For the first time in my life I was not earning a wage and I found asking Phil for housekeeping money embarrassing. To be fair, he quickly set up my own bank account and ensured that a monthly standing order more than sufficiently covered all our expenses, plus a generous personal allowance. My upbringing had taught me the value of money. Prudence could have been my middle name. I formed the opinion that Phil had never had to scrape for dough and, as a senior partner in his firm, he expected us to live a lavish lifestyle with dinner parties on most weekends, either home or away. The problem of transport was also rapidly solved when Phil bought me a new Austin Mini Cooper. It was not the most practical car when you have to hump a pushchair around, but it gave me so much freedom whether going to Richmond, Reading or anywhere in between.

Finding a babysitter was never a problem; neither in the evenings when I would meet Phil in London to take in a show, nor at weekends. Phil, being an only child, meant there was no competition for his parents' services. They were both retired and lived a short distance away near Guildford.

On the evening we arrived back in the UK, they met us at Heathrow. Phil had tactfully explained to me before leaving Australia that I would be introduced to them and his friends as a recently bereaved widow whose husband had been killed in a surfing accident soon after Matt was born. He told his father that he had changed Matt's surname by deed poll. I had initially been reluctant to accept this subterfuge, but after discussing it with Liz, I agreed it made sense.

For the first three or four years of our marriage, however, whenever I was introduced to strangers in this way, it always grated. Rather than erasing the memory of Mike, it did the opposite. Memories of how we had conceived Matt in Jenny's cottage that Easter Monday would flood back. For a few fleeting seconds, I would see myself lying on the floor in front of a roaring fire wrapped in Mike's arms. An ice-cold shudder would go down my spine. I imagined my cheeks were flushing, though they probably weren't. My conscience would make it difficult to affect an air of normality during the conversation.

Phil's parents were to remain ignorant of the truth about Matt's biological father until the day they died. Mike was, therefore, officially written out of my life by my husband. I had agreed to the deviousness, but what alternative was there? Mike's son had become a Cookson and he, too, would never know the truth; at least not until after I had died. I had decided I would then come clean with him in a letter lodged with a solicitor who worked for my old company in Douglas. I continued to live with this chicanery for the rest of my life. It wasn't easy. Occasionally, I would admit my deception in the confessional. The priest would give absolution, but I never fully forgave myself.

Fortunately, Phil's parents accepted Matt as if he was their true grandson. Phil's dad decorated the small bedroom as a little boy's room – pictures of spaceships on the wall, the ceiling painted with planets and stars, and he built a bunk bed that looked like a rocket. Their enthusiasm to babysit allowed Phil and me to maximise weekends away, often playing golf. During the week I would drive Matt to places such as Windsor, or push him around Virginia Water. Nonetheless, becoming a full-time housewife took some getting used to, despite not wanting for anything.

After four months, I had found a routine and Mum flew over to stay with us for Christmas. I took her to see the touristy sights, such as Beaconsfield's model village and Windsor Castle.

'Are you happy?' she asked at one point.

Her question threw me for a minute and I queried, 'What do you mean?'

'You know what I mean,' she replied in her typical mother-to-daughter, down-to-earth tone.

I knew what she was implying, but I didn't want to admit it. I hadn't expected her to mention Mike, as I thought she would have long forgotten him. And yet, here was my mother indirectly quizzing me about him. I knew I had betrayed her, as well as Phil's parents. The deception was compounded by the fact that Phil didn't know about my lies either. For some reason or other, Phil, his parents and my mum never confided in each other about Matt's background. It was as if none of them wanted to know the truth. Mum was to take to her grave the belief that Mike had raped me. My consequent pangs of conscience have haunted me ever since. Praying for absolution at church never wiped away my iniquity.

'Yes, of course I'm happy,' I replied.

'Then you must make the most of what you've got. Have more babies, don't allow Matt to be on his own.'

Her wish was to fall on deaf ears. Although Phil and I had a full and active sex life, I never became pregnant again. I often wondered if it was God's retribution. Was I getting my just deserts? I was to discover many years later that Phil had seen a specialist in Harley Street who had assured him that all was well. It was just one of those things that Matt was destined to remain my only child.

As Matt grew up, he accompanied me to church and attended the nearest Roman Catholic junior school in South Ascot, two miles away. He became an altar-boy at the Sacred Heart Church in Sunningdale. Phil's Catholicism could best be described as secular. He once admitted his attendances in Sydney had been purely for social purposes.

Smiling, he added, 'And it worked.' However, he had no hang-ups over my strict upbringing of Matt. Phil's parents were also 'high-days and holidays' Catholics. Their attitude to my raising Matt in the Roman faith was one of inactive co-operation.

With Phil's company doing well around the world, he frequently went on secondments to South Africa, Australia or America. On shorter trips

I would accompany him for up to two weeks while Matt would stay with his grandparents. We moved up market to a larger house on the edge of the golf course at Wentworth. Its back garden edged onto the fifth fairway on the east course. Neighbours included Danny Blanchflower and Eric Sykes. All were keen golfers and became friends with whom we regularly had dinner parties. Everything was rosy in the garden.

When Matt reached eleven years of age, Phil decided to send him to Wellington College, about twelve miles away, as a boarder. Phil was an Old Wellingtonian himself. Initially, I was very reluctant to go along with this decision, as I didn't want Matt becoming too secular and losing his faith. However, Phil persisted and he started school in September 1975. I now freely admit that the public school lifestyle suited our son; he was both intelligent and athletic. It gave me freedom to accompany Phil when he was abroad, often for several months. On one occasion, when we were in Sydney, the last apartment in a block of flats designed by his firm was left unsold. Phil bought it at a knock-down price and registered me as the owner.

'Why did you do that?' I asked.

'For tax purposes,' he replied grinning. 'It will be an investment for you should anything ever happen to me.'

It was the beginning of Phil building up a portfolio of properties both at home and abroad. After Mum's first visit to Sunningdale, Matt and I began going home to the Isle of Man and staying with her for the long summer holidays, sometimes for three or four weeks. Phil would join us for ten days. We had become high-flyers in all senses of the word. Phil's clients included pop stars and the nouveau riche who were buying large building plots in exotic places such as the West Indies and the Greek Islands. They all wanted their villas designed and built by Beaumont, Cookson and Lord. Consequently, Phil acquired apartments as investments, usually with me or Matt as owners, as far apart as Bermuda and Corfu. I became accustomed to travelling to such places and partying with the famous.

It was an enjoyable period of our lives, but only at a superficial level. The gloss shone on the surface, but underneath it was brittle and artificial. Backstabbing and plotting were rife. Agents would buy thousands of their stars' records or books to ensure they made the top ten. The wealthier the client, the more difficult it was to receive payment. Backhanders to agents, who made as much, if not more than, their clients were considered par for the course. I began to suspect Phil was tiring and noticed that he sought the peace of the Isle of Man more and more. Eventually he admitted he wanted to retire to the island sooner than later. We began seeking suitable properties and, without telling me, one day he flew over on the morning flight from Heathrow, viewed a large bungalow in the parish of Maughold that overlooked the lighthouse, paid the asking price by cheque, and came home that evening to give me the news. I was not best pleased that I hadn't been consulted.

Matt meanwhile was growing up and preparing for university. He had shown more interest in the sciences than the arts at school. On odd occasions I wondered if he might read mathematics like his biological father. In the end, he chose to study civil engineering at Imperial College, London, beginning his course in October 1982.

He would rib his father, 'I want to build bridges and tunnels, Dad, not poxy, flashy villas.'

'Ah, but you'll need an architect to design the bridge first,' Phil would reply. Secretly, Phil was very proud of Matt and gave him every encouragement, arranging several work experiences for him with a large firm in West London.

My mother died after Matt had gone to university. Osteoarthritis had taken its toll and she had slowly become less and less mobile. I had gone to the island for her final three weeks to help look after her. I was at her bedside when she passed away. The family priest, no longer Father Johns, who had retired, left around eleven o'clock having given her the last rites. I cried myself to sleep holding her hand. I awoke feeling very cold, still holding Mum's hand at 3.00 am. She was dead. All my memories of the good and bad times we'd had together flashed through my mind. I remembered swinging on the garden gate as a youngster waiting excitedly for the postman to arrive, hoping there would be an envelope with Mum's £2 allowance from my father; there rarely was. She had refused to get divorced. We would have been better off if she had.

The postman would show sympathy. 'Nothing today, love.' He knew what it meant to David and me. There would be no spare pennies for us to get a bottle of pop. I remembered Mum taking Jenny, David and me to the shore for picnics. She had knitted us swimsuits; when wet they weighed a ton! Perhaps their weight helped to make us stronger swimmers. I remembered her initial fondness for Mike and how disappointed she had been when she thought he had raped me.

I looked at her lying in bed and whispered, 'Mum, Mike never raped me; it was my fault.' She never heard my confession; it was too late. I remained with her, talking to her – 'Do you remember...' – until it was dawn before contacting her doctor. I had never felt so low since returning Mike's engagement ring in the packet of Woodbines.

Liz came from Australia for the funeral and it was the first time all four of Mum's children were together in one place since Liz had left almost twenty years previously. Then later that year, Phil's mum passed away and his father came to live with us. This curtailed my mobility. Going abroad with Phil had to be planned around his father's needs. It had been a bad year for the Cookson household.

When in 1988, Phil's dad was diagnosed with bowel cancer, I became a full-time carer. I nursed him for seven months before he went into a Macmillan Home for his last few months.

With Phil approaching sixty, one evening he confided, 'When Dad has gone, I want a simple, quiet retirement in our bungalow.'

I could see my husband had aged. I encouraged him to have a full medical before investing his pension funds in an annuity. He had always been fit and healthy. He was told that his occasional pain, from which he had been suffering for some years, was only mild angina. Phil shrugged it off as old age, but I was determined to watch his diet and curtail his drinking from then on.

'The late-night parties are going to have to stop,' I said, giving him a bonfire look and putting my foot down.

'It will be a relief. I haven't enjoyed them for years,' he admitted.

In the autumn of 1989 we sold up at Wentworth, getting double what we had paid for the property, and moved permanently to the island. We were on our own as Matt, having graduated with honours, had taken a job in Sydney.

Phil and I settled quickly into the slower pace of life. We joined the Ramsey Golf Club, a nice, laid-out, flat course, and the local Royal Bridge Club. As golf became slowly more strenuous for Phil, we joined the South Ramsey Bowling Club and found ourselves enjoying this game even more.

However, our Darby and Joan lifestyle was not to last. In October 1999, Phil had been persuaded to play in the Captain's Prize at the golf club. It was an awful day: wind and heavy rain. It was the type of weather in which we would normally stay at home rather than venture out. I had suggested he ring the club and tell them he had a stomach bug and couldn't play. However, he insisted he wouldn't let his pals down.

When the phone rang that fateful afternoon I knew something was not right. It was his pal, Frank Smith, a retired schoolmaster. 'Mia, you'd better come quickly. Phil fell over walking onto the eighteenth green and we had to call an ambulance.'

'Why, what's the matter?' I asked.

'He's been taken to the cottage hospital in Ramsey. I am ringing you from there. They have him on a ventilator. Please drop what you are doing and come at once.'

I have never driven the four miles to Ramsey so quickly, but I was not to see Phil alive. He'd had a heart attack and died soon after reaching the hospital. A post-mortem revealed a weakness in his heart that he'd probably had all his life. I was decimated. Matt was in Australia and I was glad I had David, my brother, to help me with the arrangements for the service: contacting our friends in England, organising the wake's catering and so on.

Matt and his wife, Lisa, came home for the funeral. Afterwards we discussed the future and somewhat reluctantly I agreed it would make sense to emigrate to Australia. I put the bungalow up for sale and left a few weeks later. The summer climate out there was wonderful. I stayed with Liz and Darika. Helping in the restaurant acted as a pick-me-up; it was almost as if I hadn't been away. Where had thirty-six years gone? I saw the new millennium come in while watching the fireworks on Sydney Bridge. The plan was to move permanently into one of my apartments in Sydney, but after nine months away I felt I was in the wrong place. Despite being with Liz and regularly seeing Matt, I was missing the Isle of Man. In our ten years living in Maughold, Phil and I had made many friends. On top of that there was David and his family as well as Jenny and George. Eventually, I convinced myself that running away was not the answer. The bungalow had not been sold and, in July 2000, I returned to an empty house, full of ghosts and memories. I was sixty-two and decided I must face up to being a widow for the rest of my life.

I found myself going to church more often than for many a long year. Catholicism can give great comfort to a grieving widow. As Father

Bernard began to know me better, he asked me to help with transporting elderly parishioners to Mass, and I joined the group of ladies who 'did' the flowers.

I would visit Phil's grave at Maughold Church every week to keep it tidy and talk to him for ages, reminiscing and telling him how Matt was doing in Australia.

Friends had initially invited me to dinner parties, perhaps hoping to act as matchmakers. In time they left me alone. A year had gone by and I was, to all intents, socially becoming a recluse. I saw Jenny and David regularly, but it only reminded me of our early family hardship in Stanley Square. I was having difficulties readjusting to island life. I was finding living on my own depressing after my busy life with Phil.

Then one day in the local paper, *The Examiner*, there was an obituary for Mike's father. It triggered memories of Mike. I realised I hadn't thought about him for at least twenty years. I decided to go to Mr Moore's funeral at Rosemount Church in Douglas. I arrived in plenty of time to be able to sit in the back row. The church was packed and I recognised quite a few Isle of Man Bank employees. Memories of their staff Christmas ball almost forty years previously flashed through my mind. Mike entered the church behind the coffin with his wife, two children and two grandchildren. He gave the eulogy in a most professional manner and looked as handsome as he had done at The Palace in 1963. Although he had lost some hair, he hadn't put on weight and, clearly, kept himself fit. Throughout the service my mind drifted backwards and forwards, hardly hearing what was going on. I smiled as I remembered our high hopes of living together with ten children. Neither of us had been so prolific after all. When the coffin was taken from the church with Mike and his wife following, I wept. I remained in my pew for some minutes and prayed for the first and only time in a Protestant church: *Dear God, why did we have to fall out over something as trivial as a lack of money?*

As I slipped away quietly I kept wondering, *What would have happened if Mike and I had married each other?*

Chapter 16

September 1968

There she was in the staff room: all smiles, joie de vivre, stylishly coloured coiffured hair, a fine pair of legs beneath a knee-length, tight-fitting skirt, and the centre of attention among an otherwise dull group of tweed-jacketed males and plain women. He guessed she was about thirty. She turned out to be nine years older than him at thirty-six. She came over to him, her eyes sparkling.

'I'm Joyce Harvey, the headmaster's secretary. You must be the new maths master, Mr Moore?'

Strange – I would have thought the first person to introduce himself when I arrived would have been the headmaster.

'Please, call me Mike. You're not the school secretary, then?'

'The bursar also has a secretary. We split the duties.'

But I'll bet you're in charge, he thought.

'Let me introduce you to some of the others,' she said and immediately called across the room. 'Mr Jeffries, here is Mr Moore.' She turned to Mike, 'Mr Jeffries is head of physics and the science department.'

'I'm Jeff Jeffries.' He smiled and they shook hands.

Within five minutes, Joyce had introduced Mike to most of the other members of staff. Then he followed her upstairs to the principal's office to meet him for the first time.

'It's unusual for us to appoint a member of staff without interviewing him ourselves,' explained the head, after Joyce had introduced him. 'But as you will no doubt find out, your predecessor was fired at the end of last term when it was revealed he had been having an affair with a sixth former and her parents made a complaint. Your references with Gabbitas-

Thring were excellent and I see you have recently returned from Bolivia. That must have been quite an experience.'

'It was different. I saw much of the country during the holidays and, although half of the staff were locally recruited, everything was taught in English to the Overseas Oxbridge Syllabuses. It is a beautiful country, over twice the size of Britain, and the Bolivians are delightful. My Spanish is now quite fluent.'

'What are your domestic plans?'

'I'm staying in the Queen's Head until I find a place of my own.'

'I see you were a housemaster in La Paz.'

'Yes, but I would prefer to live off campus. It will give me more time to settle in and find my way about.'

The head laughed. 'I know what you mean. My job is 24/7, as it is for the heads of our six houses – two girls' houses and four boys' houses.'

The head gave him a brief summary of the school. It had 460 pupils aged from eleven to eighteen. Girls in the sixth form had been introduced three years previously and there were now girls in the first and second forms. The school strengths were music, rugby and outdoor pursuits. It was organised in departments such as science, maths, English, and social sciences such as geography and history. The strong languages' department taught Latin, French, German and Spanish.

'Day children are bussed in from as far away as Kendal and Penrith. We have almost forty Chinese boarders,' he added.

Over the next three weeks Mike concentrated on getting up to speed with his job. The most difficult class was the upper sixth who were half way through their "A" Level syllabus. He was to discover that one of the pupils in the mixed class of eleven was the girl who had been having the affair with his sacked predecessor. Mike could understand why; she was forward for her age, but a talented mathematician. The other ten were potentially chemistry, physics or medical undergraduates. He could see how giving her extra tuition to take the double maths syllabuses, separate pure and applied, to get to Cambridge university could easily have led to an ill-fated relationship. He approached the head with his quandary.

'She'll need extra tuition if she's to do well in pure and applied, but in view of what happened I feel I should not be alone with her.'

'What do you suggest?'

'I think you should explain to her parents that I think she can pass sufficiently well to get to Cambridge, but that I am only prepared to give her extra tuition in the presence of a responsible chaperone.'

And so Joyce and Mike were flung together. When the girl was given extra lessons, usually concluded with a half-hour problem to solve, Mike would sit with Joyce at the back of the classroom and they would converse quietly.

They were approaching half-term when Mike asked Joyce innocently, 'What are you doing this weekend?'

'Not a lot. I expect you're off for a dirty weekend?' she replied with a grin on her face.

'No such luck. I'm flying over to the Isle of Man from Blackpool to see my Dad.'

'Why not come around to my place for a meal before you go?'

'I'd love to, but as I've just said, I'm off to the Isle of Man. I'm catching the evening flight on Thursday and will be slipping away from school pronto.'

'I've never been to the island.'

'You could come with me if you like. There's a spare bedroom in Dad's house.'

'I'd love to.'

'That's all arranged then. I'll be leaving immediately after school finishes.'

They were interrupted by the sixth former. 'Mr Moore, I've finished.'

He looked at his watch. He whispered to Joyce, 'She's good. She's done the example in twenty minutes. It should take longer.'

While Joyce resumed reading her novel, a Mills and Boon book, Mike sat down next to his star pupil to go through the problem and comment on her solution.

'I've brought a friend over with me, Dad, who hasn't been to the island before. This is Joyce.'

His father's eyes lit up as he gave her the once-over.

The old man fancies her himself, thought Mike.

'Joyce could have the front bedroom and I'll have my old room.'

His father nodded approvingly.

'Tonight, I thought the three of us could go somewhere nice. How about The Groudle Glen? The restaurant is supposed to have a good reputation.'

Joyce's presence was a tonic to his father. He smartened himself up in his best suit, a clean shirt with a collar and tie before they went out.

Conversation never slackened as Joyce regaled her colourful past. Married at eighteen, she was divorced at twenty-one, remarried at twenty-three and re-divorced by twenty-seven. There seemed to be no holding back her libido. The absence of children was explained.

'My ex-husbands had big plonkers, but no balls.'

Mike expected his father to choke. Instead he roared with laughter. He was smitten by her joviality and vivacity.

I've not seen Dad so cheerful – ever!

It was no real surprise when after being in bed for half an hour and with snoring coming from his father's back bedroom, Joyce appeared in front of Mike wearing a see-through, pale blue nightie.

'I want you to prove you're not gay.'

Three years of pent-up passion in Bolivia was released over the next three hours, during which time he realised he hadn't had sex with a woman since Wendy. However, this was different. Joyce was much more experienced. Mike found himself in positions that were, presumably, in the *Kama Sutra*, but novel to him. Joyce was taking him in her stride. He was the pupil. She was the instructor.

And yet Mia flooded his thoughts. He fantasised he was with Mia – educating her in the new tricks Joyce was teaching him. Whilst actively embracing Joyce, his mind was in Andreas on Easter Monday, four years previously. Mia was in his arms, not Joyce. He was apologising profusely to Mia, asking her where she had been, probing to find out if she had made love to anyone else.

Did you miss me?

Am I the best lover you've ever had?

I'm going to give you ten babies.

And so his confused brain carried on, until he was exhausted. It dawned on Mike that inside him there remained a permanent link to Mia that would never be broken. He was still bonded to her, his one and only Mia.

Where are you now, Mia?

Thereafter, Mike's love-making became evermore experimental with Joyce and Mia slowly receded from his thoughts. Mike had never imagined there were women like Joyce. Her appetite seemed insatiable. He visualised he and Joyce becoming porn stars, so good were they in bed. He moved out of his digs into Joyce's terraced house, five miles from school. At Easter, they drove to Scotland and were married before the summer term resumed. They kept their association secret, even driving to school in separate cars until a member of staff met them together by chance at Sainsbury's in Kendal. The following Monday the staff room erupted with the news and an overdue party was hurriedly arranged the following weekend in the Queen's Head by the principal's wife.

By the summer holiday, however, Mike was beginning to realise that their relationship had been based solely on their sexual compatibility. They had little in common, but it was too late.

Marry in haste, repent at leisure; I can't be the first to make that mistake, he thought.

Joyce was pregnant; there was no retreat. Golf, badminton and bridge could fill Mike's week. For Joyce, reading romantic novels, often with a historic flavour and listening to popular music on the radio seemed to satisfy her spare time. In common there was the love of good food and wine. He acknowledged she was an exceptional cook. Their sex life remained exciting, exotic and erotic, but evenings before bed began to revolve around the TV.

As the New Year approached, they discussed the requirement for a bigger house. It was a commitment Mike didn't want to make as he saw it would create problems if he wished to cut their marriage ties in future and make a run for it. He had £2,000 saved from his time in Bolivia, but was loath to put it towards a mortgage. However, as Joyce's home was too small for a family and was taking some time to sell, there was little alternative but for him to buy the bigger home they needed. He became the owner of a £6,500 detached property with a £5,000 mortgage. It seemed a huge amount to a teacher earning £1,500 per year. However, by the time their daughter, Christina, was born, they had moved to their new home in Grange-over-Sands, twenty-five miles from school.

Joyce had given up her job to be a full-time mum. Her parents, living in London, could catch a train easily and visited two or three times annually. Within another year a second child was on the way. Matthew was born in 1971. There was no going back. Mike had become like the other masters – a Harris Tweed jacket with leather cuffs, baggy cavalry twill trousers and Hush Puppies. The only consolation was that he was an exceptional maths teacher, achieving outstanding results in the external exams. His pupils at "A" Level had a 100% record. By now he had acquired his own chair in the staff room and was on his way to becoming one of the crusty, cantankerous schoolmasters so loved in comedy sketches.

As the years wore on, he and Joyce settled into a dull domesticity: always short of money, but never quite having to borrow from the bank. Sex, still adventurous, kept them together. Holidays had to be camping. Initially they travelled to Scotland, but later they graduated to ready-erected tents in France. The two children grew up wanting for nothing as, somehow, Joyce found the resources to spoil them. Then, as she approached forty-five, Joyce began to complain about menstrual pains. The doctor recommended a full hysterectomy. The result was disastrous. She put on weight, no longer took care of herself and dedicated herself to the children at Mike's expense. Sex slowed to a stop. He had been married to Joyce for almost ten years, but now the only sexual excitement was to begin discreetly ogling some of the sixth-form girls.

Terms came and went. School years came and went. Children whom he had taught in the first form came and went with their "A" Levels. Nothing much changed. He watched his own children pass through school. Fortunately, school fees were waived in his contract – the big perk of teaching in a private school. He still had a 100% success rate at "A" Level. Half a dozen of his students had gone to study maths at Cambridge. It was a record second to none at the school. However, Mike's home life was routine, boring and badly in need of a buzz.

It was at the staff Christmas party, when in his late forties, that a corner was turned. While drinking his second glass of red wine with one of the younger members of staff, the junior English teacher mentioned that the two female lab technicians were waiting to be picked up.

'They want to be taken to a pub for further drinks. Are you game?' Willie asked.

Mike had been daydreaming that the next two weeks would mean living with Joyce 24/7. It was not a prospect he was looking forward to as he couldn't think of what to buy her for Christmas and her parents were coming up from London.

God only knows what I am going to do, he had been reflecting to himself.

'I'm game,' Mike replied without thinking through the consequences.

The two technicians were Viv, who was a married thirty-five-year-old, and Sandra who was in her early twenties and single. In Sandra's car, they followed Mike and Willie to a remote country pub near Rigmaden. They split up after downing a drink or two, and Mike found himself in a quiet lane with Viv. There was no slow build-up, nor a gradual approach to a climax. It was frenzied; their hands were inside the other's clothes within minutes. Her passion for lust was uncontrollable. She was doing it for the love of doing it. Viv didn't seem to care that Mike was married to the former principal's secretary, nor that she had two children of her own. She knew what she wanted from him and made sure she got it. For Mike it was like travelling back through time. Viv was a young version of Joyce. He'd hit the jackpot.

Their affair was to continue, on and off, but mostly on, for the next ten years. It kept Mike sane. It allowed him to tolerate Joyce so that whenever he wanted to strangle her, he could release his frustrations with Viv.

'I love you dunking me,' Viv had remarked early on in their liaison. The simile of dipping ginger snaps into tea didn't go amiss. Mike realised she was a vamp. He wasn't the only man in her life, but he didn't care. Consequently, they found themselves dunking in the lab storeroom, or driving into the country for a quickie during the lunch break. She always left him totally satisfied for another week.

In 1999, he had just turned fifty-eight. The school's nominal roll had fallen. Money had to be saved. The older, expensive teachers were targeted. A few days before the Easter holiday was due to begin the newly appointed head asked him whether he would like to consider taking early retirement at the end of the summer term. He discussed it with Joyce.

He knew he would miss the run-of-the-mill teaching that he secretly enjoyed. But could he survive without Viv? That really would be a drag. Grinding her regularly kept his prostate fit and him mentally young. He kidded himself he could still pull the birds and would find a new Viv nearer home. If nothing regularly got him out of the house in future and away from Joyce then he knew retirement would drive him insane.

He pondered the future. This, in turn, led him to reminisce about the past.

I wonder what happened to Mia.

He began fantasising about the wonderful times when nothing else mattered except being with Mia. During their year together, they had lived through the Profumo affair, Kennedy's assassination and the imprisonment of Nelson Mandela without as much as a blink. He realised he hadn't daydreamed about her for ages. He could still smell her perfume, feel the hair lacquer on his cheek, look into her mesmeric green eyes and remember the smoothness of her thighs as she resisted the advance of his hands.

Over the Easter weekend of the millennium, a year after retiring, he visited his father, now eighty. He had gone alone. Joyce had driven to see her parents who were retired in Torquay. While in Douglas, he sought out his old friend, Terry, and persuaded him to meet for a drink in The British, a pub on the North Quay on Easter Monday. The Dog's Home had long gone – knocked down to make way for a new Marks and Spencer's.

'Do you remember the day we went to play golf at Rowany, and we stopped at the airport?' Mike asked.

Terry looked at him, initially quizzically. Then after a short pause, he replied, 'The day you saw Mia? It must have been about, what, thirty-five years ago?'

'It's thirty-seven years ago – almost exactly,' Mike enthused. 'I often wonder what happened to her.'

Terry had followed a career in the Manx civil service and was about to retire as the head of the General Registry, the department that handles land deals and property sales.

'I can help you there.' He smiled. 'About ten, or maybe twelve years ago, she became the owner of a property in Maughold.'

'How do you know?'

'A bungalow that fetches £500,000 and was paid for by cash attracts the attention of the finance department's fraud investigators. It turned out that the guy was an architect in a big London firm. When he put the property in the name of Ms Mia Yvonne Mylrea, the investigators wondered why. They discovered she was his wife, and was Manx by birth. They delved into the sale and concluded it was for tax purposes, but wasn't illegal as she was registered as his secretary. When I saw Mia's name going through our books, it rang a bell. So I checked her out at the births, deaths and marriages registry next door. It was your Mia all right; they were married at St Mary's, here in Douglas. I remember you getting engaged.'

Terry added, as an afterthought, 'She was a stunner.'

'I knew Mia had married someone well off and lived in Berkshire. George, her brother-in-law, told me when I met him by accident some years ago. Perhaps they've bought the house as a holiday home? Any chance you could get me the address? I'd like to see it before I go back.'

'No problem. I'm back at work in the morning. I'll give you a ring first thing. What's your dad's phone number?'

The following afternoon, Mike drove to Maughold and found the bungalow. It was clearly empty. There was no sign of life. A *FOR SALE* sign hung outside. He noted the name of the estate agents, decided he would get the property's details, and drove to Ramsey.

'Can I help you, sir?' asked the assistant.

'I've seen a nice property at Maughold and would like the details, please.'

She smiled, asked for its location and nodded after Mike described where it was. She returned from a filing cabinet with the blurb and began the sales pitch.

'It has four bedrooms, two with en-suite facilities, a large lounge with views to Maughold Head, a thirty-foot breakfast kitchen … and a triple garage in half an acre.'

He waited for her to finish. 'Can I have a viewing?'

'The owner, a widow, has emigrated to Australia to live with her son. We can only give viewings with a member of our staff present. If you give me your details, I could arrange for someone to show you around. Tomorrow, perhaps?'

Mia's gone to bloody Australia again.

'I am staying in Douglas, but am going back to the mainland in the morning. I might arrange to come back next week. Thank you, I'll be in touch.'

He left with the glossy pamphlet, thinking, *I'll never see her again.*

A feeling of despondency had overwhelmed him by the time he reached Douglas. He was returning to his father's house in deep despair. He thought whether he should try and contact George. *He might give me her address, and I could write to her now that she's a widow.* However, his father was going downhill rapidly and a month later he had to move into a nursing home. Mike travelled to the island fortnightly to see him. Having celebrated his eighty-first birthday in September 2000, he died a few days later. Mike's black dog was consuming him. He had forgotten Mia – again.

Chapter 17

June 2003

Almost three years had passed since his father had died. Mike was still living with Joyce. The consolation was that she spent a lot of time in Torquay with her parents, who were aging rapidly. To keep her sweet, Mike accompanied her to Devon every couple of months, but life had become more and more monotonous and colourless. There was little to look forward to: golf on Tuesdays and Fridays, bridge on Wednesday afternoons and Sunday evenings, a Probus lunch on alternate Mondays. When he'd had his second cup of coffee in the morning and finished the crossword and Sudoku in the newspaper, he would sink into a pit of despair and ask himself, 'What is the point?'

Pouring his energies elsewhere had only served to increase his frustration. At the golf club his cronies believed differentiation was something to do with immigration. In the bridge club the women were overweight, wore ill-fitting bras and were old before their time. He'd sought a suitable middle-aged mistress in various clubs and societies – to no avail.

U3A – the University of the Third Age – with two-thirds of the membership female, should have been productive. The sections he'd tried – badminton, bowling, table tennis and rambling – brought no success. At the history society half the members would fall asleep before the guest speaker was halfway through the talk.

He'd had enough.

He looked at what he had laid out on the bed.

Not much to show for sixty-two years, he thought.

Where did it all go wrong?

He didn't answer his own question, but began to pack his small holdall, mentally checking off everything he would need for the next few days.

He knew he hadn't forgotten anything. He'd deliberated about this day, on and off, for some time. He began at his feet – a trick his father had taught him when he went away from home for a camping weekend with the boy scouts, aged eleven.

What? Fifty-odd years ago?

He smiled at the memory of his first night under canvas at the scout jamboree in the grounds of The Nunnery – a large, private mansion on the edge of Douglas. Six boys in a bell tent that leaked. It had poured all night and he had the wettest place in the tent. With his sleeping bag soaked, he'd walked the two miles to his home the following morning, annoying his parents who had planned being on their own for the weekend

Shoes? Yes.

Socks? Yes.

And so he carried on until…

Washing kit? Yes.

There was no one else in the house. Even his faithful cat had gone. The intense heat of the previous summer had been too much for her. With temperatures in the mid-thirties day after day, week after week, she had become more and more lethargic as she became dehydrated. He had tried bathing her with a sponge soaked in cool water. She had drunk very little and sunk into a coma. The vet had been unable to revive her, even with a saline drip. Mike had wept when she was put-down. He was ashamed to admit it, but he cared more for his cat than for his wife.

God, what an existence!

You work hard all your life and you end up like this.

Finally, when there isn't a money problem, there is nothing to spend it on except a wife who you can no longer bear looking at across the breakfast table.

He blamed all his difficulties on politicians whose only ambition was to get re-elected. The recent invasion of Iraq was typical – an exercise conducted by arrogant, self-important idiots who knew nothing of the lessons of history. He held the view that politicians had deliberately dumbed down society to the point where the masses couldn't see they were being conned by a bunch of incompetent clowns. All they cared about was power.

Forty years previously, as a young man, he had converted to Catholicism when he had fallen hook, line and sinker for a beautiful air hostess. Despite his education being steeped in logic, to win her hand in marriage, he had accepted the principles laid out in the Catechism, including the irrational belief that only Catholics could enter heaven. Over the intervening years, he had become increasingly cynical regarding the mysticisms of the Roman church. Now an agnostic, the thought of ending it all gave him great comfort, in spite of the possibility of an indefinite period spent in purgatory. He'd decided to go home for one last time. He would spend three days on the island where he'd been born, gone to school, played with friends and experienced his first taste of passion.

Since retiring, nostalgia had become his major solace – *the good old days.*

He would take one last look by going back in time. Then he would see if he had the courage to end it all.

He looked at his watch.

The bus stop was a five-minute walk. He locked the door.

He had sent Joyce and his daughter away to New Zealand for a three-week trekking holiday. Both had wanted to see South Island after watching the first *Lord of the Rings* film. He had seen this as the opportunity he had waited for. He had all the necessary letters explaining his actions in his overcoat pocket. He hadn't stamped them as he intended to post them from the Isle of Man, which had its own postal service. Five letters: one for his wife, two for his children, and one each for his solicitor and his bank manager.

As he walked to catch the bus, he continued asking himself, *Where did it all go wrong?*

He showed his senior citizen's bus pass to the driver and walked towards the back of the single-decker. There was the usual mix of passengers. All had one characteristic in common; *They can't look you in the eye.*

Are they too embarrassed to look at me?

Have I left my flies undone?

He glanced down.

No, they're OK.

What an uninspiring bunch.

Two scruffy kids busy tapping on their mobiles – probably texting each other. Three women, probably no older than him, wearing drab coats that suggested they no longer cared about their appearance. They hung onto their wheeled shopping baskets for grim death and stared blankly out of the bus window. There were two obese middle-aged men with thighs larger than his waist hidden beneath a protrusion that could only be their gross stomachs.

Why can't older people look smart?

I dig the garden dressed better.

He sat down and his mind went back to class 3B at junior school. Aged eight in 1949, he remembered his teacher, Miss Cubbon, giving the class an essay to write: *My Birthday Party.*

He had sat at his desk thinking, *What is there to write?*

Sucking his pencil, he had what authors call writer's block. There was nothing to write: *jelly, cakes and pop.*

What else is there to say about birthday parties?

Sitting next to him at their double desk was Hoggy Horton. He was busy scribbling away and had already covered half a page.

Mike screwed up his eyes and read that they'd had a chimney fire during Hoggy's party.

Brilliant!

He began writing, occasionally squinting to see if there were any more juicy bits that had occurred at the Horton household.

Half an hour later the teacher collected the scripts.

The next day the proverbial hit the fan. Both were called out in front of the class and accused of cheating. Neither would own up and both received smart smacks on their knuckles with a two-foot ruler.

I'd become excellent at lying and cheating, at only eight years of age.

The bus pulled into the railway station.

He bought his ticket – a first-class single to Liverpool. There was little point in saving pennies at this stage of his life by travelling second-class; and anyway, he was a snob. It was a trait he'd caught from his mother. She'd had delusions of grandeur – aspiring middle-class with no time for the hoi polloi.

Comfortably ensconced in the first-class compartment, he began to think of other instances where he had shown his true colours.

He remembered how useless he'd been at French in secondary school. In later life he would blame his performance on his poor hearing. He wasn't deaf, but his ears were insufficiently tuned to distinguish between the finer points of French pronunciation. He remembered an occasion in Nice, on the Cote d'Azur, when he'd been trying to find the railway station and had asked a stranger in the street, '*Excuse moi, monsieur. Ou est la gare?*'

The tall, distinguished gentleman looked at him, summed him up correctly as being British, and replied in perfect English, 'There is no war, monsieur.' The subtle difference in pronunciation between *gare* and *guerre* had clearly failed him.

His mind went back further to lessons with their French mistress and how some of the boys in his class, himself included, would drop their pens on the floor, so that when retrieving them, they would attempt to look up her skirt to gape at her fine pair of legs. He was on the road to becoming a pervert.

In his first French exam, just before Christmas, a question asked: *Translate into French: 'Let us go.'* He could remember the verb *Aller,* but little else.

He resorted to whispering to his best pal sitting next to him, whose mother was French and who, consequently, was much better at the subject than him, 'What's "Let us" in French?'

'*Laitue,*' was the barely audible reply.

He wrote, *Laitue nous allons.* And thought, *That's one question I'll have got right.*

Wrong!

The train pulled into Lime Street. He chose to walk to the Pier Head, a journey of about one mile. The fast Seacat ferry had already arrived from Douglas and boarding was rapid and simple.

He settled into the first-class lounge, accepted a free cup of coffee with a daily paper and made himself comfortable for the two-and-a-half-hour journey.

His mind continued to wander through his schooldays. He'd been average at most things. In the top class of a seven-form entry comprehensive school he'd usually been in the middle half of the class for most subjects, except maths which he'd found easy. His reports generally rang with the phrase, *Could do better.* This brought a regular admonishment from his father at the end of each term. Laziness was one of Mike's traits.

At sport he had been reasonably proficient. His best events were long distance swimming and cross-country running. He possessed stamina rather than speed and dexterity. He was the school cross-country champion for several years and swam in the Douglas Cross Bay Swim of two and a half miles. At school, when teams were being picked for games and the two captains could choose their side from the boys lined up against the wall, he was usually picked early on. He felt a deep concern for the regular last men. They were always the overweight intellectuals, invariably wearing glasses, who ended up playing outside-left and never getting the ball passed to them. A natural empathy for the underdog was one of his few positive characteristics. It may have explained his tendency to be something of a maverick and always playing the devil's advocate – speaking up for the rebel. Instinctively, he had always been an awkward bugger.

When he was fifteen, his father had been promoted to the position of branch manager in the Isle of Man Bank at Castletown. This necessitated Mike moving ten miles away from Douglas with his parents. A new mixed school awaited, where there were girls in the same class. These 'things' in skirts, with bumps on their chest, were a new breed. He'd last socialised with them at junior school where girls were boys with longer hair, could outrun most of his mates including himself, wrote neater, and read quicker. Now something had changed: their hair was still longer and they were, in general, cleverer, but they couldn't run as quick, didn't play football, and did cookery instead of woodwork.

Prior to going to his new school, his father had given him his one and only sex lesson.

'I suppose you know about girls, do you?' he'd asked.

Embarrassed and unsure what to say, Mike had replied, 'Yes, Dad.'

'That's all right then.'

End of tutorial.

The memory of the conversation that lasted less than thirty seconds was the only occasion he'd ever heard his father discuss sex and he'd not even said the 'S' word. Mike wondered if this lack of communication between himself and his father had been the cause of him being largely gauche with members of the opposite sex.

He pondered about his sex life at school. His only girlfriend, Helen, was chosen because she could partner him at badminton. A year younger than him, their friendship had developed slowly: taking her to the Picture House at Port Erin, then on long walks with her dog – all innocent events that gradually over a period became ever more intimate. Their relationship had been one big experiment that took several years to lead to its natural conclusion: firstly, holding hands in public; then a simple kiss that led to a French kiss; then pressing his chest against her's, which led to his hand fumbling under her coat and the associated increase of heavy breathing;

then learning to skilfully unhook her bra, which eventually led to each other's hands prising themselves between their thighs and achieving mutual satisfaction. As a result of his experience with Helen, he'd concluded that seduction was simply a matter of promising everything until you get what you want.

At Manchester University, she had remained his steady, always waiting for him when he came home. However, in Manchester his eye had wandered. He'd attempted to play the field behind her back, using his theory of seduction: flatter them, make them laugh, and then ply them with a gin and dry martini.

His system of sexual luring, ironically, had been a failure. The few girls that were added to his tally had disappointed him: too quick, too easy and too casual. He discovered that achievement was only enjoyable after a good chase. He'd learnt that to travel hopefully is a better thing than to arrive. Women confused him. They were a total paradox. He was never to fathom them out. During his three years as an undergraduate, girls came and went at parties, but sexual fulfilment eluded him.

After graduating at Manchester, he had gone to Leicester University, at the time the centre of excellence for research into the newly emerging comprehensive schools, to undertake teacher training. Throughout the first two terms of his PGCE year, he tried it on with several girls on his course, but to no avail. His lack of success had made him depressed. He'd changed his hairstyle – trying out a 'Tony Curtis' – but to no avail. He'd splashed more Old Spice on himself, even putting some on his underpants – it hadn't worked. Until that fateful day in April forty years ago when he'd seen Mia at the airport. And with that, his memory went into overdrive as he began thinking of the only woman who had stolen his heart, who was now living on the other side of the world, who he would never see again.

Chapter 18

June 2003

Mike began his first full day on the island exploring all his old haunts in Douglas. From The Sefton Hotel, he walked up Broadway to Murray's Road Junior School, which he'd attended for six years. The Victorian buildings had long been replaced by a flashier, brighter building that would not stand the test of time like its predecessor. Already it was looking shabby, resembling a cheap factory rather than the church-like structure it had replaced. Nevertheless, the playground was the same. In 1946, aged five, it was the site where he'd seen what appeared to be a fight at the bottom of the yard. A circle of noisy youngsters had congregated. He'd rushed to the scene to discover a boy eating a yellow tube – *a large lollipop*, he thought. None of the others who had gathered around, perhaps as many as thirty children, all excited and shouting, had seen such a thing. He had gone home at the end of the day to be told by his mother that it must have been a banana. 'They must be coming back into the shops,' she had remarked.

He retraced the route he must have taken a thousand times towards his first home in West Douglas, a distance of a mile and a half. He passed Salisbury Street Methodist Church Hall, where 3A and 3B were taught in what was the annex to the main school. It was in 3B that he had cheated poor Hoggy Horton. Nevertheless, although Miss Cubbon had punished him, she remained one of his favourite teachers. He had done well with her, and been moved up to 4A for the following academic year.

His old home hadn't changed; even the front door was the same. He went around to the back of the terraced houses. From the rear lane, the garden looked smaller, but was much neater. As he wandered around his old neighbourhood it struck him that the major difference was the number of cars. The houses hadn't changed, but in the whole of Westbourne Drive as a boy he could only remember two cars. One belonged to a taxi driver and the other to the father of one of his pals who managed the largest garage in Douglas. Now the road was full of parked cars, making it almost impassable.

His childhood, he recalled, had been generally happy. There had been plenty of boys in the neighbourhood about his age. As he grew up, he had been in a friendly gang that made the empty field at the bottom of the drive their own. It was the site of the annual bonfire on 5th November where a rival mob from nearby Tynwald Street would come and try to set alight, a day or two early, the fruit of their labours. The consequent warfare was largely throwing stones at each other, but occasionally hand-to-hand fighting would break out. The field had since become the site of an extension to Noble's Hospital.

Nowhere for the kids to play now, came to his mind.

The dozen or so members of his band attended one of two junior schools: his own, Murray's Road, or St Mary's Roman Catholic. The fifty-fifty mix of Catholic and Protestant children integrated fully. The common foe was the Tynwald Street mob. The families living on either side of his home were Catholic. For him, it was a meaningless label. The only discrimination, that he could see, was on a Sunday when the Catholic boys were allowed out to play after they had attended morning Mass whereas the Protestants, who were split evenly between All Saints C of E and Rosemount Methodist churches, had to go to Sunday school and afterwards were compelled to stay indoors. This practice he accepted begrudgingly, although a sympathetic mother would often see Sunday afternoon as a chance for her to take him to visit his maternal grandparents in the nearby village of Onchan.

Too young to understand the religious differences, he was brought up without any preconceived ideas. Billy and Anthony were his Catholic pals just as Terry and Peter were his Protestant ones; there were no differences. All were equal.

Next, he meandered up the drive to his first secondary school, Douglas High School for Boys. It was only three hundred yards away. This too looked very much as he remembered it, although new classrooms had been built in the playground.

However, as he grew older he realised that in the small island community, where everyone knew everyone else, religious status was important. If 'they' didn't know you, or your family background, 'they had to place you'. Where you lived was an indicator of your social standing. It gave you a status in the pecking order. There were three main council estates in Douglas. Isolated on the edges of the town were Pulrose, Spring Valley and Willaston. The oldest estate, Pulrose, consisted of perhaps no more than 150 houses, all built pre-war. However, there were sufficient Catholic families living on the estate for it to have its own RC church. Although he could never recall anyone spelling it out, a process of osmosis meant that by the time he was at secondary school he was becoming aware of group differences. The Catholic boys did not attend prayers at morning assembly, they frequently were in lower forms, and they appeared to be less well dressed. He never thought to ask why. These were facts of life that you accepted without question as a teenager.

When he was eighteen and preparing for university, he began to discover that there were wide-ranging religious prejudices in the police, the banks, the civil service and especially the judiciary. It never affected the friends whom he had befriended in his mid-teens, as they were all in his top class at school. In his class of twenty-eight boys in 1955, when he was aged fourteen, there was only one Roman Catholic. With his Catholic pals from Westbourne Drive, he would walk to school. However, they were in lower forms and socialising with them mysteriously lessened. He never thought to query this. By the time they were fifteen and eligible to leave school, they had mostly left to follow differing careers such as apprenticeships, the merchant navy or the army. Few, if any, remained at school to go into the sixth form.

By the time he was his early twenties, he'd heard of the Freemasons. His father was not a member, but he had explained to his son that membership endowed special privileges that were denied to Catholics.

'If you want to get on, you'll have to join them,' his dad had said on one of the few occasions when they talked about his future.

'You're not one and you've done all right,' Mike had replied.

'I could never bring myself to join a society that had secrets. I wouldn't have known what I was letting myself in for. Furthermore, I don't agree with discrimination on the grounds of religion. Do you remember Mr Higgins and Mr Cromwell, our next-door neighbours in Westbourne Drive?'

'Yes, of course.'

'Well, they would not be allowed to join simply because they were born into Catholic families. It's all wrong. Who knows, if I'd been a Mason, I may have gone further in the bank.'

Until 1960 there had never been a single policeman in the island's force who was a Catholic. A new, enlightened Deputy Chief Constable that year saw that this wrong was put right and two Catholic PCs were appointed.

On the second day of his nostalgic visit to the island, Mike travelled to see his second high school, Castle Rushen, where he had taken his "O" and "A" Levels prior to going to university. This school, too, had been largely rebuilt; only the original gymnasium remained. The bright spot, in an otherwise disappointing visit to the south of the island, was Port St Mary where little had changed. It being a fine day, he decided to wander along the coastal path towards the Calf of Man, the small island at the tip of the island. Memories of walking the route with his first girlfriend, Helen, and her dog came flooding back.

I wonder what happened to her after she got married.

He passed the Sound and carried along the coastal path towards Port Erin, stopping to search for the footprint of St Patrick that he remembered seeing almost fifty years previously. The footprint had been surrounded by a three-foot-square, two-foot-high brick wall with a thick glass plate to cover it. A penny was required to illuminate the internal light that revealed the indent in solid stone. However, he could find no sign of the saint's relic.

As the path descended into Port Erin, he passed a small cottage, Darragh, which had been the home of the island's finest artist, William Hoggatt. The artist had been a good friend of his father through their common love of bridge. Mike remembered taking his onetime fiancée, Mia, to see Hoggatt's widow, Daisy. They had gone to invite her to their wedding. Months later they had split up. The thought made him feel despondent.

I must have been mad to let her go.

I should have searched the world to find her. I should have given up my job in Bolivia and gone to Australia. There must have been some clues in Sydney as to where she was.

Whenever they had been together, they had been alone. The room could have been full of people, but the only one he could see was Mia. Mia had been something special. A bond had joined them together that was unique. Thinking of her further blackened his spirits.

I wonder what she looks like now.

I'll bet she's still a stunner.

Years later, having been married for six or seven years, he had been out for a walk with his father when his dad had asked, 'Do you still think about Mia?'

The question had stumped him. It was not in his father's character to ask questions of such a personal nature.

'Of course I do. She was so hard-working and determined in whatever she did. She would have made you a wonderful daughter-in-law.'

'Despite everything stacked up against her, I was very fond of her.'

'Why did Mum dislike her so much?'

'I shouldn't say this, but there were times when your mother couldn't see beyond the end of her nose. To be fair to her, she had regrets about the way she behaved towards Mia after you went to Bolivia, because she realised she would never be a grandmother. I think she saw Mia as a threat – losing a son instead of gaining a daughter, that sort of thing.'

He'd never heard his father be so critical of his mother before. He never forgot his dad's comment, and wondered at the time if his father had begun to see through Joyce.

The third day, intended to be his last, was to walk through Strand Street, the main shopping centre in Douglas. There, melancholy overtook him again and he began to drown in hopelessness. The once bustling street had changed. Woolworths had gone, the old Marks and Spencer's had gone, the Palais de Danse had gone, Tossie Cowin's ladies shop had gone, and some shops were boarded up. In the 1950s and 60s, he would have known most people in the street. Now, he knew no one. He made his mind up. It was time to carry out the plan that had brought him to the island.

He swung around to return to his hire car when, ahead of him, his eyes were drawn to the back of a girl walking in the same direction. She was about ten yards ahead.

She must have come out of a shop that I've just passed.

It wasn't her curvaceous build, or her petite frame highlighted by a figure-hugging two-piece suit, or the fact that her hair was fair, thick and shoulder-length. It was the way she walked.

God, it can't be Mia.

The walk is identical.

Anyway, Mia didn't have that colour hair, but the legs are the same.

Her height is the same.

118

Could Mia have had a daughter?

The young belle turned into Waterstones book shop and he hurried to catch up. From the doorway he saw her talking to an assistant who retrieved from under the counter a book; presumably she had ordered it previously. She nodded and it was put in a bag. She paid by cash, thanked the shop attendant and ascended the stairs to the upstairs café. Intrigued, he cautiously followed her to the first floor. She was sitting with her back to him and talking to a young man in his early forties.

Her husband?

Mike sat five yards away, ordered a coffee and watched. She was showing her companion her recent purchase. He examined it and nodded without enthusiasm. Mike still hadn't seen her face, but her figure and bearing suggested a woman in her forties.

Like Mia: trim and elegant, he thought.

She has to be Mia's daughter.

Then he noticed that beyond her table were the toilets.

When I come out, I'll be able to see her face.

He stood up, passed the couple without looking and entered the gents.

A minute later he came out, and stopped in his tracks. He blinked and stared. He couldn't believe it. In front of him was Mia, looking hardly any older than when he had proposed to her forty years previously.

He approached her table. 'Mia?'

'Mike? It can't be?' Her eyes widened with surprise, her mouth agape. She stood up, and opened her arms to give him a welcome hug. They embraced for what was probably only a few moments.

'I can't believe it,' he said. 'I thought I'd never see you again. I understood you lived in Australia.'

'Why did you think that?'

'It's a long story, but three or four years ago I was on the island, met an old friend and he mentioned you'd acquired a house in Maughold. I went to find you, but it was up for sale and the estate agent told me you had moved to Australia.'

'When Phil, my husband, retired we came back to the island to live permanently in Maughold. He died suddenly, four years ago.' She stopped, clearly upset.

To counter her emotion, she turned to the young man sitting with her. 'This is my son, Matt.'

Mike smiled at the forty-something stranger who looked nothing like his mother.

They shook hands and Mia explained to her son that she and Mike had 'once known each other'.

A rather euphemistic way of putting it, thought Mike.

'I came over to your table because I followed you from the street. I recognised your walk and wondered if I was following your daughter.'

Turning to Matt, he quickly added, 'Please don't think I follow young girls around the streets, but your mum has a unique gait.'

Matt smiled, clearly embarrassed by the enthusiasm Mike and his mother were showing for each other.

'That walk of mine; it got me into trouble forty years ago,' she laughed.

'I can't believe you still walk the same way and don't look any older.'

Instantly, Matt joked, 'Don't worry, Mum and I often get mistaken for a married couple. You'd never think she was sixty-six.'

Mia gave him a swipe of her hand, deliberately missing. 'Less of your cheek, young man, or you'll go hungry this evening.'

Mike took his coffee to their table and conversation was largely outlining what had occurred in the thirty-nine-year gap since last seeing each other. Half an hour had passed and Matt was showing unrest.

'I am on the island for another day,' Mike lied. 'I hate eating alone. Would you like to have dinner with me tomorrow evening?'

He looked at Matt. 'I promise to bring your mum home in one piece.'

Without hesitating, Mia replied, 'That would be lovely.'

'Wonderful. If you choose where you would like to go and make a booking, I'll pick you up at about seven o'clock.'

He arrived to pick up his former fiancée bang on time at the small village in the northeast of the island. She invited him into her house and Matt offered him a glass of wine.

'I have booked a table for eight o'clock,' she said. 'There's a new bistro in Ramsey that is supposed to be very good. Is that OK?'

He nodded. 'You look lovely.'

She seemed embarrassed by the compliment in front of her son, and excused herself. 'I didn't know what to wear as this will be the first time I have been out alone with a man since Phil died.'

'Then there's something wrong with the men around here,' Mike replied instinctively. 'You haven't changed in forty years.'

'Don't be daft.'

'I mean it. I wouldn't have said so otherwise.'

Matt stood looking at him, saying nothing. He was smiling awkwardly as the stranger heaped praise on his mother.

The three chatted amicably, but conversation was somewhat stilted until it was time for them to leave.

Mia and Mike talked politely as he drove her to the restaurant. Having parked the car, he wondered if he should hold her hand or put his arm around her shoulder as the short walk to the restaurant was poorly lit. He did neither, but wondered how he could show she had rekindled his feelings for her.

They were shown to a quiet table at the edge of the seductively lit room. Attention from the staff was efficient and sensitively diplomatic. They appeared to sense that the pair wanted seclusion. Their nostalgic reminiscing never stopped.

They didn't know it, but their lives were about to change.

June 2003

The privacy of their table in the corner of the restaurant, and the discreet lighting coupled with the tasteful décor, meant they could relax. It was conducive to talking freely. Mia had chosen well. The ambiance reflected her. His imagination was asking whether she had she deliberately chosen a seductive setting. In anticipation of an evening reminiscing further about their engagement year, he was feeling nervous. He was wondering if she had forgiven him for their break-up.

He cautiously asked, 'Do you realise today is exactly forty years since we became engaged?'

'Is it? Meeting you yesterday has been something of a shock. My mind has been harking back ever since. Some events are very vivid, such as the evening we met in The Palace and the picnics we used to have with your parents, but there are huge gaps in my memory. I guess my mind blocks out what I don't want to remember. Not everything was a bed of roses, was it? You never really came to grips with my Catholicism, did you?'

He immediately felt awkward. She had not forgotten his blasphemy nor forgiven him.

Her eyes were focussed a long way away: in a different world and a different time. He left her for a while to think about her rebuke.

Meanwhile, he was considering the wisdom of his conversion to the Roman faith. *Perhaps Catholicism was our downfall? Maybe we could have had a successful mixed marriage.*

When she came out of her spell, she changed the subject, as if not wanting to know the answer to her own question.

'It was madness to pull down the Palace Ballroom,' she said.

'It's typical. They did the same thing with the Derby Castle.'

'Not to mention the Regal and Royalty cinemas.'

'Our first date was at the Regal. I took you to see *Come Fly With Me*. I never forgot that night. I can remember what you were wearing.'

She smiled, as if pondering what she had worn.

'Afterwards you took me to the Villiers for a drink. It's a bloody bank now.' She began laughing. 'They love pulling things down in the island. My husband, who was an architect, was asked by the Isle of Man Government to draw-up a list of buildings that should be classified as Grade-1 Listed. And guess what?'

'Go on.'

'Of the forty that he listed, eight have already been pulled down.'

'Such as?'

'Well, the Peveril Hotel has gone, it's now another bank. The Noble's Baths in Victoria Street is an insurance company. St Barnabas' Church is a car park and my old school, St Mary's, is a concrete extension of Tynwald. The beautiful arched frontage of the Westminster Garage has become just another faceless shop made of steel and glass. There seems to be no end to so-called progress.'

'Perhaps it's us getting old,' he sighed.

She stared at him, seemingly baffled by his remark, as if to say, *I'm not old!*

Her bright green eyes, the eyes that had ignited a spark within him as a young graduate, were the same. She could still give him a bonfire look – that stare which pierced right through him. *The eyes age least*, he thought.

Her glare, however, was rekindling a flame. His pulse had begun to race, and his ears burned. He sensed they were two peas in a pod. There were other pods in the room, but he couldn't see any peas. His eyes remained focussed on her impish face.

He couldn't understand how she hadn't changed. She was facing him full-on and he noticed the subtle cut of her dress. And there it was – the small mole on her left breast that he had never forgotten since Blackpool. He tried hard not to gape, but it winked at him.

I'm not seeing her as who she is, but as who she was.

Try and concentrate on what she is telling you.

Their conversation moved on as she explained how long she had been a widow and how her late husband had died suddenly. As he listened, he continued to think of other things.

Is she slimmer?

Mike must have looked as if he wasn't listening, for she paused and asked, 'Are you all right?'

'I'm sorry. I was miles away listening with astonishment to your life with your husband. I've never been to Australia and I was asking myself why we ever fell out.'

It was a question to which he knew the answer, but was afraid to admit it. He hadn't the courage to acknowledge he'd allowed rumours, innuendos, the religious divide, the social differences, paternal pressures and his immaturity to build up to that fateful day when he'd used the lack of money as an excuse to break off their engagement. Like all cowards, however, he sought to avoid confrontation. He waited to see her response.

She never replied. Mia was sufficiently canny to realise silence is golden when a trap is set.

Reluctantly, Mike had to make the first move. 'When you went away, I was devastated. Your mum and David accused me of raping you. I went to see George, but he didn't know where you'd gone. I went to Jenny's house, but she told me to bugger off.'

He noticed Mia grin, as if the phrase amused her.

'I wrote you a letter after I received your engagement ring from Manchester. I gave the letter to George, asking him to give it to you when he next saw you. Did you ever get it?'

'No, I didn't see him for four years until I came back to the island. What was in it?'

'Nothing much. It was just a feeble attempt to apologise. I guess George must have forgotten it. I moped around that summer holiday, playing a lot of golf. There was nothing else I could do. In the end I had to return to Blackpool for the autumn term. By then I'd decided to go abroad. Why did you leave the island?'

'I told Mum you'd got me pregnant against my wishes and had raped me.'

'But that's not true.'

'I know. I'm sorry. I panicked after that row over money and the fact that we were going to have to postpone the wedding for at least a year. When you said, "Is there any point in our getting married?" I believed you no longer loved me. I remember clearly replying, "This is not working out." You then exploded. I'd never seen you cross with me before. I was devastated. You practically threw your signet ring at me.

'Then you blasphemed our church. I couldn't believe you did that. After all, you were a Catholic; whether you like it or not, you still are.'

Once a Catholic, always a Catholic, he thought.

'I ran into our house, and cried all night. I didn't know how to explain to Mum that you no longer loved me nor wanted to get married.'

She stopped, as if expecting him to defend himself.

'I don't know what to say, except sorry. When we were together, we were always alone, just the two of us, even in a crowd. Wherever we went, I can't remember anyone there. It's a cliché, but we only had eyes for each other.

'This restaurant is three-quarters full, but there's no one else here. All we wanted was to be together. I never dreamt I could have got you pregnant that day at Jenny's cottage. I still find it hard to believe. I might have been naïve, but I'd attended Catholic birth control classes and learned about the rhythm method. You assured me you were safe and I believed you.'

'I know. I'm sorry. I never did get pregnant.' She was lying through her teeth. 'I realised after our argument that I had made a mistake and used pregnancy as an excuse to get away.'

'What do you mean "made a mistake"?'

'Mike, you were too young for me. I eventually married a man ten years older. I had always been determined, after seeing how my mother had struggled to bring David, my sisters and me up without any money, that I would never allow myself to be financially insecure. Sometimes my father would only send my mother £1 a week, often nothing at all. You were earning a pittance – less than £50 per month after tax, if I remember rightly. Furthermore, you kept harping on about money and I could see us living together in a small, dingy, rented apartment in Blackpool with too many kids and no cash. It would have been like living in Stanley Square all over again.'

'Was I that bad?'

'The son of a banker, what do you expect?'

She laughed and he smiled at the subtle dig that had more than a grain of truth in it.

'I'd no idea. I wanted us to have a happy, fruitful life together. I'm sorry I overplayed the need for money.'

There was a lull in the conversation and wanting to change the subject, he asked, 'So, when exactly did you get married and have Matt?'

'I married Phil, who, as I've said, was ten years older than me, about a year after arriving in Australia. He was a senior partner in an international company of architects, with his own house in Berkshire. Matt was conceived on our honeymoon in Tasmania.' She knew her deceit was getting her further into the mire, but reckoned Mike would never find out.

It dawned on her that she had now betrayed the three dearest people in her life: her mother, Phil and now Mike – all with different stories.

I'll be damned to live the rest of my afterlife in purgatory, she thought.

Mike quickly worked out that if she had married soon after arriving in Australia, then she could have been sleeping with Phil shortly after leaving him. The thought disappointed him.

How could she forget me so quickly?

He tried not to show he was upset. 'Lying to your mum; telling her that I raped you was unfair. I would have been a good husband who would have gone everywhere with you, whenever you wanted. I converted to Catholicism for you. OK, so I never followed the faith, but had we stuck together, I'm sure things would have been different.'

She didn't react.

She's never forgiven me for my tirade about her religious beliefs that night. Catholicism was our stumbling block, not the need for money.

'Of course, money would always have been tight, but we knew that all along. If only you'd told me to come down from my high horse, I would. We'd have worked something out.'

He was fishing to see if she felt the same way.

She was keeping her cards close to her chest, not taking her steely eyes off him. He remembered Mia's mother, who had similar eyes, giving him a similar look the first night they went to the cinema. Mia was weighing him up, giving him the 'once-over'. He felt uncomfortable.

'There's nothing I can say, except to remind you that you said you didn't want to marry me anymore.' She spoke forcefully, even though she knew she was on a sticky wicket.

Although she was right, her assertion shook him. He was now on the back foot. 'I might have said that, but I never meant it. You must have known I wanted to marry you from the moment you agreed to dance with me at The Palace. That night you were the most beautiful girl in the world. You still are.'

She ignored him. 'Our marriage would have been a stormy relationship. Maybe everything worked out for the best.'

His shoulders sank intuitively. He was disheartened because he knew Mia was right. He said nothing. Her bungalow in Maughold had already told him one thing: Phil had left her well-off and she was in a different financial league to him. Her enthusiasm about her successful married life, as opposed to his dismal affair, deepened his gloom.

She began to press him about his marriage. 'I've told you about Phil, when did you marry Joyce?'

'When I returned from Bolivia. She was the school secretary where I was to spend the rest of my career. I'd gone to South America to get away from Blackpool. It had too many memories.'

He was deliberately vague as he didn't want to give Mia an excuse to think she was the sole reason for him going abroad.

'And you're still married?'

'Yes, but we've lived like brother and sister for twenty years.'

'Why?'

'I guess we drifted apart after Joyce had a hysterectomy. Thereafter, for some inexplicable reason our love-life dried up. We never split up for the sake of the children. Then, when they had left home, we just carried on doing our own thing.'

'That's sad. Phil and I never stopped loving each other.'

'Then you've something to grateful for.'

'Tell me about Bolivia.'

'There's not much to tell. It's a beautiful country with warm, friendly people. I bought a Honda motorcycle and saw most of the country during the school holidays. Getting to sail on the upper reaches of the Amazon and seeing a forty-foot anaconda was probably the highlight.'

'What do your children do?'

'Christina studied pharmacy at Nottingham University and works three days a week for Boots in Norwich. Matthew...'

She interrupted. 'Your son is Matthew?'

'Yes, like yours.'

'We never forgot the names we were going to give our kids, then?'

'No, I guess not. Matthew works for the Financial Services Authority in the City. He did economics at university.'

There was a pause in the conversation; long enough for Mike's mind to drift. His strict Methodist upbringing, a father who worked in a bank and thought the greatest crime of all was to be overdrawn on your account, his frequent harping-on to Mia during their engagement that they had to save harder – it had all contributed to the breakup. He knew the foundations of their relationship had always been fragile and he had failed to cast them aside for the girl he loved.

He pushed his hand across the table. She examined the peace offering. She took it, smiling. She had the most beautiful eyes of anyone he'd ever seen.

God, why did I ever let you go?

'We would have had fun making up after our stormy rows.' She squeezed his hand.

'I always loved you, Mia.'

She said nothing. There was the faintest trace of moisture in her eyes. If she felt the same way, she wasn't going to admit it; certainly not on their first date in thirty-nine years. They remained motionless, holding hands, for several minutes.

Then without warning she asked, 'When I sent you our engagement ring from Manchester Airport, what did you do with it?'

'I kept it safe and I know where it is,' he enthused. 'I stuck it under the bottom of a drawer in my bedroom with a piece of Elastoplast. I forgot about it until I was clearing our house in Cronkbourne Drive after Dad had died. It was still where I'd left it.'

'It's as well your parents never got rid of the dresser.'

'I suppose so, but you'll remember what they were like – never throw anything away. It took me ten days to clear the house. I filled two large skips with rubbish. The ring is now in a safe-box in our attic.'

He saw his chance.

'If you like, I'll send it to you.'

'No, it's yours now. I returned it to you.'

'Would you like to see it?'

'Of course.'

'Then I will send it to you wrapped inside a packet of Woodbines.'

She laughed. 'I'm not sure you can get them anymore.'

Looking at her, he'd made up his mind. She'd shown few signs of frostiness. He wouldn't have blamed her if she had. He wanted to begin courting her again and relive their youth. He had to see her again and find out if he could win her back. His plan to finish his miserable future had to be cancelled.

On the spur of the moment, he continued, 'Look, I have to go back to the mainland in the morning. Meeting you again has been a revelation. I would love to keep in contact. I have to come over to the island before the winter.'

He didn't explain why as he couldn't think of an excuse. He hoped she wouldn't ask why.

She didn't.

'I could stay for a few days and we could see each other. What do you say?'

'I would like that very much.'

'I will text you and, if you confirm it is convenient, then I'll ring you.'

They finished their meal and Mike drove her back to Maughold. She invited him in for a coffee.

'I've brought your mum home safe,' Mike said to Matt, who smiled awkwardly. He seemed unhappy that his mum had dated a married man.

June 2003

As soon as Mike returned to his home in Grange, he checked when his wife and daughter were due back from New Zealand. They weren't scheduled to return for another week. Excited, he texted Mia:

CAN YOU MEET ME NEXT W/E?

His hopes were crushed when she replied:

I WILL NOT MEET YOU

He thought, *What the hell?*

He looked at his text.

She's taken it the wrong way.

He amplified his intentions:

I THINK YOU MAY HAVE MISUNDERSTOOD. I COULD FLY OVER FOR A DAY AND TAKE YOU OUT FOR LUNCH

Her reply was curt and to the point:

MATT FLIES BACK TO AUSTRALIA THAT W/E AND WE WILL BE BUSY

He wondered if his high hopes for a future with Mia were misplaced. Had he misinterpreted her reactions at the restaurant? There was a simple solution:

I'M SENDING YOU YOUR ENGAGEMENT RING FIRST CLASS TRACKED POST TOMORROW. YOU WILL RECEIVE IT BEFORE 1.00 PM NEXT DAY. HOPE IT STILL FITS

There was no reply for three days.

FORGOTTEN HOW BEAUTIFUL IT WAS. FITS WELL, BUT A TAD LOOSE. MUST HAVE LOST WEIGHT

GLAD IT'S OK. PLEASE KEEP IT. IT WAS ALWAYS YOURS. WILL WRITE LATER

THANK YOU. LOOK FORWARD TO LETTER

He sat down and wrote a rambling letter by hand.

My one and only Mia,

I feel strange writing to you for the first time in thirty-nine years. I guess my handwriting has changed since I was in Leicester and Blackpool. Putting pen to paper somehow feels odd in this day of emails and texting.

On the boat back to Liverpool I thought about how things used to be between us, and of the wonderful times we had together. I know we reminisced at dinner, but more memories have since come flooding back. There was the time when we got into the wrong car. We had parked Dad's grey Standard 10 while we went shopping. Afterwards, we went back holding hands, with eyes only for each other. I unlocked the car and we got in. It was then that you noticed the steering wheel had a fur cover. The two cars were identical in every other way, including the locks. We laughed for ages that we could have driven away in someone else's car. There will be so much to talk about when we next meet.

I have been thinking of that Easter Monday in Jenny's cottage. Has she still got it, by the way? I loved you that day more than I knew it was possible to love. Our worlds collided when we met at The Palace, and although we didn't remain together, some remnants endured. Whatever they were, they must have self-sealed and hibernated. Now they have opened, what will happen?

During those thirty-nine years, a trigger would spark a memory such as when I met George twenty-odd years ago and he told me you were living in Berkshire. Then your old school friend Margaret came to live next door to my father. I would pop-in to see her whenever I was on the island. Over a bottle of Rioja, we would reminisce about the 50s and 60s. I would always ask how you were doing. Margaret knew we had been engaged and that I had converted to Catholicism to marry you. On one occasion she told me you had bought a holiday home on the island. Four or five years ago, she told me your husband had died. However, I never thought we would meet again.

Mia, I now realise I squandered the best years of my life. I have not stopped asking why I cocked-up our engagement. I can only apologise for being such a prat and not realising how important you were to me.

When looking for your engagement ring, I came across the only photo I ever had of you. You probably don't remember giving it to me. Unknowingly, I had kept it safe tucked away inside an old film album. You were so beautiful; don't get me wrong, you still are. You were without doubt the prettiest, most sophisticated girl I ever knew.

I can't believe I overplayed the need to save harder and get more money for our wedding. I must have been mad. I should have insisted we marry in a register office. At one point I did write to you c/o George to this effect, but I guess it was never passed on. As man and wife it may not have been recognised by our church, but we would have survived in our flat in St Anne's – not rich, but happy.

Please forgive me for all the pain and trauma I gave you. Did I really say, 'Bugger off and get lost'? For you to concoct the story of rape and pregnancy, you must have been frantic. To upset your mum could not have been easy, as I know how close you both were. She must have been devastated; going to the grave not knowing the deception – thinking you were pregnant when you weren't. And it was entirely my fault. If I could put the clock back, I would. My only consolation is that from what you told me, you and Phil had a marvellous life. It's no less than you deserved.

Your one and only,
Mike

The letter arrived the following day and Mia realised what a fraud she was. She had tricked her own mother into thinking Mike had raped her, she had deceived Mike into thinking she wasn't pregnant when she was and that his son was another man's child, and she had bluffed her parents-in-law about being a widow. She slept badly, but decided she had to continue with the pretence or lose her second chance with Mike – a man she now wished she had married. She put pen to paper.

Dearest Mike

I don't know where to start, except to say I love you. Since our meeting and receiving your letter, time has been going backwards. I never thought nostalgia could be so wonderful. I have been remembering some of the daft things we did together. Do you remember the barbeque we had at Ballaugh beach when we set the cliff alight? Or the night we were in the back of your dad's car parked somewhere near Onchan and a policeman knocked on the steamed-up window, wanting to know what we were up to? Or the day we bought an Elvis record and were entangling romantically on the floor of our front room to its music when Mum came home unexpectedly and caught us? After marrying, I lived happily and contentedly with Phil and Matt. Like you, there was a part of me that, unknowingly, must have forever been yours. Our bond was frozen in time. Now it has defrosted, my mind keeps harping back to 1963.

I loved you so much and, when you deserted me, I was heartbroken. Yes, you did say, 'Bugger off.' I swore that if I could get even with you I would. I would have happily stuck a knife in your ribs and sworn, 'Die, you bastard.' But now you've woven that spell again and my heart has come to life. People have remarked in the village shop, where I go for my newspaper, that I am looking younger. I feel like I am walking on air.

Every day I seem to be remembering more and more. I can picture our first date when we went to The Regal cinema to see Come Fly With Me. I remember what I wore – a black coat with an astrakhan collar. We sat upstairs near the back row and I remember not letting you kiss me as I thought it was inappropriate on our first date.

When you returned to Leicester, I wondered if you would come back. I prayed that your feelings for me were as strong as mine were for you. Then you bought me a pair of navy-blue court shoes for work and sent them to me. Do you remember that? I was over the moon and Mum remarked, 'He must love you to do that.' When you came to Blackpool for the day, I thought my prayers were answered. I reckon we could only have been out half a dozen times before we became engaged. Were we both mad? Were we in too much of a hurry? Or was it that neither of us had experienced such intense love before?

Our year together was the happiest of my life. Why didn't we just accept what we had? We should have slipped away quietly like you suggested. I would have made you a wonderful wife and we would have still been together. Don't get me wrong, I lived life to the full with Phil, but I would have loved life to the full with you. Now it is too late; all we can hope for are fleeting moments together whenever you can get away from Joyce.

Please keep in touch.

All my love,

Mia

My Dearest Mia,

Joyce returns from New Zealand tomorrow with our daughter and, frankly, I'm not looking forward to it. I can't help thinking of you and wishing I was with you instead.

I agree we must take every opportunity to share our time together with the few years we have left. What a mess we've made of our lives. How can a couple who have lost thirty-nine years make up for it?

Can I come over to see you in three weeks' time? I need to tidy up my parents' grave. I do this annually, normally flying over and returning the same day. However, I can always make an excuse to stay a night and I could take you out to dinner. It would give us a chance to catch up further with our memories. Text me and let me know.

All my love,

Mike

LOVE TO SEE YOU. MAYBE WE COULD GO FOR A WALK IN THE AFTERNOON, IF THE WEATHER IS NICE. THERE'S A NEW INDIAN RESTAURANT OPENED IN RAMSEY. SHALL I BOOK A TABLE?

WONDERFUL. I'LL FLY OVER ON EARLY PLANE FROM BLACKPOOL, PICK UP A HIRE CAR, ATTEND TO THE GRAVE IN THE MORNING AND THEN COME TO YOUR PLACE.

CAN'T WAIT. TABLE RESERVED.

He immediately booked his flight, his hire car and his hotel in Douglas.

He met his wife and daughter at Manchester Airport the following day. They enthused about the scenery of New Zealand's South Island, but he wasn't listening. He was composing his excuse to visit the island.

A day or two later, he brought the subject up. 'I was thinking of going over to the island to tidy up the family grave.'

'When?'

'The week after next, if that's OK?'

'Suit yourself.'

He had chosen a perfect day – rare in the island, even in July. An azure blue sky was reflected by the sea, which was as smooth as a mill pond. There wasn't a breath of wind, and the temperature was in the mid-twenties. He bought several bags of white chippings and a weed killer en route to his parents' grave in Onchan. An hour later he had finished and continued to Maughold. Mia opened the door and greeted him with a hug. Even wearing jeans and a sloppy sweater she looked a million dollars. They had coffee in her back garden and she outlined a plan: a light pub lunch at Andreas and a walk from Bride to the Point of Ayre lighthouse, returning along the beach.

'It's a round trip of about three miles. Will that be OK?'

'Are you suggesting I may not be capable of walking that far?'

'No, of course not,' she laughed.

Conversation centred on their memories of times past. 'Do you remember...' began sentence after sentence. Frequently the response was 'I don't remember that.' Much giggling and smiling would ensue as embarrassing or even unpleasant details emerged. All the while Mike was realising what a fool he had been. Here was his girl, his Mia, looking no older than when they had split up. Her figure and her face, bar a few wrinkles around those fabulous emerald eyes, were still those of a twenty-five-year-old.

They drove through Ramsey to a pub in Andreas, a journey of six or seven miles. He noticed she was wearing their engagement ring, but he said nothing. They ordered some sandwiches, a plate of chips and a beer.

'Do you still drink a pint of Guinness?' he asked. 'It's what you had in The Dog's Home the day we got engaged.'

'Fancy you remembering.'

'I remember how beautiful you looked and can tell you what you wore: a royal-blue dress with a matching jacket that had a Kashmiri collar.'

'I kept that dress and jacket for years.'

They drove to the thatched cottages at Cranstal, beyond Bride, and parked. As she was leaving the car, she remarked that their engagement ring was a little loose and she didn't want to lose it. 'I can only assume I have lost some weight.'

'Can I hold your hand?' he asked. 'I'll make sure it doesn't fall off.'

'My hand or the ring?'

Typical Mia.

She smiled and held out her hand. It occurred to him that he was having physical contact with her for the first time in thirty-nine years. It seemed so natural to hold her dainty hand. They sauntered along the side of the road, heading north. There was no traffic. The only sounds were the Arctic terns and the wailing of the herring gulls as they squabbled on the shore beyond. He couldn't take his eyes off her. She was as classy as ever. Her hair, minimal make-up and poise oozed class as they always had. Wearing flat walking shoes she seemed smaller than he remembered, but her saunter was the same – that unique walk that was so different.

Nearing the lighthouse, they spotted a bench that faced the sea. Visibility was excellent and they could see the hills of Cumbria. They sat down in the warm sunshine and he hesitantly put his arm around her shoulder. She didn't resist and he moved closer.

'It's peaceful here,' she observed as if to distract him from any ideas he was getting. He drew her closer so that her head rested on his shoulder. She didn't withdraw, and he remembered their first date in the Regal cinema. For both of them, memories kept flooding back. They were alone again and he was happy. They remained motionless for ages until from nowhere a Manx cat jumped on Mia's lap.

'Where have you come from?' she asked.

The cat purred a reply.

'It must live in the lighthouse,' suggested Mike.

The cat settled down. They were, presumably, sitting on his seat.

Mia queried, 'What do we do now?'

'I guess we'll have to stay until it gets fed up.'

'It's nice being here on our own – well, almost.'

'Almost nice or almost alone?'

'Clever Dick, you know what I meant.'

'I can't believe we've found each other after so long.'

She turned to look him in the eye. 'I love you,' she said out of the blue.

'I love you too,' he replied as he leant across the cat and kissed her forehead. 'Mia, I have lived most of my life not realising how much I loved you.'

She smiled. 'Someone once said, he who has not loved, has not lived. I feel the same.'

And with that he put his right hand around her waist, drew her as close as he could with the cat still on her knee, and they kissed for the first time in thirty-nine years.

Chapter 21

July 2003

Her response surprised him. It was distant; there was no passion. Her reserve stunned him. She didn't exactly push him away, but she recoiled after a few seconds.

Thinking he had upset her, he apologised. 'I'm sorry, I shouldn't have done that.'

There was a faint glimmer of a smile, dampened by a look of regret. 'It's OK, but you must give me time.' After a pause, 'I do love you, you know.'

'I love you too,' he whispered. 'When I saw you in Waterstones bookshop, I realised within seconds that I still felt the same way about you that I had all those years ago.'

She said nothing, her mind forty years away, as she stroked the cat asleep on her knee. She turned to look him square in the face. 'When I drove home after meeting you, my heart was thumping so hard it hurt. I'd realised at your father's funeral that there had been something special between us.'

'You were at Dad's funeral?'

'Yes, I sat in the back of the church.'

'You should have come to the wake.'

'No; it wouldn't have been right, but I was fond of your dad. We had some great times on those picnics.'

'Yes, it was my mother who was sniffy and the thorn in our flesh.'

'Her dislike of me never went away, no matter how hard I tried to please her.' Her beautiful green eyes misted.

Mike knew there was no answer. What could he say? It hurt him as much as it obviously hurt Mia. They sat on the bench in a world of their own, soaking up the warm sunshine, each with their own thoughts. He moved closer to nestle her and to try and express his regrets for what had occurred so long ago.

Mia was thinking that God had, at last, answered the prayer she had made when she had arrived in Australia: *Please let Mike someday return to me.* She was wondering whether she should tell him that Matt was his son.

Mike was, yet again, deliberating as to whether the root cause of their problems had been Catholicism. *How many other young couples have had their lives ruined by religious bigotry: Catholic–Protestant, Hindu–Muslim and Jew–Gentile?*

He wondered, *Am I a bigot too?* The awful possibility made him cringe.

'It's good to be together again after all these years,' he eventually said. 'Somehow it seems right. It's not perfect – me still being married – but I'm so thankful we have met again. I feel my life has a meaning once more.'

She looked him squarely in the face. 'After we bumped into each other in Waterstones, I was excited, but I spent most of the evening regretting the fact that I'd agreed to see you. If I'd known how to contact you, I would have done so and made an excuse for us not to meet.'

'Why?'

'I was afraid this would happen.'

'What?'

'This. I've got used to being a widow. I've found myself a small circle of friends at the golf club, the bowling club and the church. I've a very comfortable lifestyle. I vowed after losing Phil that I could never survive having to go through such despair and despondency again. Somehow, the thought of being alone in the future gave me solace. I've grown to like my own company. I can do what I like, when I like. Since Phil died, I've wintered in either Australia or the Bahamas for three months. I vowed I would never lose another close friend again, providing my son outlives me. Does that make sense? Now you've come along and upset the apple cart. I couldn't stomach having to lose you and go through all that misery again.'

'When I look into your eyes, I see a channel that I can slide into and discover your feelings. You don't have to say a word. We were pre-programmed so that we can read each other's mind. You experience it too, don't you?'

She never replied as she stared out to sea. He knew she was sensing it, but wouldn't admit it.

'This has not happened by chance. It's not our fault that we met at The Palace. That evening something rammed us together. I don't know how to describe it, but we never totally split apart. After we broke up, I had a few girlfriends, but none lasted. There was always something not right.

'You radiate something undetectable that is more than the sum of its parts and I feel stronger. My nerves line up like iron filings in a magnetic field. When we went out for dinner last month, I wanted to shout to everyone in the restaurant, "Come and look. Mia is radiating energy. Can you feel it too?"'

She looked up at him and smiled uncomprehendingly.

She thinks I'm a nut-case.

I probably am.

'I love being with you,' she whispered. 'Hold me.' She buried her head in his shoulder.

He drew her even closer. He could smell her perfume and feel her hair on his cheek.

'Surely, we're not the first couple to experience this? All I want is to comfort you for evermore.'

'I am yours,' she murmured, almost inaudibly. 'There's no going back this time. Wherever you go from now on, I'll be with you.'

'Is it because we are now mature enough to realise what we have been missing all this time?'

She shuffled uncomfortably, reluctant to make a similar admission that her husband could, unknowingly, have been second fiddle.

Her movement woke up the cat. Disgruntled, it expressed its disapproval by jumping down and striding away. They took this as a signal to begin walking back. There was a period of silence as they ambled, hand in hand, towards the foreshore; each speculating on what their lives could have been.

As they walked south, Mike decided to come clean about his fits of depression.

'I came to the island last month to commit suicide.'

She stopped dead in her tracks. Her eyes opened wider than he'd ever seen them before. Her gaping mouth and stance demanded an explanation.

'I'd had enough. I get the black dog badly and had been on a downer for years. I'd decided to come up here to the Point of Ayre and swim into the sea. That way no one would have the unpleasant experience of finding my body. I've had four friends over the years who've taken their own lives, two by walking in front of a train and two in a garage with the engine left on. When you get to the stage where you believe there's little point to it all, then as Nietzsche famously said, "*The thought of suicide is a great comfort.*"'

'You know it's the church's gravest sin?'

'Of course, but I never go to church. After we broke up, I never practised the faith because you were not there to give me guidance. I'm sure, if we'd remained together, you would have kept me going straight.'

She made the sign of the cross. 'Mike, you must promise never to kill yourself.'

'Yes,' he said somewhat sheepishly.

'*Promise,*' she said loudly, her eyes blazing.

He could feel she would know if he lied.

'*Promise,*' she repeated, even more loudly.

'Promise,' he replied. He was unsure if he could mean it.

They walked back to Mike's car in silence. On their way to Maughold, they stopped at a café in Ramsey's Mooragh Park for afternoon tea. They resumed their blend of wistful longings and the wonderment of rediscovery. The subject of suicide had been dropped.

He left her at her bungalow and drove back to his hotel to change for their evening date. 'Don't overdo it,' she said as she was getting out of the car, 'smart casual will suffice.'

'I'll pick you up at 7 .30.'

Driving back to Douglas on the coastal road through Laxey, he began to think over the consequences of what he was doing. There was a big difference in their circumstances. Whereas his feelings for his wife had waned and passion had been non-existent for over twenty years, Mia didn't hide the fact that she and Phil had remained sexually active throughout their marriage. Mike found the discrepancy an enigma. He wondered if she had been the pro-active partner to keep Phil from straying. Or was she simply good in bed? Could she have been the one to stray, like him? Or was she was hiding the truth? The possibility that Mia had been unfaithful with Phil intrigued him. Memories of the innuendos made about her forty years ago flooded back. Had she been more experienced then than she let on? No, he assured himself; he had been the first. He told himself to stop worrying.

As a widow she had every right to fall in love with another man and, according to the rules of her church, could re-marry whereas his hands were tied. More than anything else, he now wanted to spend the rest of his life with the first girl with whom he had fallen in love. The problem was, how?

Apart from arranging Joyce's murder – impractical, the only alternative was to leave home – expensive. It would entail giving up his house, his children, his grandchildren and his small circle of friends. He would become a social pariah. Where would he live? He could afford a small apartment in Ramsey – necessary as he couldn't simply move in with Mia, at least not immediately. If in the longer term Joyce would divorce him, he was unsure that Mia would want him in her house where she had lived happily with Phil.

He resolved to bring up the delicate subject of their future that evening, if the opportunity arose.

The food was good, but the ambiance was poor – spoiled by a noisy party at the far end of the restaurant. Mike and Mia didn't hang around. It was a cloudless night and by the time they left Ramsey it was dark. The sky, once away from the urban street-lights, was brilliantly lit by the starry heavens.

'Do you want me to take you straight home, or would you like a little walk?' he asked.

'That would be nice,' she replied and they parked in the empty car park at Maughold church.

'Shall we just talk?' she suggested. 'I have been wondering where this is leading.'

'I have been thinking about it too,' he replied. 'I've decided I will leave my wife and find a small flat in Ramsey.'

'*No*,' she replied. The forcefulness of her reply surprised him. 'I'm not going to let you do to your wife what my father did to my mother. It's wrong for us to share our happiness as a result of the misery of others.'

He was dumbfounded for some moments.

'Mia, you and I were meant for each other. I understand your conscience telling you it's not right. I get a feeling of guilt too. In my case I have no feeling of remorse. My affection for Joyce disappeared long ago. For twenty-odd years we've gradually drifted apart. More and more we do our own thing, with little or no involvement in each other's interests. We co-exist under the same roof. I have wondered for years what we have in common and concluded – nothing. You've given me more happiness in the last four weeks than Joyce has in the last twenty-four years. When we're together, I become who I was; not who I am. So please don't think you are breaking something up. It's been broken for a long time. I guess the only reason we've not split up is pure laziness and a hope that the kids will somehow draw benefit from it. When I'm with you, I feel younger; the world changes and there's no horizon.

'I know I let you down. If I could, I'd put the clock back. Your life would not have been as glamorous, but I would have been a good, loving husband.'

Her eyes were filled with moisture. 'I'm sorry Mike, but two wrongs don't make a right. I'm glad we've found each other and I'm quite happy to see you whenever we get the chance, but I'm not going to be the direct cause of a divorce. Call it my Catholic conscience, if you like, but that's final.'

She had put her foot down and he knew not to argue. He had insulted her church thirty-nine years previously. He had learnt his lesson the hard way and would not repeat the mistake. They were both staring out of the windscreen in deep thought when a meteor shot across the sky.

Mia reacted first. *'Catch a falling star and put it in your pocket,'* she crooned quietly.

'For love may come and tap you on the shoulder,' replied Mike.

'It's an omen,' said Mia. 'Put your arm around me and hold me close.'

His mind went back to where he had kissed her passionately for the first time after their date at The Highlander. How little Mia had changed. Her waist was as slim as ever. His hand between her ribs and hip felt as if it had never left.

'I love you, Mia. I always did.'

He made to kiss her lips, but she moved her face away.

'Not tonight, next time.'

'I'm not sure when that might be.'

'I'll be ready.' She smiled. 'I won't let you down.'

'The golf club are having their annual September weekend in Scotland. I could tell Joyce I'm going. She won't care and I could come over here.'

'You could lose your balls here instead,' she laughed.

'Did you say, "lose" or "use"?'

They both laughed.

Chapter 22

September 2003

By the time September approached, they had texted dozens of messages and made frequent phone calls. Mia, possibly feeling guilty at refusing Mike's advances, agreed to fly to Blackpool where they would spend the weekend. Mike's pretext of going to golf in Scotland had given Joyce an excuse to visit her parents in Devon.

Mia was excited at the thought of revisiting old haunts from her days as a Britair stewardess. She hadn't visited the seaside town since 1963 and wondered how much could have changed. However, there was a tug-of-war going on between her Catholic morals and her rekindled love for Mike.

She conceded, during one of their regular phone calls, that Mike could book a double room, although he detected a certain amount of uncertainty in her voice. To his amusement, she asserted it was conditional on her remaining out of range in bed.

'I will only sleep with you if it's a six-foot bed,' she said over the phone.

Mike assumed she was joking, imagining the smile on her face, but there was an element of doubt too. He assured her that his intentions were honourable – a remark uttered with tongue in cheek that had Mia giggling at the other end of the line. They both knew, but weren't prepared to admit, that they wanted to relive their long-lost affair. Blackpool would be the first time they had ever curled up between the sheets of a bed.

'We've never been to bed together,' he pointed out.

'No, I don't suppose we have, but don't get any ideas,' she replied.

The concern that his libido may have been tempered by years of inactivity since his affair with Viv worried him. He was sufficiently anxious to approach his GP.

'What can I do for you?' the doctor asked. Mike's appointment was with the senior member of the local practice, a man of similar age to himself.

'I'm having trouble getting it up,' he replied.

His family doctor stared at him, looking him up and down. He didn't know Mike from Adam, despite Mike having been registered at the practice for over thirty years. This was only the second visit Mike had made in a decade – the last occasion being due to a minor hernia, when he'd been seen by one of the junior doctors.

'What can't you get up?' the GP asked.

'You know,' he replied, embarrassed by the direct question. 'When I try to do it.'

'You mean when you make love to your wife?'

'Something like that.'

The old boy smiled. 'Ah, it's like that is it?'

'Yes.'

He took Mike's blood pressure and 'ah, ah'd several times. He picked up his pen and scribbled on a pad. 'Take one of these two hours before doing it. It should do the trick.'

'What if it doesn't?'

'Then take two.'

'And if there's still a problem?'

'Then it's time you settled down!'

September 2003

I didn't know if Mike was having doubts about our forthcoming weekend, but I was in a quandary. I knew the outcome of sleeping with Mike could be disastrous if it went badly. My love life with Phil had been regular, if unspectacular, until he died. Even after thirty years of marriage, we made love at least once a week. Whenever he came home, having successfully negotiated a big contract, and was full of beans, I knew he would give me what he called 'a what for'. It was always frenzied and frantic. But the last occasion had been over four years ago. My body had been more supple then and able to cope with the rough and tumble. I was slowing down. I knew it might be difficult to accommodate Mike. As I remembered him from all those years ago, he was well endowed. I decided to travel to Douglas, where I was less well known. I visited a small independent pharmacy, situated in a group of shops locally known as The Terrace, in upper Douglas, not all that far from Stanley Square. I looked around the shelves, but couldn't see what I wanted.

I approached an assistant and asked in a whisper, so as not to be overheard by other shoppers, 'Have you got KY cream?'

'The KY jelly is over there,' the young girl shouted loudly and pointed. The other shoppers turned around and looked at me.

Embarrassed and not knowing where to hide, I announced loudly to all and sundry, 'I'm getting it for a friend.'

No one believed me. I paid up and ran out of the shop.

Chapter 24

September 2003

Mike initially thought about booking their weekend at the hotel where Mia had stayed when he'd travelled from Leicester forty years previously. However, although he could remember where it was, he couldn't recall its name. Instead, he chose The Imperial, a five-star establishment on the North Shore, as it offered a twenty-four hour room service. His hopes were high, now that he had been given lead for his pencil, that he and Mia would spend all the weekend in bed.

Enthusiastically, he turned up at Blackpool Airport early to meet Mia's flight. Waiting, he became restless. He kept looking at the arrivals' screen, hoping that the flight wouldn't be delayed.

It should have left by now, he thought.

I don't care if Mia gets stuck here with me, but for her not to arrive would be a disaster.

He sat in the arrivals' hall – a new building that had replaced the wooden, World War Two-era hut that had survived from the days when the airport had been RAF Squires Gate. He asked himself how he came to be there. Had meeting Mia been random chance? Or were all things predetermined? Had they been destined not to marry? It didn't make sense. They'd not had things easy forty years previously. They were no easier now. If there was a God, why did He let them meet in the first place?

He consoled himself that everything in life is random. Any other explanation was religious hocus-pocus.

He pondered how he had fallen in love so quickly. It had been spontaneous combustion when he saw her at Ronaldsway. A minute had been long enough for him to burst into flames. He had never been the same again. Yet he couldn't understand how he'd managed to live without her for nigh on a lifetime. Yes, he'd thought about her on and off during those years, but he'd survived. Then one look in Waterstones and instantaneous ignition had occurred once more. He was in love all over again. To explain the conundrum needed an intuitive, emotional brain. To Mike, it defied logical analysis.

In his first year at Douglas High School for Boys, the physics master had boiled some water in a tin, sealed it with a cork and the class had watched and waited for something to happen. As the steam cooled inside, the tin began to crumble because of the pressure of the air. It was magic! He'd been hooked. The realisation that there was an invisible force all around them that he couldn't see mystified him. From then on his favourite subjects were physics and mathematics. Thereafter, he grew up believing mathematics could explain everything in the universe including the weather, but not, he now concluded, falling in love.

Consequently, he had developed inter-personal relationships on the basis that they had a function. When he'd needed a partner in badminton, Helen had been chosen. Subsequently, other things happened that satisfied their adolescent needs. Without realising it, Mike had become a cold fish. Friendships had a reason: to fulfil his needs. It could be a partner in the physics lab, someone with whom to play golf, a partner for bridge or a girl to fulfil his sexual appetite. He never saw them until the next requirement. He had no friends for friendship's sake. That would have been illogical.

As he waited for Mia's plane to arrive, he realised this had been true with Joyce. She had satisfied his needs. He'd married her because he was twenty-seven, hadn't gratified his libido for over four years and Joyce had put it on a plate. He'd liked the taste. She was a good cook, ironed his shirts and looked after his children. But she had never become his friend. Although married for thirty-four years, they had never done anything for the fun of doing it together, such as playing bridge or golf. Even when on holiday with the children, the friendship had been functional. Family holidays were something everyone did, so they did them too. There had been no logical reason for holidaying in France; it was just what the other school staff did.

The theory that an ordered society depended on a stable family, he believed, was the consequence of propaganda pumped out by centuries of church dogma. It ignored the reality of the struggle of bringing up a family: a lack of money, a mortgage to pay and the ever-increasing demands that youngsters make when they think money grows on trees.

For Mike, there were only three logical necessities to sustain life: water, food and sex. All three had to be satisfied regularly.

So what made Mia different? He had asked the question hundreds of times. His mind harped back to the year of their engagement. That year, he wanted Mia to be his friend for life because she made him happy. It dawned on him that their relationship had been blissful until they had sex that fateful Easter Monday. Then he had become dissatisfied. Like the apple on Adam's tree, it had been the ultimate goal, but it turned out to be the poisoned chalice. It wasn't logical. He deliberated on why it had changed everything. He wondered whether their love could have survived if they had waited until they had married. Perhaps the church's teaching that sex outside marriage was potentially disastrous was right after all.

As the clock in the hall ticked away and there was no update on the arrival time he wondered if Mia was his first friend for friendship's sake. Why? Because she had always made him happy. He could measure the width of a human hair with a micrometer, but there was no gauge with which he could measure love or friendship.

He concluded he never wanted to be apart from Mia. In her company the sun always shone. When together, their mutual contentment and happiness kept the unwanted outside at bay.

Chapter 25

September 2003

At Ronaldsway Airport, I was having second thoughts. My Catholic upbringing was kicking in and making me doubt the wisdom of going for my first ever dirty weekend. The possible outcome of what I was about to do was worrying. I saw the ghost of my mother warning me: *His tea leaves are all wrong.* I remembered our day at Jenny's cottage and how Mike had got me pregnant.

I began thinking about the boys I'd known. I wondered what had made Mike so different. Yes, he was the most handsome boy I ever knew, but surely, that wasn't the reason? Determined to improve my professional qualifications during my late teens and early twenties had meant my social life had been dramatically curtailed compared to friends of my own age. I hadn't kept count, but there must have been half a dozen different boys over a ten-year period who'd taken me out on more than one occasion. Some friendships lasted longer than others, some made my blood simmer more than others, some had rattled the lid on my pan, but it was Mike who was the first to make me boil and had lifted my lid off.

For over thirty years of marriage, there had only been Phil. There had been opportunities to err at weekend parties, when on more than one occasion I had been propositioned. Men who've had several glasses of wine don't half fancy their chances. They all think they're James Bond. Some wouldn't take 'No' for an answer and would turn up at our home the following week when they knew Phil would be at work. Getting rid of them could have been difficult if it hadn't been for Hua, our Chinese domestic, who worked for me three days a week. Fortunately, the cads would always turn up on one of the days when she was with me.

I would be lying if I didn't admit that I had been tempted to stray. With Phil my love life had slowly become routine. Phil always made the lid rise, steam would escape and I would be left satisfied. Afterwards, I would feel content in that wonderfully exhausted way, but the lid always fell back. When I met Phil, I'd wanted a new life with a father for Matt. During our marriage I'd tried to give him one hundred per cent of my affection, but deep inside, I realise now, I'd never stopped grieving for Mike. After all, Mike was Matt's father. Phil had deserved all my love, but he had only received ninety per cent. The thought that I had not given my husband everything he'd deserved was depressing me.

With Mike, from our first date I'd begun to learn to boil. It took us a year before I experienced the lid flying off my pan, but that was my fault. It was on that ill-fated Easter Monday that he'd blown my lid away.

All sorts of ideas were passing through my head.

Should I come clean with Mike and admit Matt is his son?

What if our libidos no longer click?

Is his only motive to get inside my knickers?

I love him and don't want to lose him again.

If I feign illness and don't go, then he may never want to see me again.

I thought of my sister, Liz, and the advice she had given me when I was in a dilemma as to whether I should marry Phil.

'Go for it,' she had told me. 'You may never get a chance again.'

Sorry, Mum. Liz was right.

It turned out OK with Phil.

Now I've got to take a chance with Mike.

But I kept coming back to the same question: what made Mike so different? We had fallen in love so quickly. It had been like two cars crashing and their bumpers becoming entangled. His car had been so different to mine: his university education, living away from home for four years, and a family life that gave him everything on a plate. Me? I'd left school at fifteen, had a parochial upbringing where money was scarce, always had to work – everything was so different. And yet, we had become stuck together, at least for a year.

Then a crack in our bumpers must have appeared. Our two cars had separated and we had driven away as if nothing had happened. However, something had happened: our bumpers were missing. And just as cars can function without bumpers, so too, we had functioned without each other for forty years.

I wondered if our hugely different backgrounds, cultures and experiences would ever have allowed our marriage to work.

Now we had crashed into each other again, but would our different cultures blow us apart once more? Or could our maturity save the day this time, allowing us to remain joined together? Would our second collision be more successful than the first?

Determined that I would do my damnedest to make some sort of a future with Mike, I heard the flight being called and went to the departure lounge. My heart was pounding in anticipation of the weekend ahead.

September 2003

Finally, the tannoy announced the flight's arrival twenty-five minutes late. Mike's heart began beating rapidly; his loins began to stir. He put his hand in his pocket and felt the magic pill. *As soon as the plane lands, I'll swallow it.*

He gasped as he watched her enter the arrivals hall. Coming toward him was a twenty-six-year-old wearing a navy blue, figure-hugging, knee-length two-piece suit. It was the girl he had fallen in love with. Her gait, or was it a swagger, hadn't changed.

This is Ronaldsway 1963, he thought.

She spotted him, smiled and ran toward him. He put his arms around her waist, kissing her while at the same time lifting her seven-stone frame from the ground. 'Your outfit, it's beautiful. It makes you look twenty-six again.'

'I'm chuffed that I can still squeeze into a size eight. Do you like it?'

'It's fantastic. It's the same shade of blue as your Britair uniform.'

She posed, drawing attention to her slim, girlish figure. He noticed she was wearing their engagement ring and her court shoes matched her dress.

She's as elegant as ever.

Hand in hand they walked to his car. They drove out of the airport, passing the ex-RAF Vulcan gate guardian, passed over the bridge at Squires Gate railway station and onto the South Shore promenade.

'Where are we staying?' she asked.

'The Imperial,' he replied.

'Oh, I thought it might have been the Red Court.'

'Was that what it was called? I thought about it, but for the life of me, I couldn't remember, the hotel's name. The Imperial should be comfortable as we have a sea view.'

She smiled and began chatting; telling him how much she was looking forward to rediscovering Blackpool. As they passed the Pleasure Beach, she reminded him that they had ridden the big dipper '...that night when I stayed at your digs'.

He turned his head and, puzzled, remarked, 'I don't remember that. I thought we went to the pictures.'

'You're hopeless. I'll bet you can't even remember when you first kissed me,' she laughed.

Embarrassed to admit he had no idea, he fumbled for an answer. 'It was the night we went to The Highlander for a meal and we stopped on the way home.'

'There, I knew you'd forgotten. It was the night we saw *Come Fly With Me*.'

'You wouldn't let me kiss you in the Regal.'

'It was outside my house as we said goodnight. You pushed me against the gate and took me by surprise.'

'Really?'

'Yes, really. I nearly told you to bugger off there and then, and never come back.'

'I'm glad you didn't.'

'Same here.'

They booked into the hotel and were shown to their suite. It didn't disappoint. Their large room was furnished with a super king-size bed. Mike smiled and looked at Mia to see if she had noticed. It appeared she had not. The usual tea-making facilities, minibar, television, easy chairs and fully equipped writing desk completed the room. However, in the bathroom the striking feature was a double bath with headrests at each end, next to a panoramic window. They would be able to sit in the bath and look over the promenade towards the sea.

'I always like having a bath before going to bed,' she remarked.

Thinking this was an invitation, Mike suggested, 'Let's have one now.'

'Later. I would like to see where you took your confirmation lessons, and your old school.'

'What? Now?'

'Yes, it's a lovely evening. A walk along the front will work up an appetite.'

'It must be a couple of miles to St Theresa's.' He was thinking he didn't need his appetite working up. Remembering the wonder drug in his pocket, he tapped it to make sure it was still there and thought, *I'll take it later.*

'If you don't mind, we'll get the tram to Cleveleys,' he added.

Within twenty minutes they were looking at his old school. It hadn't changed except for a few more Terrapin classrooms in the playground. He noticed his temporary classroom was still there.

At St Theresa's people were beginning to arrive for the 6.30 pm Mass. 'I would like to go,' she said.

He felt guilty, hardly having been inside a church since taking his Catholic vows. 'I won't be able to take the sacrament,' he replied defensively.

'It will be nice for me to see where you were confirmed after all this time.'

They entered hand in hand. She crossed herself with the holy water. He did likewise. She led the way to an empty pew, genuflected and sat down. He could tell she was totally at home while he followed, feeling uncomfortable and thoroughly out of place. The church could have been anywhere. He couldn't remember any details of what it was like forty years previously. Somehow it seemed bigger and starker.

I could have sworn there were far more statues and stained glass. It used to be darker and more sombre.

His mind drifted as he looked at Mia next to him, still kneeling in prayer.

From a distance you would swear she was a teenager. This is not why I brought you to Blackpool, he said to himself.

Realising what he had thought, he added, *God forgive me.*

Throughout the service, in English, he found himself remembering the Latin Mass. Somehow, the English version wasn't the same: not so mysterious, not so poetic, and not so awe-inspiring. As they left, the priest greeted them at the exit and, seeing Mia wearing her late husband's wedding ring, made the wrong assumption.

'Welcome to St Theresa's,' he said.

'Thank you, Father,' Mia replied, 'but we're only here for the weekend.'

'Then I hope the weather will remain pleasant.'

He shook hands with them and greeted the next couple. Mike breathed a sigh of relief.

Thank heavens he didn't ask any questions.

However, as they walked towards the sea to catch the tram back to Blackpool, Mia asked, 'If we had married, would we still be together?'

'Why do you ask?'

'You were uncomfortable in church. You became a Catholic, but you don't believe in the Eucharist – the belief that the bread and wine are transubstantiated into the body and blood of Christ.'

'Do you?'

'Of course, it's what makes Catholics different from the other Christian faiths.'

'Mia, it's completely illogical. I can accept the bread and wine representing Christ's wish: *do this in memory of me*, but that's about all. Are you telling me the bread suddenly tastes like meat?'

She stopped in her tracks. She looked up at him. Her eyes had welled up. She was shaking with rage. She wiped her eyes; they were on fire. 'Our marriage wouldn't have lasted five minutes, would it?'

'It would. I'd have accompanied you to church on Sundays.'

'You're a fraud, Mike Moore. You blasphemed the night we broke up. Now you've done it again.'

'Mia, I've said this before. As long as you live your life without harming others, then that's all that matters. I'll bet Phil didn't go regularly to Mass with you. Did he?'

She didn't answer. She turned and continued walking towards the tram stop. Mike followed, a yard behind.

They had decided to see if the restaurant where they'd had lunch, when Mike had come from Leicester, was still there – it wasn't. They found an upmarket Chinese just off Talbot Square and by 9.30 pm were heading back to the Imperial, with Mike having surreptitiously swallowed two pills during the meal.

Chapter 27

September 2003

Persuading Mike that we should go to see his old haunts before dinner had been my ploy to postpone the inevitable for as long as possible. Frankly, I was frightened by the potential outcome of the weekend. Unbelievably, my conscience was telling me I was letting Phil down. Since his death, I'd been true to his memory, so how could I be betraying him I asked myself? I had visited his grave every week and prayed for his soul while replacing his flowers. The dichotomy between my Catholic upbringing telling me one thing and my rekindled love for Mike telling me something else was agonising. I had reached a crossroads in life and there was no going back. It wasn't as if I'd gone looking for an affair with a stranger. Mike had always been there. Finding him had been a stroke of luck; finding that we'd remained in love for forty years had been even luckier. I breathed in hard, asked Phil for forgiveness, and resolved to make the weekend a success.

We had an awkward moment after Mass while walking to get the tram. I'd asked Mike about his Catholic beliefs as I'd felt that in church he'd been uneasy. I was upset, but shouldn't have been, when he admitted he couldn't believe in the Blessed Sacrament. Transubstantiation is the most fundamental Catholic dogma of all, yet he saw it as just another ritual like incense or holy water. Phil had been a sceptic too, but our marriage had survived. It was my fault for asking Mike whether our marriage would have stood the test of time. We walked to the tram stop without saying a word, but held hands in silence during the fifteen-minute ride into the centre of Blackpool. I realised I shouldn't have called him a fraud and had no rights to try and control his opinions. He was a good man at heart and if we had married, then he may have turned out not to be such a cynic.

He knew he had hurt my feelings, but had enough sense to know that, at moments like these, silence is golden.

After unsuccessfully looking for the restaurant where we had lunch the day he had driven from Leicester, we found an up-market Chinese. Things were back to normality when over our meal, I asked, 'When did you realise you still loved me?'

'When I looked into your eyes at Waterstones, I couldn't believe what I saw. Not only had your walk not changed, but your eyes hadn't either. Your bonfire stare still frightens me. Strangely, it reminds me of snakes and ladders.'

'The board game?'

'Yes. The notion came to me that I had so nearly won you by getting to the top of the board in 1964. Then, when we argued in Dad's car that fatal evening, you gave me a glare. It was my last throw of the dice to win you. Instead, I fell back to square one.

'I'd forgotten what an ass I'd been all those years ago. At our meeting in Waterstones, I told you a porky – I planned to stay another day. I hadn't. I wanted to find out if you felt the same way as me. Mia, you've given me something to live for. Since retiring, I'd felt life was pointless and plodded along with nothing to look forward to. Now you've rekindled my energy and I am a different man. I'm happier than I've ever been. All I want is to be alone with you, to look into your eyes, and hug you.

'Waiting to call for you and take you out the day after Waterstones was endless. Then, when I arrived, there you were looking a million dollars. You don't know it, but you're caught in a time warp. How can you possibly be in your sixties when you look as if you are thirty-five? When you told me you hadn't been out with a man since your husband died, I couldn't believe it. I thought, *What's wrong with the men around here?*'

His compliments made me feel uncomfortable, but Mike hadn't changed much. Thinner on top and going grey around the temples, he still walked upright and was about the same weight. The subdued light of the Chinese restaurant hid his wrinkles, and he was still that handsome man I'd met at The Palace.

When we arrived back at the hotel, I insisted on a bath before going to bed. My plan was to secretly use a little of the KY jelly. However, Mike decided to get into the bath with me. I had never shared my bath with Phil. This was a new experience, only made possible by the size of the bath. Mike ran the water, sprinkling liberal amounts of bath foam while

I undressed. I felt exposed as I entered the bath, but Mike showed no embarrassment. He undressed in front of me, folding his clothes neatly over one of the chairs. I stared at his naked body as he entered the bath. He had a slender torso. His stomach muscles were sufficiently taut to give him a waist, below which hung his utensils. I thought how beautiful he looked and began drooling at the fate that awaited me. And yet, I still worried. Since Phil died, I hadn't even thought about sex, but here I was getting excited – as if I was sixteen, not sixty-six. Curiously, I thought that if I told my best friends in the golf club about this, they wouldn't believe me.

We sat looking at each other across the foaming, warm water. He lent forward to kiss me. I moved toward him and we kissed across our bended knees.

I leant back against the bath's padded back and felt him rubbing his toes on the inside of my legs. It was an erotic experience. Spasms were shooting up my thighs. We continued to gaze into each other's eyes. I knew then, if I didn't know already, that I was head over heels in love with him again. My longing to have him to myself was greater than it had ever been. This time I would not let him go.

At St Theresa's, a few hours earlier, I had prayed for Phil's soul, but here I was, sitting in a bath, wanting another man to make love to me.

Am I being immoral?

God, please forgive me, but can it be wrong to love Mike?

He was my first lover and the father of my only child.

The tingling intensified as his toes moved slowly towards their target and I questioned if there would someday be a retribution for my sins. I decided I didn't care.

I wanted him.

His rhythmic trigger sparked the wildest feeling. I began gasping for air. My whole body went out of control. Even the tip of my nose tingled. I grasped the sides of the bath with both hands to steady myself. The cocoon that I had felt when dancing with him at The Palace had returned. Everything was right with the world. We were alone and inside my citadel. We were floating through space. We were heading for paradise. My blood was boiling. My lid had been blown away.

My fears for the weekend and my Catholic hang-ups disappeared. His tempo speeded up and I exploded as I passed through the clouds. I couldn't wait any longer.

'The water is getting cold. Let's get into bed.'

We dried each other with the biggest towels I'd ever seen, and snuggled under the huge duvet. We lay together, partially damp.

'I just want to lie here and look at you,' he whispered. 'Seeing what I have been missing all these years makes me want to weep. You have the most beautiful eyes God ever created.'

He took his time as his hands moved tenderly over my body, enticing extraordinary, tantalising feelings. His taut body pressing against me heightened ever more passion.

Bizarrely, I thought, *Go easy, Mike, I'm not used to this.*

I had entered Utopia. My eyes were closed as I hung on to him for dear life.

As his tongue moved downwards, he pushed his face firmly into my stomach. I could feel his facial features and the day's growth of his beard against my skin.

For the rest of the evening, I remained in a fanciful trance and only have the vaguest recollections. My mind was a vacuum. Whenever I came round, his beautiful dark blue eyes were smiling at me. He was enjoying looking at me asleep. We would then begin again. On each occasion the intensity of our relationship increased. Where his stamina came from, I don't know. However, by the morning, neither of us had slept much. I was not only tired, but I ached. Everywhere felt tender.

'I'm sorry, Mike, but I'm sore all over. I need a rest until this evening.'

'It's OK, Mia, I understand. I shouldn't have taken that pill.'

'What pill?' I asked.

'I was afraid I might disappoint you,' he explained, 'so I took two.'

'You didn't disappoint,' I assured him, laughing at the irony of my forgetting the KY jelly.

'They say you can't turn the clock back,' he began, 'but those pills make me feel as if I could make love to you all day.'

'Well, you're not going to. Take a cold shower instead.'

We began laughing that we had beaten Old Father Time and had become love-torn teenagers.

We planned our day over breakfast. We went to the Tower Ballroom, but there was no Reginald Dixon. He'd been dead for eighteen years, but both of us sat for a while reliving the moment when we had heard the maestro practising on that fateful Sunday morning after church. We walked hand in hand, in a dream, to St Cuthbert's. It was open and we ventured inside.

To my surprise, Mike announced that he would like to return for the following morning's 10.30 service.

'After all,' he explained, 'this is where it all began.'

'What?' I asked.

'My conversion to Catholicism for you.'

'But you never go to church.'

'Maybe, but converting was a hell of a big step. If there was one indicator of my love for you, then that must have been it. I've never been the same since. The conversion left me in limbo: a non-practising Catholic torn between Methodism, Catholicism and secularism. I guess I'm a genuine agnostic who really doesn't know what to think anymore.'

We had an early lunch in a nearby pub and spent an hour or two at the Pleasure Beach. The rides were bigger and more frightening than in 1963. Mike remembered we had gone to the pictures with me wearing one of his sweaters over my Britair uniform. My overriding memory of that evening, when I stayed at his digs, was travelling down the promenade on an open tram admiring the illuminations, then riding the big dipper at the Pleasure Beach. Weirdly, Mike couldn't recollect the rides, only that we ended up at the cinema. Not for the first time, our memories were playing tricks.

I'd agreed at breakfast to accompany Mike to see Blackpool play Notts County that afternoon at Bloomfield Road. We sat in the warm sunshine and saw the home team win 2–1 in front of a crowd of six thousand. I'd never been to a professional soccer match before and couldn't help thinking it was a long way from Douglas, when as a youngster, I would sometimes go with my brother to watch St Mary's play in the Manx league and shout abuse at the visiting side.

That evening we dined in the hotel. At a quiet, corner table, with a bottle of Moët, we continued to reminisce about incidents long forgotten.

Out of the blue, he asked about his signet ring. 'Do you remember buying it for me when we became engaged?' he queried.

'Yes, why do you mention it?'

Oh my God, he's going to ask what happened to it.

'It was engraved with my initials and I seem to remember your initials, MYM, were on the inside of the ring.'

'We had it engraved while we went up Douglas Head.'

'What happened to it?' he asked.

I still vividly remembered him tossing it at me the night we split up.

I hadn't the guts to hurt his feelings and tell him I knew where it went. Soon after I left for Australia, my mother had found it in a drawer and sold it to a scrap dealer.

'I don't know,' I lied. 'It must have got lost when Mum moved to a smaller house after David got married.'

That evening I made sure I used the KY jelly. Although it eased my problem, I still ached. Fortunately, we were both tired from the previous night. When we fell asleep in each other's arms, we remained unconscious until Sunday morning. I reminded Mike that if he wanted to go to St Cuthbert's we would have to get a move on and didn't have time for anymore 'you know what'. My ploy worked and we arrived in time for Mass.

My flight home left at 1430 hours, just giving us time after church to visit St Anne's where Mike showed me 'our' flat. We stood outside, hugging each other and wept silently. Both of us were alone in our thoughts, imagining what could have been. Minutes passed before Mike looked down at me, tears in his eyes.

He wiped his face and sniffled, 'I love you Mia. To me, you are who you were. You always will be my little Mia. Maybe it was meant that we shouldn't have spent our lives together.'

Holding hands, with tears running down my face, we drove silently along the front toward King Edward School and found a café to have a 'lite bite' before returning to the airport. Seeing where we should have spent our early married life dampened the weekend's enjoyment, but I promised myself that next time I would be better prepared to withstand his ardour.

Chapter 28

October 2003

After Blackpool, their texting and phoning increased. Mike's weekly letters were frequently augmented by adding copies of old photos. Mia could not reply by post as her Manx stamps would have been a giveaway if Joyce picked up the mail. Their surreptitious affair was to neither's liking. Mike was only too aware that he was trapped. He had always been one for postponing making a decision and believed prevarication was, in itself, a form of making a choice. Admitting to Joyce that he had rediscovered his long-lost love would be impossible. He, therefore, set about plotting a way out of his dilemma.

My one and only Mia,

I am constantly thinking of you. Do you remember our playing golf at Port Erin? You taught me that a properly crafted swing beats muscle every time. Wouldn't it be marvellous if we had an apartment near the Rowany Course? One of those new converted flats in the former hotels that overlook the bay towards Ireland would suit us perfectly.

We can't go on like this indefinitely. At some point something has to give: either you sell up, come away and we elope to the North-West of Scotland or I get rid of Joyce and join you on the island. Which is it to be?

Your one and only,
Mike

The following week Joyce had gone to the theatre to see a play being given by a local theatre company. On the phone Mike probed Mia's views on the idea of leaving Joyce. As usual, she was vehement with her reply.

'*No!*' she emphasised. 'I am happy that we can arrange to meet two or three times per year. There is no way I am going to be held responsible for the breakdown of your marriage. Our happiness can't be at the expense of Joyce's misery. I saw what my father did to my mother when he deserted her; I'm not letting you do it.'

'But our marriage is broken already.'

'I know it's far from ideal, but if Joyce was to sue you for divorce on the grounds of your affair with me, then she could take you to the cleaners. She would get half your teacher's pension for a start. As you would have abandoned her, she would get your house. Your children and grandchildren would never speak to you again. Need I go on?'

He knew she was right. There was no point in arguing.

She continued, 'We've got to be realistic. We've never lived together. Two or three days together in a hotel is one thing, but living in the same house, day in, day out, week in, week out is something else. After forty years apart we both have habits that will annoy each other and are too ingrained to change. You like a shower; I like a bath. You eat fish and poultry; I prefer beef and lamb. You listen to Classic FM; I like Radio Two. You read *The Guardian*; I read *The Mail*. You hate Marmite; I love it. We'd get on each other's nerves after a month. Then, there are the neighbours. What do you think they're going to say? Within an hour of you moving in, it would be all around Maughold. By the end of the day, half of Ramsey would know. You know what people are like: "She's in tow with a married man." My friends at church and the golf club would shun me. They're happy for me to be an ageing widow, but they wouldn't approve of me being shacked up with a toy boy... oh dear, no. That would be too much for them.'

'They'd probably be jealous.'

Mia began laughing. 'I do love you, Mike, maybe even more now than when we were engaged. I am old enough now to appreciate what you are. I would marry you if you were free, but you're not. Unless something happens to Joyce then our destiny is to remain apart. We will never be united.'

'Mia, I'm not sure I can carry on without you. I've heard of people having a split personality, but I'm living a split life. My body is in Grange, but my heart is with you. Not a moment goes by when I'm not wondering what you are doing. It's tearing me apart. I've started to draw up a list of things that I would want to bring with me if I left Joyce. I've identified paintings, books, files, bank statements, as well as clothes. I've drawn up a list of organisations I'd have to inform about my change of address. I'm torn between reality and illusion. All I know is where I want to be.'

'Look, Mike, you've got to see your glass as being half-full, not half-empty. Before we met, we both had nothing to excite our libido. We never missed each other because we never had each other. Now, and especially after Blackpool, we have something to look forward to. OK, so we don't know when we can next meet, but I am sure it won't be long. Then we'll enjoy each other's company like we did three weeks ago. You must count your blessings, Mike.'

Over the next few days, he thought about her words: *Unless something happens to Joyce, then our destiny is to remain apart.*

How could Mia arouse such uncontrollable passion in him? What made her different? For weeks he had thought of little else. He had come to no conclusion other than there was no answer. He wanted her all the time. She was eating him alive. It had been like this in 1963. Then, he had been warned that she was not good for him. Now he could see a similar problem. If he pursued her to its logical outcome – leaving Joyce – then it would not be good for him. But the ardour she aroused in him overruled logic. He knew he had to go the whole way. Previously, he'd made the error of not allowing his instinct to rule his head. He wasn't going to let it happen again. In 1964 he'd wanted Mia more than anything else, but he'd been pathetic. He'd allowed the pressures to build up and lost the only girl who ever made him happy. He'd been weak and allowed others to sway his judgement. He'd travelled to South America to forget her. It hadn't worked. He was resolute that he wouldn't lose her – again.

He'd never taken drugs, but suspected he was suffering from some sort of withdrawal symptom. He had to escape from Joyce, one way or the other. Like a bar of his favourite chocolate, once started he had to consume it all, even though he knew it wasn't the right thing to do. Mia was his bar of Toblerone and he had to finish it – court her, marry her and live with her until he died.

He began planning.

Joyce's parents were elderly. They had retired from their jobs as civil servants in London twenty years previously and moved to Torquay. Her father was now eighty-four and had suffered several minor strokes. All his life he had been the type of man that expected his wife to run around after him: meals on the table at set times, washing and ironing done regularly. He never went shopping with Millie, his wife. She even ironed his trousers and cleaned his shoes. Recently, however, Millie's dementia had worsened and she had been diagnosed with Alzheimer's. A crisis loomed in their household and, as their only child, Joyce had little alternative but to spend ever more time in Devon.

He drew up plans that he knew were wrong. Mia would not approve, but the void in their lives would be filled. He would rid himself of Joyce. It would be a matter of careful timing and attention to detail.

JOYCE'S MOTHER IS NOT WELL AND SHE PLANS TO GO HOME FOR A WEEK NEXT FRIDAY. HOW ABOUT ME COMING OVER FOR THE W/E?

WONDERFUL. WHERE WILL WE STAY?

THERE MUST BE SOMEWHERE – PORT ERIN, PERHAPS. IF YOU SEE A HOTEL YOU LIKE, BOOK IT. I WILL ARRIVE AT 1605 HOURS ON THE BLACKPOOL FLIGHT.

Chapter 29

October 2003

I met Mike from the plane. He had a grin on his face a mile wide.

'You look fantastic,' he said and we hugged in the arrivals hall with no self-consciousness whatsoever. I was grateful there was no one around who knew me. In the car we embraced for several minutes before he asked, 'Where are we staying?'

'Port Erin. There is an upmarket B&B on Bradda Head.'

'A bed and breakfast?'

'It comes highly recommended by a friend in the golf club who had a weekend there last month. She's not the sort to endorse anything but the best.'

And so it proved. At the Arches, we were given the Mauve Suite with its own balcony overlooking the bay and a view of the coast towards the Calf of Man.

'There can't be many B&Bs with a jacuzzi, a gymnasium and a swimming pool,' remarked Mike after we had been welcomed and shown around.

Alone in our room he held my shoulders and, looking directly into my eyes, purposefully pressed me carefully backwards onto the bed.

'You look ravishing, and I am going to roger you,' he said.

My eyes and mouth must have opened in surprise for I wondered what he meant. I nearly asked him what Roger had to do with it. I soon found out, as he immediately began fumbling under my blouse.

I hadn't expected such an immediate ambush. I couldn't believe what was happening to us. It had taken him forty seconds to put the clock back forty years. I found myself breathing heavily, gasping for air and my body stiffening as shivers smartened my nerves in anticipation of what was to come. With my blouse half-undone, my skirt tugged up over my waist and my knickers pulled to one side, he rogered me. Never before had I experienced the joining of bodies with clothes on. The earthiness added excitement – a coarseness that was so fresh that I was exhausted, but high on the drug of contentment that extended from top to toe. I lay by his side recovering my breath, unable to speak, thinking that if rogering meant doing it fully clothed then I wanted to be rogered more often.

After cooling down, we bathed together in the swimming pool and, feeling hungry, walked into Port Erin, found a pub that did food, and strolled back in the dark.

Some days later, I asked my best friend, who had been married twice and had had children with both her husbands, 'Have you ever been rogered?'

She answered, 'I don't think so, what is it?!'

Sitting listening to our conversation, her thirty-something son began laughing. Doubled up and with his eyes steaming, he choked, 'But Mum, every fifteen-year-old schoolboy knows that!'

The weekend was paradise. We were never out of each other's sight. We spent much of Saturday in the Manx Museum in Douglas researching through old copies of *The Isle of Man Times*. We found our engagement announcement, as well as several photos of our attending functions during the Christmas – New Year period of 1963–64. That evening we reminisced as we lay in bed. We remembered things that we had both long forgotten. It was dreamland being with Mike. We were alone and could have been on a desert island. There was no one telling us we were unsuitable for each other.

I felt we had become a permanent couple, but I'd felt that way before. Was my forty-year wait finally was over?

We had both spent the intervening years in a wilderness and all because I hadn't had the courage to tell Mike that he'd got me pregnant. Being inflexible over the idea of a register office wedding had been the biggest error of my life and I cursed myself for being so stupid. I had been more concerned about upsetting my mum and our priest than loving Mike. I knew, as I lay next to him, that he would have stuck by me even though all of Douglas would have known we were having a shotgun wedding. So what? My mother and his parents would have come round. They always do when they see their first grandchild.

Yes, I'd been lucky finding Phil and had enjoyed our life together. I was a wealthy widow thanks to his brilliance as an architect. I'd been to places with Phil that Mike had probably never heard of, mixed with celebrities whose wealth made them powerful, and met international politicians. And yet the man lying next to me was the simple man I'd fallen in love with – a gifted schoolmaster who would have made me happy, given me too many children, and made me return to work to pay the bills. *It's ironic*, I thought, *but the life and love I truly wanted began at The Palace Ballroom.*

Lying next to me was the father of my only child. How could I tell him without upsetting him and possibly risk losing him? I was in a quandary that I knew I had to resolve sooner or later. Timing would be crucial, but now wasn't the time.

Chapter 30

October 2003

When Mike returned to Grange-over-Sands from the Isle of Man there was a message on the answerphone from Joyce. Her father had died suddenly from a stroke and she was remaining in Torbay to organise his funeral. He returned the call, excused his absence by saying he had been playing golf, and promised to drive down to Devon the following day. However, the news was just what he wanted. His scheme to free himself from Joyce had suddenly been given a boost. He saw a way out.

The following evening he arrived in Torbay. He had not expected to see his mother-in-law in such a bad state. Whether the sudden death of her life-long partner had exacerbated her dementia or not, he didn't know, but it was obvious Millie was incapable of looking after herself. She was going to require full-time care.

That evening, Joyce raised the subject of their future. 'There are three alternatives,' she said. 'Firstly she could come and live with us...'

'No way,' he replied, not giving her a chance to finish the sentence.

'Secondly, she could go into a nursing home...'

'And the third?' he asked.

'We could move down here to be near to her.'

'You mean we move in with her,' he corrected.

'Not necessarily.'

'Joyce, I don't see why we should move. We've got the house in Grange the way we want it, especially now we've had the new bathroom fitted. We've got our friends up there. You've got U3A and your volunteer work with the National Trust at Sizergh. I've the golf club, the bridge club and Probus. It only took me seven hours down the M6 and M5 to get here and I wasn't rushing. I think your mum needs round-the-clock attention. If we can find the right care home, she'll be happy. She has her pension from the Home Office, and will get half of your dad's Ministry of Defence pension as his widow. On top of that she has her Old Age Pension. I wouldn't have thought it'd be necessary to dip into her savings or the proceeds from the sale of the house to pay the nursing home fees.'

The following day they discovered they were spoilt for choice. The Torbay area was full of nursing homes. In general, the greater the fees, the better the quality. Mike's figures suggested that his mother-in-law's total income from the three pensions would amount to £2,400 per month. The home they chose charged £3,200 per month, but the shortfall could be met from her savings. On top of that, her detached bungalow in Babbacombe would probably realise something approaching £300,000.

They stayed in Torbay for three weeks, during which time Joyce's mother was settled into the nursing home and her bungalow was sold for the first offer of £290,000. Five years previously, Joyce had been made Power of Attorney and it made the administration of the estate relatively simple. Mike began firming up his scheme to split from his wife painlessly.

When they returned home, Mike kept in touch with Mia as before. He never mentioned his intentions, but quietly began implementing his plans. Joyce was telling her acquaintances that her mum was in a care home and, therefore, she would regularly need to travel south to visit her. Mike, meanwhile, was spreading a slightly different story. He was telling friends that because his mother-in-law no longer knew her own daughter they had decided to move to Torquay permanently so they could be near her at all times.

When Joyce travelled to Devon for her first visit to her mother, Mike approached a local estate agent. A realistic price that should ensure a speedy sale was agreed, but there was to be no advertising. Interested purchasers could only visit when Mike was present, so that he could ensure Joyce was absent. He had sole ownership of the house, having bought it when they had moved thirty-three years previously. It dawned on him that Joyce had kept the profit from the sale of her small two-up-and-two-down in Kendal that had not sold until the year after they moved to Grange.

All fair in love and war, he consoled himself.

With Joyce away, he flew with Aer Lingus to Dublin from Blackpool for a day. An early morning flight and a return in the late afternoon met his requirements. He took a taxi from the airport into the centre of Dublin.

'There's a generous tip if you take me to a postal forwarding office that doesn't ask too many questions,' he said to the driver.

'I think I know what you want,' replied the cabbie.

They headed towards one of the less salubrious districts – a cobbled street on the south side of the River Liffey, off Wellington Quay. Mike noticed several middle-aged 'heavies' in leather jackets and jeans hanging around on the street corners. They watched him like Hawkeye. In the street there were several shady shops. He was uncertain of their precise merchandise, but thought, *Probably porn, drugs and prostitution.*

He was dropped off in front of a window that advertised: *Postal Forwarding Service, Confidentiality Guaranteed.* He entered and made enquiries. He discovered that mail could either be collected (the usual method according to the owner – a seven o'clock shadow, liberally tattooed, shaven headed man who looked sixty, but was probably in his mid-forties) or forwarded to your chosen address.

Not an advert for healthy living, thought Mike as he looked at the fag hanging from the corner of the proprietor's lower lip, as if stuck there with super-glue.

'How much?' Mike asked.

'€30 per month in advance if collected, €40 if sent on.'

'I'll always want mine sent on. The address might change from time to time.'

'No problem.'

Mike placed two €20 notes on the counter.

'Minimum contract is three months.'

A further €80 went on the counter. 'Suppose the police come snooping and demand to take away the correspondence?'

'They'll need a search warrant and I'll have been tipped off.' He raised his forefinger to his nose and grinned, revealing a set of green teeth that did not enhance his appearance. He then scribbled the address to be used:

C/O Box 14,
15 Back Chester Street,
Dublin.

'We need to agree a system of passwords,' the man added. 'If you phone to change your forwarding address, you'll need a password and a six-digit code to confirm your identity. Your password will be in lieu of your real name.'

It then dawned on Mike that he had not revealed his name.

'For my password, what about *Quo Vadis*?'

'Where are you going? A most appropriate and interesting choice,' the man replied.

Mike watched him scribble the password, spelling it correctly.

Perhaps he's not as dim as he looks; he must have been taught Latin at school, he thought.

'And your six-digit code? Most use a memorable date.'

'260663.'

'What happened then?'

'I got engaged to the girl I should have married. There is another service I want.'

'Go on.'

'Shortly, I will begin sending you letters inside envelopes. The inner letter will be addressed to my home in Grange-over-Sands. I want you to put an Irish stamp on it and send it back.'

'That's OK.'

The first letter arrived at Grange from Dublin a fortnight later when Mike was playing golf with his usual Tuesday afternoon four-ball cronies. Joyce picked up the post and sorted her correspondence from Mike's. She noted the Irish stamp and looked at the handwriting that seemed vaguely feminine. Puzzled, she thought no more about it. When he got home he saw the letter, smiled to himself and made a display of folding it and putting it in his pocket.

'Aren't you going to open it?' asked Joyce.

'I'll read it later,' he replied, trying to act embarrassed.

She scowled, but said nothing.

Two weeks later another Irish stamped letter arrived. Intrigued, Joyce carefully steamed open the envelope. Inside, she read…

My dearest Mike,

How much longer are we going to continue like this? Since our last weekend together, I miss you more than ever. I know I said I would be happy to simply meet you two or three times each year, but it isn't easy. Since our first meeting last year, when we met by accident, I never thought that someday I would have to go through the agony…

And so the letter went on…

All my love, your one and only,
    Bridget.

The bastard has been having an affair.

She confronted him when he came home. 'You effing git,' she began. 'How long has it been going on?'

'What's being going on? What are you talking about?'

He smiled to himself. *It's worked.*

'You've got some Irish tart in tow.'

'Oh, so you're opening my mail now, are you?'

'It's as well that I did. How long has it being going on?'

'Look, woman, we've not been intimate for over twenty bloody years, so don't give me the high-and-mighty. Just look at yourself. You could fit into a size ten when we got married. Now you're a size twenty…'

'I'm only an eighteen.'

'Well, whatever. You let yourself go after that damned hysterectomy and became a bloody old woman. When I met you, you had shoulder-length fair hair, dressed nicely and I was proud to call you my own. Now you're a dowdy, old frump, always fretting over something insignificant. Why do you think I've not had a prostate problem? Because I've been shagging regularly for the last fifteen years to keep myself fit. Men with prostate problems lose it because they don't use it.'

'Rubbish!' she yelled. However, it stopped her in her tracks – the thought that her husband had been having an affair, or even several affairs, behind her back for so long.

The wife is always the last to know!

'I want you to leave straight away.'

'Like hell I will. I think you'll find I own this house. I've sold it already and accepted an offer. You've got a week to clear out. You can afford to buy an apartment for yourself in Devon with the proceeds of the sale of your mother's house. So pack your bags and bugger off.'

'You're not going to get away with this. I've lived with you for over thirty godforsaken years, borne your children and brought them up. No judge is going to let you walk away scot-free. I'll make sure I get half this house and half of your bloody pension. Anyway, where do you think you're going to go?'

'To Ireland, property is cheaper there. I'll be outside the British judicial system and you won't be able to get a penny of mine. I don't care as long as I don't have to see you over the breakfast table again. This is my contact address.' He gave her a slip of paper.

C/o Box 14,
15 Back Chester Street,
Dublin.

'It's a private postal service, so you will not be able to follow me. When you leave here you will never see me again. I've hired a van tomorrow to take my stuff and put it into storage until such time as I've an apartment of my own. What's left is yours, so you'd better get yourself organised.'

She left the room, slammed the door and drove away in her small car. She didn't return that evening. He'd no idea where she went and he didn't care.

The following day, Mike drove to a nearby branch of a van hire company, left his car and returned home in a white transit. He removed all his personal files and belongings, including his golf clubs, took several paintings from the walls, packed his clothes, put books that he wished to retain in boxes, and wrapped delicate breakables such as glasses, a china tea service and sufficient day-to-day crockery and cutlery.

He never saw Joyce again.

Chapter 31

November 2003

Mia was woken by a banging on the door. She looked at her bedside clock. It was only seven o'clock.

Who the hell is that?

She looked through the curtains. There was a white van in her driveway. She couldn't see anyone. She went into the hall and saw a figure through the frosted glass of the front door. She cautiously opened the door, having forgotten to put on her dressing gown.

It was Mike.

'What the hell are you doing here?' she asked.

'Can I come in?' He looked terrible. 'I've just come off the midnight boat. It was a bloody rough crossing.'

Her face registered astonishment. She was flabbergasted at seeing him.

Surprised, she didn't move, but repeated, 'Mike, what are you doing here?'

'I've left Joyce and am moving back to the island to be near you.'

'I thought we agreed it wasn't a good idea.'

'I know, but we can't carry on the way we are. We can't wander around in never-never land continually. We are neither here nor there. I plan to buy an apartment and will begin looking later this afternoon for somewhere suitable. But first of all, there are some hard questions to be answered. Do you want me to be with you for the rest of our lives? We've got what, fifteen active years at the most?'

'You know I do.'

'Then, can I come in and explain?'

'Yes, of course, I'm sorry.' She stood to one side to let him pass. She suddenly realised it was cold outside.

They moved into the lounge. She lit the gas fire; the central heating had only just come on.

'Don't get me wrong,' she began, 'but it was a shock seeing you at the front door.'

'I know there's no way I can begin living with you straight away. Joyce has said she is going to sue me. However, she's got to find me first as her only contact is a forwarding address in Dublin. She thinks I've gone to Ireland to live and, therefore, I will be outside the British legal system. Nonetheless, I will have to be prudent until everything gets sorted. It could take a year, or even longer. I've been looking on the web. There are plenty of one or two-bedroom flats on the market in Ramsey that I can afford and still keep a reserve of cash in case things go wrong.'

'Are you implying that at some future date you will be able to move in here?'

'I thought you said that is what we both wanted.'

'It wouldn't work.'

'Why?'

'Phil bought this bungalow in my name. In a way it's his house. He bought it without me seeing it. I would have chosen somewhere with a bigger kitchen, a smaller garden, nearer the shops and without a triple garage and workshop. I'm sorry, Mike, but if I lived here with you, I would end up seeing Phil's ghost and comparing you with him.'

He nodded silently. A black dog had appeared in front of him.

'If I was free of Joyce would you marry me?'

'Yes, you know I would.'

'Would you then sell this place and go fifty-fifty with me on somewhere else?

'Of course I would.'

The black dog began to fade.

That afternoon Mia drove him in her Porsche 911 to the biggest estate agent's office in Ramsey. Within an hour, they were able to view three flats. Mia turned her nose up at each one.

In the first, 'The kitchen is too small.'

'But there will only be me to cook for.'

In the second, 'The bedrooms are pokey.'

'I will only need one for myself; the second can be a study.'

In both, 'There's no en-suite.'

'Do I need one?'

It began to dawn on Mike that their roles had been reversed by the passage of time. When they had broken up, Mia had shackles chained to her feet.

There was the Stanley Square factor: *You're NOT going out with a girl from there?!*

The single-parent family factor: *Where's her father in all this?*

The lack of a formal education factor: *She left school at fifteen, she can't be very bright.*

The age factor: *She's four years older and has been around a bit.*

The Roman Catholic factor: that equated to the Manx social order factor.

The lack of money factor... and so it went on.

It had all added up. Although any single factor on its own would have been insignificant, when added together they created an obstacle that he was unable to hurdle. Since meeting Mia again, he had kicked himself every day for being such a prat, but as she kept repeating, 'Get over it, Mike. Let's make the most of our time together while we can.'

Now, however, the shoe was on the other foot – or, more precisely, the shackles were chained to him instead. Mia had married a wealthy man who had left her considerably well-off. She lived in a bungalow in 'Little Rhodesia', the name given by the locals to that area of the parish of Maughold where wealthy families had settled in the mid-60s after fleeing Ian Smith's Rhodesian Unilateral Declaration of Independence. Mike had never discussed money with Mia, but estimated that she could be a millionairess. She wintered in Australia and the Caribbean. Many of her friends lived in large houses with acres of ground, ran expensive cars, entertained each other with stylish dinner parties and had helicopters. They reflected a social class far removed from his.

How the tables have turned, he thought.

However, there was a hell of a difference. Whereas Mia's chains had been an accident of birth and no fault of her own, his were self-inflicted. He had been born intellectually gifted into a middle class family, but had wasted his talents. With a 2:1 degree in maths from Manchester University, the world should have been his oyster. Computers were in their infancy in 1962 when he graduated. Manchester University was the world's leading research centre into the new science. Turing had worked at Manchester's

Newman Laboratory in the 50s. The father of computers, Professor Tom Kilburn, had given several lectures to Mike's final year group. Instead of embracing the digital future, Mike had drifted into teaching because it was easy. He was good at it and it didn't tax him. By contrast, Mia had maximised the use of her talents while he was squandering his. He bet himself that she'd had more than a hand in helping Phil's career by successfully entertaining his wealthier clients.

The paradox reminded him of St Matthew as he paraphrased the Bible: *a prophet has honour, except in his own neighbourhood.* Away from the small-minded people of Douglas, Mia had been accepted for what she was by those she met – beautiful, talented and hard-working. The Sunningdale and Wentworth sets would not have seen her as a penniless girl from a single-parent, Catholic family living in a run-down apartment.

Travelling around looking at properties at the bottom end of the market with such a glamorous, elegantly dressed woman began to depress him. No wonder she was so sniffy. He wondered if she was recalling her start in life and whether she had also noticed that their relationship had been reversed.

She must love me to even think of renewing our relationship.

'Now, this is much better,' she remarked when viewing a seventh-floor penthouse.

'It is too expensive. I can't go over £120,000. Allowing for a buffer in case Joyce finds me, that's almost half the price I'm getting for my house in Grange.'

'You need to speculate in order to accumulate.'

'Mia, that's all very well, but I'm afraid I'm going to have to be financially cautious until Joyce gives up trying to find me and our separation is finalised.'

Then, brooding on their role reversal, he added, 'I've been thinking…'

'Oops, that's dangerous.'

'No, seriously. You and I were always like milk and cream.'

'What do you mean?' she asked with a puzzled look.

'You're the cream and I'm the milk.'

'You mean I'm thick?'

'No, you've risen to the top.'

She understood the implication. She held his hand and looked him squarely in the face. 'Don't worry, Mike. The flat will only be temporary until everything is settled. Then I'll sell up and we can move to somewhere that'll suit both of us. That apartment you wanted in Port Erin overlooking the sea, perhaps?'

Mike felt his eyes welling up and pulled her close. With his arms around her shoulders they stood in silence for several minutes. It was all he really wanted – to hold her close whenever he could.

He settled for a two-bedroomed apartment costing £90,000 on the fourth floor of a purpose built block. He paid a ten per cent deposit, accepted the name of a local solicitor recommended by the estate agent and was promised completion within three weeks. He emptied the contents of his white van into Mia's garage, noting how big it was – probably the same size as his newly acquired home. That evening they drove to Douglas in his empty van and booked into the Sefton Hotel.

Their room overlooked the promenade and Mia stood in a trance looking at the panoramic view that swept from the imposing war memorial on her left to Victoria Pier on her right.

'Mia, are you OK?' he asked.

She turned, shook her head and came out of her stupor.

'Sorry, I was miles away.' She paused and asked, 'Can I get you a cup of tea or something?'

He smiled. 'I wouldn't mind the something.'

She got the message and began laughing.

He put his arms around her slim waist and looked into the face that never tired him. She reached up and closed her eyes as they kissed. When he held her close, a process of absorption occurred and she would become a part of him. He recalled the first time he had held her in his arms at The Palace Ballroom – only half a mile away along the promenade. He had been so careful not wishing to cause discomfort to her dainty, shapely figure.

Moments later, they were lying on the bed. She had her eyes tight shut as they pressed their bodies as close together as possible. She was with her champion. He with the only girl for whom he would give up everything.

'I prefer your something to your tea. We'll have to do it more often.'

'From now on, we can do something whenever we want,' she replied. 'I feel satisfyingly drained. Do we need to go down to dinner, or can we order room service?'

The following day Mia accompanied Mike back to Lancaster from where he had hired the van, swapped it for his car, a three-year-old Ford Fiesta, and the pair made off for a short holiday to the North of Scotland. Mia didn't seem to mind Mike's car despite it being in a different league from her 911. She was overjoyed to be with him and showed her feelings in all sorts of tiny ways. Mike's blues had lifted as he looked forward to a happy future with his one and only Mia.

Chapter 32

November 2003

Mike and I had a wonderful week in the Scottish Highlands: walking, talking, coupling and decoupling. We were a good match. I had never been so happy. Our years apart had brought us closer together. We both agreed that our feelings for each other had never died; they had merely been put on hold. I didn't care that Mike hadn't made much of his life. Let's face it, he hadn't made much progress in his career. I remembered our expectations when he had gone for an interview at Blackpool for his first job. Then came our euphoria when he told me of his success on the Victoria Pier, as he came off the boat from Liverpool. The day we became engaged was hardwired into my heart. In Scotland we were reliving the days of the 1960s as if there had never been a gap in our lives. My heart was pounding against my ribs again every time he held me. I'd forgotten how it felt.

I became convinced that Mike's limited career progression was not for a lack of talent, but for an absence of ambition. Living with Joyce had drained him. She had given him no encouragement to seek something more demanding. I discovered, for example, that she never returned hospitality. When invited to dinner parties, she never reciprocated by asking people back to their home. Invitations soon dried up and their mutual social life withered on the grapevine. By contrast, I had always taken the initiative for Phil and ensured his important clients came to our house parties at Sunningdale and Wentworth. I staunchly believed that whatever the profession, in the public as well as the private sectors, advancement was as much a matter of *it's not what you know, but who you know*. Creating a wide range of acquaintances by socialising had helped

Phil's business to become one of the top architectural successes in Britain.

I resolved, therefore, that when Mike and I returned to the island I would introduce him to my circle of friends and let them see him for what he truly was. He didn't know it, but he was going to join the golf and bridge clubs. I would make sure he attended Mass with me on Sundays. I resolved to see him in more fashionable clothes instead of his Hush Puppies, baggy trousers and tweed sports jacket.

I had never been to Scotland before; ironic as with Phil I had been all over the globe and, yet, here on our doorstep was the most beautiful, wild countryside. Despite the hilltops being sprinkled with a covering of snow, the skies were blue. The sun, although low in the sky, was warm. We spent two days in Strontian; famous for being where the radioactive element strontium was discovered. The small hotel, The Ben View, served the most wonderful fresh food I'd ever tasted. We drove to the most westerly tip on the mainland of Britain – Ardnamurchan Point. That day when driving beyond Glenborrodale on the single-track road, we never saw a soul for what must have been twenty or thirty miles. Afterwards we made love in the back of Mike's car on the deserted, golden sands at nearby Sanna Bay and fell asleep in each other's arms. It was paradise on earth. Returning to Strontian, we picked our own mussels from the rocks close to the hotel and the proprietor cooked them for our starters with our evening meal.

The next day, we drove up the steepest road I'd ever seen to Applecross before finding a gem of a hotel at Shieldaig. We returned via Inverness, where Mike bought me an eternity ring. We passed Loch Ness and Loch Lomond, and stopped at Tarbet for our last night in Scotland.

When returning to Heysham to catch the boat, Mike cautiously approached his house in Grange to see whether Joyce had moved out. To his relief, she had. He was able to show me the property they had lived in for over thirty years. Joyce had left it tidy, although far from spotlessly clean. He left his keys with the estate agent. It was at that point I ventured to ask what his two children thought about him splitting with Joyce.

To my surprise he replied, 'I haven't told them. They'll find out soon enough.'

'I don't want to be nosy, but you've hardly ever mentioned your children. Don't you have much to do with them?'

'Not really. Matthew works in the city for some quasi-government organisation. I'm not sure what he does. He phones once a month. He keeps himself busy: cricket, golf, scuba diving and five-a-side football.

He's a typical bachelor whose life is too hectic for him to settle down. Christina's two kids keep her busy as well as her part-time job as a pharmacist. We have visited her occasionally at her home in Norwich, but neither Joyce nor I get on well with her husband. Don't ask me why. He's a nice enough fella, but takes life terribly seriously. I guess not seeing the grandchildren will be the biggest wrench.'

I held his hand, and suggested that someday everything might work out for him, but secretly I had my doubts. I wondered at our predicament. I was certain that our love had never died, but I kept asking myself why. It was a mystery I couldn't comprehend. How had we put our feelings for each other away into a bottom drawer? How could our affection remain hidden for all those years and never see the light of day until we met at Waterstones? The irony was that he had kept our engagement ring, while I had taken the KIGU musical powder compact with me to Australia and kept it when I married Phil. On one occasion Phil had asked me how I came to possess it, as when Matt was young he used to play with it as a toy, enjoying its musical tune. I told him it was a Christmas present from Liz, but I'm not sure he believed me. I suspect Phil realised Mike had never gone away. The fact that he wasn't Matt's biological father must have gnawed away inside him like a cancer. If it did, Phil never mentioned it. His love of Matt, who couldn't have had a better father, was never in question.

I concluded that God had blessed Mike and me with a unique bond when we met. It had remained intact. Father Time had not been able to break it. I knew, as I held his hand and looked at our old engagement ring, that he had always been my only true love. Silently, I asked Phil to forgive me.

I did try to give you one hundred per cent, Phil – honestly.

We had decided that, for the weeks before Mike took possession of his apartment, he should stay in a hotel on Ramsey's North Shore. We spent much of the time seeing what items he would require for his flat: new carpets, white goods, bedroom furniture, towels, sheets and so on. The day he took possession and picked up the keys, everything went to plan; the carpets were laid the following morning. Mike showed himself to be a dab hand at decorating and within two weeks, he had a comfortable pad. However, until he moved in, there had been some awkward and embarrassing moments. Whenever we'd met people I knew, I'd introduced him as an old friend of the family. I was given knowing looks by my closer friends. They were putting two and two together and making four.

After Mike moved into his apartment, things became easier as we had a private nest. I would spend three or four nights with him each week. We were as happy as two rabbits in a burrow when we were together. We were making up for lost time. Re-living our youth was wonderful. Discovering the joy of togetherness was exciting, as Mike never allowed our intimacy to become routine.

However, on odd occasions, I began to detect an undercurrent of despondency. I imagined his apartment might be reminding him of his flat in St Anne's and the time he spent in Blackpool scrimping and saving. I resolved to kick him out of his misery and planned a surprise for his Christmas present. I arranged for us to fly from Manchester on the 28th December to see in the New Year in Australia. When I told him, he was most unenthusiastic. He immediately expressed reservations about money.

'Mia, I can't afford to spend several thousand pounds on a holiday to Australia.'

There he goes again, I thought.

He's as bad as he always was – like father, like son!

Banking must be ingrained in his psyche.

His face reminds me of a bloody bank statement.

'We will be staying in my apartment that overlooks Sydney Harbour. The fireworks at midnight are unbelievable. You'll love the weather too; it's the height of their summer.'

'How many apartments have you got in Australia?'

'I have several. Phil bought them as a long-term investment. They are rented out and Matt lives in one. I keep the smallest for my personal use. I will claim our trip on expenses when I complete my tax return.'

'How will you do that?'

'I shall say that you are my financial adviser and I need to do an inspection of my properties.'

'I know nothing about finance.'

'You're a mathematician. You can do sums better than anyone I know.'

He said nothing for a while, and then mumbled a protest that was barely audible. 'I don't like the idea of being a kept man. I'll pay for my air fare.'

I was furious. Instead of thanking me for what would be a wonderful holiday, he was full of egocentric, self-righteous shit and feeling sorry for himself.

'If it'll make you feel better that's fine, but there isn't any need. If there's one thing Phil taught me, it is how to look after myself financially.

Mike, you're going to have to get used to the fact that I no longer live in Stanley Square. I have moved up the socio-economic ladder. I will try in future not to buy you gifts that embarrass you because you feel they are too expensive. So, please accept this holiday in the spirit it is intended. We'll have four weeks in the sun in the middle of the British winter. We'll be alone. Matt won't bother us. We can go and see Ayers Rock. I've never been. There may even be a cricket match we can go to.'

He looked sheepish after my reprimand. 'I'm sorry, Mia. It's a lovely idea. You do realise I've never travelled that far in an aircraft before?'

We spent New Year's Eve with Matt and his wife, Lisa, in Sydney's Opera House bar and restaurant overlooking the harbour. I didn't dare tell either Mike or Matt it was where I had my first date with Phil over thirty-five years previously. Consequently, I found my mind drifting back all evening to my early life with Phil. He had turned out to be a perfect husband and a wonderful father for Matt. Had Phil lived, it occurred to me that he could be sitting in Mike's place. It would have been a cosy family gathering. Instead there was an imperceptible, cold undercurrent of tension that, perhaps understandably, was radiating from Matt. It wasn't Mike's fault, I told myself, that Matt was uneasy with my having brought a married man to Australia. Whether Mike noticed the awkward ill-feeling or not, I couldn't tell, but I was determined to put it behind me and enjoy the midnight firework display. Mike agreed it was second to none and worth the journey. This cheered me up no end and we enjoyed the rest of the vacation as we were mostly alone. We took a flight to Alice Springs for four days and saw Ayers Rock in the late evening sunshine. All too soon it was time to return to Britain.

'I would like to come back someday,' he remarked while we awaited our flight back.

I thought, *I've won; he's got over his hang-ups.*

Chapter 33

February 2004

During the last week of January I invited two of my closest friends from the golf club and a further friend, who I knew from church, to come to a dinner party with their husbands the following weekend. My intention was to introduce Mike as my long-term partner and quash any rumours that had begun to circulate that I had a toyboy. Mike seemed ambivalent when I told him of my plans and I wondered if I was rushing things too much. Forty years previously I might have said something along the lines of, 'If you loved me...' Now I was wise enough to know that such an approach would be little more than a crude attempt to control him. I would have to handle him with kid gloves if I was to get him to integrate with my social circle. I suppose I still wanted control, but not of Mike – rather our lifestyle.

I went out of my way to create something special, buying the best seafood for starters, a fillet steak for the main course, and preparing Mike's favourite – a baked Alaska – to finish. I encouraged Mike to select the wines, perhaps being tactless when I told him, 'Selecting the wines was always Phil's job.' He didn't react, although I wondered later if my faux pas had a bearing on the lack of success of the party. I spent all Saturday ensuring everything would be perfect: buying nibbles, checking we had sufficient sherry, gin, tonic water, laying the table and so on.

Things didn't exactly come to a head between us, but there were times that evening when Mike made me feel uncomfortable. He appeared to have few conversational skills. There were awkward pauses at the table and despite the wine flowing, small talk was limited.

He was fine if pontificating on the merits of private education vis-à-vis comprehensive schools, or the mystery of mathematics such as when he asked my friends, 'How many numbers are there between zero and one?'

'None,' replied Jill.

'Nope,' was his reply.

'One,' guessed her husband Peter.

'An infinite number,' Mike answered with a grin.

We all looked at him to amplify.

'There's 0.1, 0.2, 0.3, then there's 0.01, 0.02, 0.03, 0.001, 0.002, and we could go on forever. There are infinite numbers, but no such thing as infinity.'

I think we were all dumbfounded. None of us had thought about it before. The silence was deafening and the party went flat.

When I repeated the dinner party experiment two weeks later with different friends, it happened again. My first thoughts were that the problem was my choice of guests. So, I tried a different formula – a finger buffet with ten couples from different backgrounds. Mike was like a lost lamb. He had no idea how to circulate, or top up the guests' glasses. I found it difficult to understand why his lack of interactive social skills was so poor.

His problems disappeared when we were alone. As a consequence of marrying Phil, I had become a social animal surrounded by countless friends from all over the world. I still received regular phone calls from friends in South Africa, the Caribbean and America, inviting me to stay with them. I could not change and become a recluse and have Mike as a monosyllabic companion. Accordingly, I was beginning to fear our relationship could end up going the same way as it had in the 60s.

All sorts of ideas began to flood into my mind. I speculated why his family life meant so little to him. Was he with me purely to get away from Joyce? Were we only living for the moment? Why was he so anti-Catholic, or was I being paranoid? Did he simply want to relive his youth by having the sex life we never had? Could our relative maturity make it last this time? Did he have any long-term ambitions? When was he going to do something about his marital mess?

Persuading Mike to make new friends was proving impossible. I guess I had always had a gregarious personality. I'd always made friends easily: at school, at work or with Phil's colleagues and clients. It had finally dawned on me, although it had taken me long enough, that Mike was an individual who liked his own company. He was, therefore, indifferent to meeting strangers. When we played golf together he was always ready to go straight home after the game and avoid the nineteenth hole. My rose-tinted spectacles were beginning to clear. The mist over my eyes was evaporating and I was seeing Mike's weaknesses. I tried to remember if they existed when I first knew him. Whether it was my imagination, or not, I don't know, but the more I thought about it, the more I came to believe they did. Although I couldn't recall any specific examples of him being antisocial, we were invariably on our own for that year when we were engaged.

After Easter, I floated the idea that we could get a cheap golf holiday in Portugal for next to nothing. He enthused at the idea. It didn't occur to me that his eagerness might have something to do with wanting to get away from my circle of friends and be alone with me.

We flew to Faro via Manchester and stayed in Lagos. The entire seven days were spent golfing in the morning, lying by the pool in the afternoon and dining alfresco in the evening. It was a tonic for both of us. I thought he came back to the island looking healthier, and with his spirits lifted.

However, within a week things had returned to the way they were. I conjectured if he had depression and needed a medically qualified specialist to diagnose his problem. I guessed that living with Joyce had gradually forced him into a shell. But then I asked myself how could he have been successful as a teacher? It didn't make sense and so I went to see my GP.

Dr Simpson had been our family doctor since Phil and I moved back to the island in 1989. He had been most supportive when Phil had died. He listened sympathetically, but pointed out that unless Mike was willing to undergo a psychiatric assessment there was little he could do. I didn't mention that Mike had once considered suicide. I had hoped our rekindled love would be strong enough to bury that possibility for ever.

'Perhaps his problem is discovering that he no longer knows anyone on the island. When you knew him in the early 60s, he had a circle of friends, fellow students, boys he had been to school with?'

He paused to accept my acknowledgement.

I nodded, but didn't volunteer to admit I couldn't remember any.

'Now the island is bigger. The population has doubled. All those people he knew have dispersed and could be anywhere. Those who stayed on the island will have their own families, and have changed addresses. Ramsey will be a foreign land to him. You told me he spent his boyhood in Douglas and the south of the island?'

I nodded again.

'There you are then. You may be worrying too much. You have a naturally optimistic and upbeat personality. I was amazed by how quickly you recovered from Phil's sad departure. You will have to be patient with Mike. It sounds as if he is something of a pessimist and a fatalist. However, maybe I can help. Has he registered with a practice?'

'No, he hasn't.'

'Then suggest to him in a subtle way that he should and I will have an excuse to give him a thorough examination.'

By the end of the week, Mike had registered and seen Dr Simpson.

When he returned, I asked how he had got on.

All Mike would say was, 'Fine.'

Mike had begun to get threatening letters via his Irish post box from Joyce's solicitors. They were demanding to know his permanent address so that they could institute divorce proceedings. Mike had been ignoring the letters, hoping the noose that had begun to tighten around his neck would go away. Six months had passed since he had moved into his apartment and, unknown to me, he had continued to use his Irish post box for all correspondence. His depression deepened further when his bank threatened to close his account, as somehow, they had started to get letters from Joyce's lawyers. He had kept his bank account at Lloyds in Douglas since he went to university in 1959 and perhaps Joyce had known this. Before travelling to see his branch manager, he asked me if he could use my Maughold address for future correspondence with his bank.

'They'll be happy if I give them a permanent Manx address. It'll only be for my bank – no one else,' he explained.

'What's wrong with your apartment's address?' I asked.

'Nothing, but it might be wiser...' He didn't amplify any further and I wasn't in the mood to push him.

Without thinking through the possible outcome, I said, 'Yes.' After all, I thought, *It can only be his bank statements that will come to my address.*

A few weeks later, after we had been for a walk down to Maughold lighthouse, I confronted him as we sat having a light lunch in the kitchen.

'Mike, you are going to have to face Joyce's solicitors sooner or later. You tell me you want to marry me, but until you've sorted this mess out, we can't move on.'

'You're right, as usual. It's just that I'm scared she'll take me to the cleaners if she finds out what I've done. I'm envious of you.'

'Why?'

'Your faith; you've kept it all these years despite the expansion of sectarianism and religion becoming unfashionable.'

'I'm more liberal now than when I first met you. Matt got married in a register office. We should have done too. Unfortunately, forty years ago I believed that would have been a sin and, therefore, we wouldn't have been married in the sight of God.'

'There you go; you still believe in sin,' he said somewhat sarcastically.

'Don't you?' I replied.

'I believe in good and bad which is all the Ten Commandments amount to. I would like to think I treat others as I would want them to treat me, but I am only too aware that my life is riddled with incidents when I have fallen well short of that ideal.'

'You converted to Catholicism. Surely, some of the promises you vowed stuck?'

'I was naïve. Much of your church is founded on myths.'

I could feel my hackles rising. 'Such as?' I demanded.

'Rosary beads, the sale of indulgences, praying to Mary rather than God, altars having to possess a relic of some kind, miracles – need I go on?'

The bastard is a fraud.

He only converted all those years ago to get inside my knickers.

He never intended to marry me.

I've been a fool not to see through him.

Maybe he's after my money.

Well, he'll not get a bloody penny.

I couldn't believe my instinctive reaction to his blasphemous rant. My mind was racing with all sorts of ideas as to how to respond. There were several minutes of silence as I agonised, thinking how to answer the man I loved. I felt intensely bitter. I couldn't help it. He was getting my bonfire look.

'But those are physical things that are only a conduit to faith. I'm sceptical of much of what my church has done in the past, or still does. Nonetheless, it doesn't dent my belief that the Pope is God's representative on earth.' I paused. I could see him wanting to apologise as he realised how much he had hurt my feelings.

Calming down slightly, I added, 'Mike, you're a great one for procrastination. I know it's a Manx trait – *traa-dy-liooar* or time enough – but you've got to get a grip. Stop running away from hard decisions. Life isn't fair, it's bloody difficult.'

'I'm not that bad,' he said indignantly.

'Look at yourself. You're a wonderful, clever, warm-hearted man who has allowed life to pass him by. Whenever you needed to do something that might prove awkward, you chose the easy option. You could have become a headmaster, if you'd put your mind to it. There can't be many schoolmasters who never had a single failure at "A" Level in thirty years.'

'I liked teaching and the contact with kids. Headmasters don't teach. They just push pieces of paper around and play politics with the school's governors.'

'Come off it, Mike. You gave in to the obstacles facing us getting married. You blamed lack of money as our problem, but we knew all along it wouldn't be easy. The truth is that your mother bullied you to drop me because I came from the hell-hole of Stanley Square, didn't have a father and was a Catholic.' As soon as I had said it, I bit my lip and regretted my outburst.

'That's unfair,' he retorted.

'There you go again – unfair. You didn't face up to your mother. Now prove to me you're a real man and face up to Joyce. Or am I going to lose you to her as well?' I'd said it impulsively, my blood was still up, and I could hardly believe my own ears.

His face dropped. Suddenly he looked like a child who'd lost his weekly pocket money. His pathetic face made me livid and I lost the plot.

'The difference between you and Phil is incredible. He would never have let Joyce get in the way. He had balls and faced up to his parents when he brought me home from Australia. He took the line, "Love Mia like I do or lose me." You couldn't do that back then and you still can't do it. Until you do, bugger off and don't bother coming back.'

I stormed down the corridor, slamming my bedroom door.

He followed me and knocked on the door.

'Go away.'

Phil would have kicked the door down and given me a 'what for'.

Instead, he pleaded, 'Please, Mia, don't be cross.'

Cross? I'm bloody fuming.

Come in and roger me.

It's what I want.

'Mia, I'll do anything you ask.'

'Then sod off and don't come back until you've sorted the divorce out.'

'It could take ages.'

'So bloody what? I want a man, not a boy.'

'It may take some time.'

The last words spoken by Captain Oates, I thought.

There was silence for a few moments before I heard him drive away.

I stood shaking with nerves, regretting everything I'd said. I tried to console myself by arguing that it needed saying. There was no way we could go on indefinitely the way we were. He had been living in his flat for six months and nothing of any consequence had happened. How long was I supposed to wait? I wanted him to marry me. I wanted us to be happy, have an enjoyable life, and be romantically active for the next ten years. Was it too much to ask?

I looked at my watch. It was two o'clock. I needed something to take my mind off our quarrel. I decided to go and get some groceries at the supermarket in Ramsey. It would give me time to cool off.

Then, I thought, *Afterwards I might go around to his flat and we can make-up in the usual, tempestuous way.*

May 2004

The Roman Catholic church in Ramsey has the lengthy name of Church of Our Lady, Star of the Sea and St Maughold, an overdone title for a church, if ever there was one. However, it is unquestionably the finest Catholic church on the island, having been designed by Giles Gilbert Scott in 1909. Its architecture and style are much admired.

Since converting to Catholicism Mike had hardly ever been to church, certainly not a Catholic one. The exception was for the wedding of his former next-door neighbour and friend, Anthony. However, since meeting Mia again, his life had changed. After accompanying her to church during their Blackpool weekend, he had wanted to convince her that his love was sincere. Since moving to the island, he had accompanied her to Mass. Slowly the rituals he had long forgotten such as the Hail Mary, the Kyrie Eleison and the Eucharistic Prayer had come back to him. However, he neither attended confession nor took communion. Mia had at no time pressured him. She understood that his forty years in the wilderness could not be washed away by reciting a dozen Hail Marys.

He had entered the empty church, crossed himself and knelt in a pew near the front. He began praying silently for the first time since he was in his twenties. His mind was in a state of flux; he barely comprehended what he was thinking.

Dear God, what a mess I've made of everything. Where were You to guide me when I needed You most? You let me find Mia, the most beautiful woman I ever knew. Mia, who did something mysterious to me that no one else has done. She changed something inside me. Only You know what it was, but I was transformed for ever. You allowed me to win her affection forty years ago and then watched me make a fool of myself. I got what I deserved when we split up, but I can't help thinking what a wonderful life we would have had together. I became a restless soul seeking an unknown goal. I'm not blaming You for that. It wasn't until Mia reappeared that my burden lifted and whatever she had done to me all those years ago started again. I lived with Joyce in the wilderness for thirty-four years. Why? If You had rescued me from the backwoods sooner, Mia and I may have had time to make amends.

We fell in love so quickly. Why did we fall out of love so quickly? Was it in Your great plan that we should never become man and wife? Did You foresee a disaster and intervene?

I remember my father telling me, that if I'd really loved Mia, then I should have searched the world until I found her. How could I? I was as poor as a church mouse. How could I have found her in Australia? Surely, You could have told me what to do? But then I was always a prevaricator. Was it Your idea to ensure Mia got the better man? The man who could give her everything: all that she deserved – travel, excitement and money? I could never have done that. With me she'd have been a school teacher's wife struggling to make ends meet. Phil metaphorically dragged her out of Douglas and opened up her horizon. Where better than Sunningdale and Wentworth? With me? We might have made a semi-detached in Blackpool? Who knows? Only You.

When Mia met Phil in Australia I guess they were a natural match. She has shown me photos of their houses. I could never have equalled the lifestyle he gave her. When I looked at her wedding photos, all I could see was my Mia. Not Phil's Mia, no one else's Mia; just my Mia – with another man. I felt so envious. There he was – a man with my Mia and she looked to be in love with him. God, how I've cursed you for letting me lose her. I don't know where she had her wedding night, but it should have been with me. Apart from Mia did I ever really harm anyone? No!

Hoggy Horton? He received a smack from Miss Cubbon.

Helen? She was temporarily upset but quickly found a husband.

Wendy? She used me as much as I did her.

Joyce? It was fifty-fifty and she deserved it.

Matthew and Christina? They'll get over it.

I've given up everything for Mia – including my grandchildren – and have nothing left.

Mia has told me I am incomparable to Phil – certainly not as good at providing the luxuries she has grown used to. God, with Phil she's been to places I've hardly heard of: Tallahassee, Curaçao, Sharjah and Quito.

And yet, did I ever really trust her? All along – all those years ago people were telling me she was not what she was making herself out to be. She was constantly a paradox. She always kept something back, but I was blinded by her beauty. If she had told me she was the reincarnation of Helen of Troy, I would have believed her.

God, have I only ever been a pawn on her chess board? How she's played with me. Now she's sacrificed me. Well, God, it's my turn and I'm going to make sure the black king captures the white queen and throws her into the chess box. And You can't stop me.

Converting to Catholicism at the time could only have been a ploy on my part to win her affection; it couldn't have been real. It was necessary for me to marry her; the only way I could have her for myself.

What a prat I was. I should have seen through her all along. That day at Jenny's cottage – was I the first? No, of course not, but I wanted to believe it. I convinced myself I was and until an hour ago I still believed she had only ever had me and Phil. But then I've always been an idiot. I was a cheat at school and university. Yes, I admit I cheated Mia, but she cheated me too. Now I'm going to cheat You.

I'm sorry I've ignored You for so long. Deep down you know I do believe in You. I was always a doubting Thomas. I believe in God, the father; God, the son; and Mary, mother of God. I believe You are all-forgiving, so I hope You will forgive me for what I am about to do.

I am going to break the sixth commandment and will die in a state of mortal sin. Meeting Mia last year postponed the inevitable. Now I will cheat her for the final time. At least this way, no one will have the terrible job of finding me – so You might give me some credit on my account.

Cheerio God, don't be too hard on me – I've been a drain on your rations, but it won't be for much longer.

He moved to the candle rack and although sceptical of the ritual, so frequently practised in Catholic churches, he lit six candles: one for Joyce, one each for his children and grandchildren, and finally, one for Mia. As he lit each, he asked their forgiveness and prayed for their soul.

His last words of prayer were,

This is the end I deserved: the end that began with cheating Hoggy Horton and will finish today with cheating You, the creator of all things.

As he turned to leave, he met the priest, Father Bernard, coming up the aisle.

'Are you all right, my son?' he asked.

It had always amused Mike that a man half his age should greet him so. They shook hands. 'It's nice to see you here on your own,' continued the priest.

'Yes, I'm fine thank you, Father,' he replied. 'Mia is shopping and I thought I'd just spend a few minutes in quiet contemplation.'

He looked at his watch. 'I'd better get a move on, Mia will be wondering where I've got to.'

'Go carefully,' replied the priest.

Too late for that, Mike thought.

Chapter 35

May 2004

Mike drove carefully out of Ramsey, deep in thought about his plan. At the top of Bowring Road, he bore right onto the Bride Road and headed for the Point of Ayre. He had little idea how long his scheme would take to come to fruition. Despite the numerous imponderables, he was certain it would happen sometime that afternoon, so he didn't rush. Unconsciously, he'd laid the trap at Mia's an hour earlier that had festered in his mind since those wretched dinner parties with her artificial, so-called friends with plastic brains. At Bride, in front of the church, he turned right and headed down Cranstal Road. He passed the traditional Manx cottages, eventually reaching the mile-long straight that led to the lighthouse. Approximately two hundred yards from the most northerly building on the island, he drew off the road and parked by the sand dunes where his car could easily be seen. It was near the spot where he had sat with Mia and the Manx cat ten months previously.

His mind continued to reflect irrationally.

What a year it has been.

Meeting Mia, realising I still wanted her.

Did I ever love her?

Are love and hate the two sides of the same coin?

Can you only love someone you hate?

Is sex the conduit that links the two sides?

Although our bond couldn't be broken by time, we sure as hell knew how to test it.

He left the car unlocked with the keys in the ignition. He placed a letter inside a sealed envelope that he had written before going to church on the front passenger seat. On the front cover of the envelope, addressed *To The Finder*, was the message:

Please take this letter to the Inspector at the Ramsey Police Station. Tell him where you found it. Its contents will explain that a letter left with the Manager of Lloyds Bank in Parliament Street can now be acted upon. You should subsequently receive a reward of £100 for your help in this matter from Lloyds Bank.
Gratefully,
Mike Moore

He walked ten yards over the dunes to the stony beach.

The sea looked cold. Despite the westerly wind at his back, the tide was ripping northwards towards Scotland. He knew it would be like this, but he was not deterred.

How long is it since Dad and I swam around the Queen's Pier in Ramsey?

I was about seventeen; Dad would have been in his forties, exactly forty-six years ago.

Not much to show for it: mistake after mistake, blunder after blunder, a liar and a cheat.

Lazy and bone idle at both school and university.

A lecher with Helen, Mia and Joyce.

What talent God gave me, I wasted.

He's going to make me spend a long time in purgatory.

Well, I might as well be hung for a sheep as for a lamb.

'Your trouble,' his maths master at school had told him, 'is that you put your pen down when you think you've done enough to pass.' His teacher had been right, but whether it would have made any difference or not, he was unsure.

He took his shoes off, along with his fleece and trousers. He folded them neatly, placing a heavy stone on top to prevent them blowing away, but in a location where they could be seen easily.

He walked over the ten yards of shingle that sloped rapidly to the waves. The first breaker came over his feet to his ankles; the second wave, halfway up his shins; the third was over his knees. He launched himself forward.

God, it's cold.

He began to swim the breaststroke and noticed the air inside his shirt helped his buoyancy. He'd swum, perhaps, less than three yards when a large wave broke over his face. It temporarily blinded him as he swallowed some seawater. He spat most of it out and continued heading away from the shore. The rip of the tide was taking him away from the land and pushing him northerly towards the area where the current from the east of the island collided with that from the west. He could see the waves in front of him rising, maybe three or four feet above him. He began to notice his movement – up and down. He knew he was no longer in control. He was being bobbed around like a cork.

There's no going back now.

You've done it this time.

Only a few more minutes and it will be all over. God, what a mess I've made of my life.

Faith, hope and love, but the greatest of these is love. Is that what St Paul said? I never mastered any of them.

Faith – I converted to Catholicism for Mia, but only took communion once.

What a fraud I was.

Hope – I was a lifelong pessimist who suffered from the black dog. If you're a pessimist, you're never disappointed.

The thought made him smile – for the last time.

Love – I'm not sure if I ever knew the meaning of the word.

Mia and I were deeply in love, always happy in each other's presence; yet I let her down badly.

How could she possibly have lived with Phil for all that time and been in love with me?

But then, I was the same.

I lived with Joyce, but unknowingly had remained in love with Mia.

Love – the greatest mystery of life; more mysterious than black matter. At least that can be explained by mathematics.

It serves us both right for not getting together after our breakup forty years ago and sorting our problems out.

We could have lived in Blackpool and learned to live on my salary.

But Mia wouldn't have been satisfied; she'd have wanted more.

'You're being unfair on me,' a voice shouted from somewhere behind him. He looked up, but he only saw a wave, six feet high, about to crash over him. He knew it would swallow him up.

He began struggling to keep afloat. Something had made him change his mind, but his frozen arms were tired and he could feel his legs giving away.

This is it.

He thought he heard Mia shouting to him to come back. His brain recognised her voice. Yes, it was Mia. He was sure it was. He tried to shout to her, but nothing would come out. He turned to see if the only girl who had mattered was there. He could only see a roller a few feet away. Instinctively he knew this would take him to the bottom.

As he went under, he grabbed at something. He didn't know what it was. He could see the bubbles exhaling from his lungs. There was no feeling; his eyes shut involuntarily. There was only an inky-black silence. His last recollections were his ears popping and having a crucifying pain in his head.

I'm sorry I hurt you Mia, please forgive me.

Everything would have been so much better if Terry hadn't asked me to play golf.

May 2004

Mia knew she shouldn't have been so sharp with Mike.

She appreciated his problems with leaving Joyce after thirty-odd years. She understood him having to take care with his finances until everything was resolved. Now her worry was that their worlds, which had twice collided so spectacularly, could explode again. On the other hand, she felt she had to take a stance. His boorish behaviour with her friends was unacceptable. It wasn't in her nature to take things lying down. She had always stuck up for herself – with fire in her eyes, if necessary.

Determinedly, she pushed her trolley around the supermarket, her mind spinning. She wasn't thinking about what she was buying. In a dither, she conjectured if she should rush over to his apartment to see if he was all right. She knew they would make-up. The thought made her smile.

But no! He had to learn a lesson. If he wanted to live with her permanently then he had to pull himself together and put his house in order. She wasn't going to nursemaid him any longer.

Her mind was drifting, flitting from wanting to keep control on the one hand to analysing her own faults on the other.

Why did I have to tell my mother that Mike raped me?

I should have told her and the priest that I had wanted him to make love to me; after all that was the truth.

Mike was my first man.

Phil had been the second – my only two lovers.

It had been good with Phil; I was lucky finding him.

Remember, he left me a wealthy widow.

But Mike envelops me when we sleep together.
We've collided again and I've merged with him once more.

Her train of thought began to upset her. Where was her loyalty to Phil? It was clashing with her feelings for Mike. The contrast was pulling her apart. She was experiencing the symptoms of a split personality – a new, uncomfortable feeling.

As she continued to wander aimlessly around the supermarket, she realised how ironic it was that she had too much money. Mike couldn't acclimatise to the fact that she could afford to keep him in the style to which she had grown accustomed. She had furtively paid for their holidays to Australia and Portugal, but it was his reluctance to accept that he was going to have to change his attitude that was annoying her. A long time ago, she had been made to feel a pauper by his parents, especially his mother. Now the roles were reversed. She had the upper hand. When they had argued, she had wanted to make her point, but realised that she may have overdone her reproof.

As she turned a corner in the one of the aisles, she stumbled on the slippery floor, and fell awkwardly. She had been too preoccupied to notice the yellow warning cones. The sudden fall knocked the air from her lungs and she began gasping as she picked herself up. A shelf-stacker nearby turned and asked, 'Are you all right?'

She looked up at him. It was Mike – young, in his early twenties; a thick head of light brown, Brylcreemed hair; of medium build with a sympathetic smile. She was back in The Palace Ballroom.

'Mike?' she queried.

'No, madam, my name is Alan.'

He sounded like Mike.

She blinked and refocused.

'Can I help you, madam?'

She stared harder. He had changed. It wasn't Mike. An unknown youngster stood in front of her.

'You've had a nasty fall, madam. Please come with me to our first-aid station and sit down. Your recovery… it may take some time.'

It may take some time…

Mike's last words were, 'It may take some time.'

It's a sign from God.

Something terrible has happened and I'm to blame.

'I'm sorry, but I must go at once,' she replied. She rushed past the startled worker, leaving her trolley, half-empty, behind.

She ran to her car. She knew what she had to do; there was no time to waste. The 911 burst into life and she screeched out of the car park, burning rubber. Some startled pensioners, who had been nattering near the exit, were left cursing something about bloody youngsters. Little did they know the driver was as old as them.

Her heart was in her mouth. She had never driven so quickly, nor so near to her limit. Speeding down Ramsey quay was not her usual style, but less than two minutes after leaving the supermarket she pulled up in the market place. She ran across the road into the apartment block. The concierge, Billy, welcomed her.

'Hello, Mrs Cookson, what's the hurry?'

'Have you seen Mike?' she asked.

'He came in less than an hour ago. Then he left about thirty minutes later saying he was going to the Point of Ayre. I saw him walking across to the Catholic church. About five minutes ago I saw him drive away. His car isn't in the car park, so he hasn't come back.'

'Did he seem his usual self?'

'Now you mention it, no. Normally he has always got something to say. We usually have a chat about nothing in particular, but today he seemed pre-occupied, as if he had something on his mind.'

'Thanks, Billy.'

Without further ado, she ran out of the reception area, quickly checking that Mike's car wasn't in the residents' car park and ran back to her 911. Slamming the Porsche into first gear, she turned on the spot and retraced her route along the quay towards Bowring Road. She accelerated hard over the bridge that crosses the Sulby River. A minute later, at the Y-junction, she took the right turn.

Hell, I'll never forgive myself for this.

God, please don't let me be too late.

I know why the idiot has gone to the Point of Ayre.

Hitting 90 mph in places, she turned right at Bride village, down the much narrower cul-de-sac that led to the lighthouse. Two hundred yards from the former keepers' houses, she could see Mike's car. She screeched to a halt next to it, got out and began running towards the sea.

She saw a pile of clothes, recognising Mike's fleece. She searched the area in front of her. She yelled at the top of her voice, 'Mike, come back. I love you. I always did. I didn't mean what I said. Matt is your son, not Phil's. Please come back.'

There was no sound, only the wind and the waves crashing on

the stones at her feet. Instinctively, she made to kick off her shoes and launched herself into the breakers as she saw his head bobbing up and down no more than seven yards away. She lashed out with her crawl stroke, but her skirt felt heavy and she realised that she was struggling.

'Matt is your son,' she yelled again at the top of her voice.

She was out of her depth, but Mike was only ten feet in front of her. A roller carried her upwards. He was in a hollow beneath her. As she plummeted downwards, he tried to grab her waist. The slope was against him. She was freezing cold. The motion of the swell carried her towards him. He lashed out to grab her and she felt his arms locking around her waist.

'I'm sorry,' he groaned and shut his eyes.

He was sinking fast and taking her under. His arms locked around her waist reminded her of their first meeting at The Palace Ballroom – a quickstep with The Squadronaires. She closed her eyes. She was with Mike and nothing would prise them apart again.

Her last thoughts were, *Mike, you were my love; Phil was my experience.*

Chapter 37

May 2004

The doorbell rang.

She thought, *Who the hell is that?*

'Matt, will you go and see who it is?'

'I'm busy,' came the reply from the study.

Begrudgingly, she dried her hands on the kitchen towel and went to the front door.

A middle-aged man stood in front of her. His face looked familiar, although she was certain she hadn't seen him before.

'Yes?' she asked, in a voice that indicated she had been disturbed. She had been busy in the kitchen preparing the evening meal.

'Is my father in?' he asked.

'I'm sorry?' she queried, not understanding his question.

'My father, he lives here – Mike Moore.'

The light dawned instantly.

My God; this must be Matthew, Mike's son.

'I think you'd better come in.' She stood to one side, but he remained rooted to the ground.

'I asked if he's in.' His stance, body language and tone of voice radiated hostility.

'He's not here any longer. If you'll come in, my husband and I can explain.'

His face immediately registered puzzlement and, although seemingly unwilling, he entered the hall.

She smiled and said, 'My name is Lisa Cookson, by the way.'

She held out her hand and the man reluctantly shook hands, mumbling, 'Matthew Moore.'

'I know who you are,' she asked. 'But how did you find this address?'

He replied somewhat hesitatingly, probably thinking, *How does she know who I am?*

'I work for the *FSA*.'

He paused to see whether Lisa understood.

She didn't and enquired, 'The *FSA*?'

'The Financial Services Authority. I am on the island, working for the British government, inspecting offshore accounts that we believe are being used illegally by English residents. I suspected my father might have kept his account with Lloyds Bank in Douglas when he left my mother. He'd opened it when he went to university in 1959. For the past six months, since my parents broke up, the only address my mother and I had for him was a dubious PO Box in Dublin. My father never returned our letters. By chance, when inspecting the list of Lloyds' customers yesterday, I discovered that the bank has recently been forwarding his statements to this address. I came today to confront the bastard and find out why he dumped my mother.'

'As I said, your father is no longer here. I'm afraid he committed suicide ten days ago.'

His face went white. He began to shake.

'Please come into the lounge and let me make you a cup of tea. You can have a Scotch, if you prefer.'

He nodded appreciatively and Lisa led him into the room at the front of her mother-in-law's house just as her husband Matt appeared from the study.

'You wanted me?' he asked his wife.

For a fraction Lisa was flummoxed as the two Matthews eyed each other for the first time. Their similarity was remarkable. *God, you can tell they're brothers*, she thought, *although my Matt must be five years older.*

Quickly regaining her composure, she looked at her husband and said, 'Matt, meet your half-brother, Matthew Moore.'

She turned to the man whom she knew to be the younger and said, 'Matthew, this is my husband, Matt Cookson. This will come as a terrible shock, but you and my husband have, or rather had, the same father.'

The two half-brothers stood staring blankly at each other for some time. The elder brother was eyeing up his sibling suspiciously, summing up his closest relative, while the younger Matthew stood open-mouthed with the sudden shock as he stared at his elder brother, whom he never knew existed.

Matt Cookson made the first move. 'Until a few days ago, I never knew of your existence either. Lisa and I live in Australia. We came over to the island last week to tie up my mother's estate. You see, my mother, Mia, disappeared the same day as your father... *our father,* he corrected himself. 'Whereas our father left a suicide note, my mother simply vanished. Their bodies have not been found.'

Matthew Moore sat down. 'I'll have that whisky, if I may,' he said to Lisa.

'Of course.' She went to the drinks cabinet in the corner of the lounge.

The younger man looked at his elder brother.

'What's been going on?' he asked. 'My mother, sister and I have not heard from Dad since he left home about six months ago. Mum initially refused to get a divorce. She hoped Dad would come back. Letters sent to a Dublin post office box, even by Mum's solicitor, were never answered. After three months I persuaded her to sue the old man for all he's got, but we've not made any progress until yesterday when I found this address being used by his bank.'

'I'm afraid this is as much of a shock for us as it is for you. Last week a policeman came to our house in Sydney. The Australian police had been contacted by the Isle of Man authorities to ask whether we knew where my mother was. Apparently, her car had been found abandoned at the Point of Ayre next to Mike's. Mike had left a note to the police in Ramsey that he was planning to commit suicide by swimming into the sea. The currents up there are vicious and his body would have been swept away in minutes. However, the Manx police couldn't explain my mother's disappearance. Lisa and I flew over on the first plane we could.'

'So what is the police's theory of what has happened?'

'They think my Mum may have dived into the sea to save Mike. She was a strong swimmer, despite her petite build. The family solicitor has told us to proceed on the assumption that both died tragically and so we are going through the house, organising her papers, that sort of thing.'

'How are you so sure we have the same father?'

'My mother's solicitor gave me a sealed envelope that he had been given for safe-keeping marked: *To be opened on the death of Mia Yvonne Cookson (née Mylrea).* It is a letter of explanation of her early life and I think she would have wanted you to read it, even though the letter is addressed to me. It appears to have been written several months ago.'

Lisa handed her half-brother-in-law a large glass of Glenmorangie along with the letter. 'I think you may need another when you've read the letter,' she said with a smile.

The letter had been typed and appeared to be over half a dozen pages in length. 'While you're reading it, we will leave you on your own. Is that OK?' asked Lisa.

'If you like, you can stay and have dinner with us this evening,' added Matt.

Matthew looked up and thanked them. 'That would be very nice. Thank you.'

He began the letter.

My dearest Matt,

I met Mike Moore at The Palace Ballroom in April 1963. At the time I was twenty-six and working as an air hostess with Britair, flying out of Ronaldsway with the Manx crew, while Mike was training to be a teacher.

We fell in love instantly and got engaged on 26ʰ June 1963. We were blissfully happy for a year. Then we fell out over arrangements for our wedding as we were not saving enough towards its costs. I had insisted all along on a Catholic wedding at St Mary's in Douglas. Mike knew this would create tensions in his family, who were strong Methodists, but he accepted the inevitable. He began his teaching job in Blackpool in September 1963 and led a parsimonious lifestyle that winter, trying to save as much as possible. He took lessons to convert to Catholicism, although I suspected he was half-hearted about it. He was baptised into the true faith at St Theresa's, Cleveleys in February '64.

The night we had our altercation, we fell out big-time. He coolly took his signet ring off his finger (I had given it to him when we became engaged) and tossed it at me. He pushed me out of the car in front of my mother's house in Stanley Square. I didn't see him again for thirty-nine years until June 2003, exactly forty years after we became engaged. That was the day you and I were having coffee in Waterstones.

That's not quite true. I had seen Mike once, but he didn't see me. I went to his father's funeral in Rosemount Methodist Church, Douglas. I sat near the back so as not to be conspicuous. I remembered his father with some affection. He was very kind to me when Mike was teaching in Blackpool. I would go to Mike's parents' house after work on Friday and have tea with them, despite relations between his mother and me being strained. Mike would ring from Blackpool so we could have a natter as your Grandmother Mylrea didn't have a phone. The only other way of communicating in those days was by writing; we wrote to each other on alternate days. I kept his letters for several years afterwards, secretly taking them with me to Australia. I destroyed them when I married Phil.

I finished my job as a stewardess with Britair at the end of September '63 and went back to work at Corlett and Kermode in Athol Street. A few days before finishing flying, however, our aircraft went u/s in Blackpool. That evening I stayed with Mike at his digs. We could have slept together, but we didn't. However, by then our love-making was becoming ever more daring and risqué. It was only a matter of time before we would be intimate for the first time.

Over the Easter of '64, the inevitable happened.

By early June, I suspected I was pregnant, but didn't tell Mike. I had intended to tell him the night we fell out, but I was so upset by his attitude over the wedding that I thought, 'Bugger you'. I kept the news to myself – at the time I was only a few weeks overdue. I cried all night in bed and never went to sleep, thinking he would come around to our house the next morning and apologise. A week went by and it dawned on me that we were finished. By then I was almost two months pregnant by a man who no longer loved me. I was deeply upset about the way Mike had treated me. I panicked and made a plan.

When the family doctor confirmed my pregnancy, I had to tell your Grandmother. She went ballistic. As I write this now, I believe Mike still loved me. Had I been sensible, swallowed my pride and told him, he would have married me. I am sure we would have lived happily ever after. We would have been hard-up, but we would have made it work. However, I wanted revenge. I decided to lie and say that Mike had raped me. Mum insisted we went to see our priest and he demanded that I should leave the island to have the baby and get it adopted.

Mum told Mrs Kermode, the wife of the Head of Chambers, that I was going to see my sister, Liz, who Mum claimed, was seriously ill in Australia. Mrs Kermode gave her the money for the tickets, providing I promised to return to work for her husband when I came back.

I lived with your Aunty Liz and when you were born in December 1964. I decided to keep you rather than have you adopted. I worked in Liz's restaurant. Times were hard, but we survived. You were baptised Matthew Mark Mylrea. Mike and I had often discussed having a family when we were engaged and we had agreed our first born boy would be Matthew. I guess I was still in love with Mike.

When you were aged two, I met Phil Cookson. He was in Australia doing some work for a London company. We met at St Michael's Church. He was wonderful and kind. Despite knowing about your illegitimacy, he asked me to marry him a few months after we met. We were wed a month later. We agreed never to tell you. Phil wanted to bring you up as his own son. You were formally adopted and legally given the surname of Cookson. He'd had to swear an affidavit that he was your biological father and your birth certificate was re-written.

When Phil's work was finished, we came back to England and moved into his house in Sunningdale.

His architectural business flourished. My Mum had forgiven me and she would join us for our holidays. Phil and I had a good life together. When Phil reached sixty, we came to retire in Maughold.

Then, almost ten years ago, as you remember, your dad had a heart attack. By then you were nearly thirty. I should have told you then who your real father was, but I was so upset by Phil's sudden death that I couldn't bring myself to do it.

You had met and married Lisa and were living in Sydney. After staying with you for three months, I lived the life of an ageing widow when I returned to the island. Then, by accident, Mike turned up that day in Waterstones. Thereafter, we saw each other secretly as often as we could and we realised that there had been a flame of love inside us that had never gone out. After five months Mike could not live his double life any longer and he left his wife to come and live in Ramsey.

When Mike and I came out to see you over the New Year, I had intended to explain that our intention was to marry as soon as his divorce was finalised. However, I detected that you were reluctant to see Mike as a future step-father and so I postponed telling you.

I know Mike and I can be idyllically happy, but he is prevaricating about getting divorced. As I write there is no progress. He has gone into a shell and refuses to answer correspondence. He has told me about his wife Joyce and their two children, Christina and Matthew. Yes, you have a half-brother with the same Christian name, and a half-sister! Maybe someday you will meet them. I cannot foretell what the future may bring. I simply want you to know that I love Mike deeply, but where it will all end, I don't know.

In anticipation that I will not live for ever, I have written this explanation for you to understand the background to my relationship with Mike. I can confirm that Mike was your biological father, but I have never revealed it to anyone – including Mike himself. All the people who knew the truth are dead: your grandmother, Aunty Liz and the priest at St Mary's. Neither your Aunt Jenny nor your Uncle David knew I was pregnant when I went to Australia, although they knew about the so-called rape.

I love you, Matt, and regret that this letter will come as a shock. Please don't think too badly of me. I have left everything to you in my will. Mike fully understands this.

Your loving mother,
Mia.

As he was approaching the end of the letter, Matthew had heard the doorbell ring and a subsequent muffled conversation in the hall. He had finished reading Mia's letter when Lisa entered the lounge with a stranger. Matthew stood up to be introduced.

'Matthew, this is Mia's elder sister, Jenny,' said Lisa.

They shook hands and Jenny explained that her late husband, George, who had died the previous year, had left considerable amounts of old correspondence in their attic. She had been slowly 'sorting things out' prior to throwing much of it away. The previous evening, she had come across an old letter addressed to Mia. The envelope was a sepia colour and according to Jenny could have been written forty years ago.

'I thought Matt should read it,' she added, looking at Lisa.

'I'll get him,' replied Lisa. 'He's in the garage.'

Matthew and Jenny stood looking at each other, unsure what to say.

Matt appeared, kissed his aunt, listened to the explanation about the letter's provenance and opened the envelope.

'Shall I read it aloud?' he asked.

All nodded.

'It's dated Friday, 19th June 1964,' he began, 'and reads as follows:

My dearest darling Mia,

By the time you get this note, you will probably have forgotten me and I wouldn't blame you if you have. However, I am hoping that someday George will be able to give you this letter and it will trigger some fond memories of our year together. They were the happiest days of my life.

I loved you very, very much and really did want to marry you. I want you to know that I would have done anything for you. I treasured you as my best friend; indeed you were my first true friend.

I wanted to come round to your house the day after our quarrel and apologise, but I was frightened in case you told me that you were finished with me. It's a poor excuse, I know, but it's true. He who hesitates is lost, and my procrastination lost you.

I have received your letter from Manchester with our engagement ring. I will put the ring somewhere safe – it will be stuck under the drawer of the dresser in my bedroom. I expect it will remain there until I die.

I intend going abroad and will not return for a long time. We will not meet again, at least not in this life. It was obviously not meant for us to spend our lives together. However, someday I hope we will meet in another world and I will be there to say how sorry I am for hurting you so much.

Please, please forgive me. You will always be the only girl in my life. You sweetened my life with your love. I will never be the same again. God bless you, Mia.

Your loving one and only,

Mike

The four stood in silence for some time. Matthew and Lisa wiped the tears from their eyes; Matt's face was expressionless.

It was left for Jenny to remark, 'Their whole affair was an enigma. That year when Mike was with Mia, the two of them were so happy they radiated light. In their presence, it was dazzling; you could feel their love. I could never understand how he was supposed to have raped Mia; he adored her. I understand now it was Mia's way of copping out of admitting she was pregnant. It's a terrible indictment of Catholicism that she was afraid to be truthful with our mum and the priest. George must have put the letter somewhere safe and forgotten about it. It was four years before Mia came back to the island from Australia. I can understand how George could have forgotten it.'

Chapter 38

December 2004

'Court rise,' called the clerk.

All present stood and the West Cumbria Courtroom in Whitehaven went silent as the coroner entered to take his place on the bench.

The coroner began, 'We are here today to determine the cause of death of the two bodies recently washed ashore at St Bees. Who is the first witness?'

'The gentleman who found the bodies while walking his dog, sir. His name is Mr Norman Stubbs,' replied the court clerk.

The retired schoolmaster gave his evidence, describing how, after his dog had spotted the bodies and barked for his attention, he had dialled 999 for the police and ambulance.

Next to give evidence were the local police.

Sergeant Gill described how he secured the area when arriving at the beach. 'It was twenty minutes after we received the 999 call in the Whitehaven Police Station,' he said.

Detective Inspector Christian, based in Workington, explained that he had arrived a further twenty minutes later with two scenes of crime officers. He clarified the procedures undertaken by the SOCO team. As officer in charge he confirmed that, after consultation with the SOCOs, he took the decision to allow the paramedics to remove the bodies, having satisfied himself that foul play was not an issue.

The ambulance crew were the next to give evidence, and told how the two bodies were in a bloated state. 'Whereas the man's face was badly bruised and cut, the woman's features were relatively unscathed,' said the senior crew member. 'Strangely, however, the man and woman, who were mostly clothed, were locked together,' he added.

'Are you sure?' asked the coroner.

'Certain, sir,' replied the paramedic. 'The man's arms were wrapped around the female's slim waist. We had a devil of a job to undo his grip to separate the bodies and put them in the ambulance. I remember thinking at the time it was like splitting two pieces of a jigsaw puzzle. We had to twist and pull at the same time. It's as if they'd been dancing together in the sea. Her face was buried in his chest with his jaw on top of her head.'

'I shall have some questions for the pathologist on this matter later,' commented the coroner.

Identification of the bodies was given.

'I can confirm the male body was that of my late father, Mike Moore,' Matthew Moore began. 'My father left my mother just over a year ago and moved to the Isle of Man. There he met his former fiancée, Mrs Mia Cookson, who was a widow. They resumed their relationship and had several holidays together. My father left a suicide note for the Manx Police. It is believed he swam into the sea at the Point of Ayre seven months ago.'

'Do you know what reason he may have had for swimming into the sea?' asked the coroner. 'It is an unusual way of committing suicide.'

'No, sir, I do not. I'd had no contact with my father after he deserted my mother.'

Matt Cookson then gave evidence of identification of his mother. 'My mother, Mia Cookson, left a personal letter to me that was only to be opened when she had died. The letter contains an explanation of her relationship with Mr Moore. I would appreciate if its contents could remain confidential to the court.'

'If I can, I will respect your wishes,' replied the coroner. The clerk passed the letter to his superior, who took several minutes reading it.

The coroner returned the letter to Matt and thanked him. 'I don't think there is any need for its contents to be made public,' he added. 'Is there anything else you wish to add before you stand down?'

'I live in Sydney, Australia. Having been told by the local police that my mother had vanished and was assumed to have drowned, I flew to the island to wrap up her estate. I was aware she had resumed a relationship with her former fiancée. I had met Mr Moore twice. The first time was about eighteen months ago when I was visiting my mother on vacation. She explained to me that Mr Moore had been her fiancé forty years previously. I never thought any more about it. Then last New Year she and Mr Moore came to Sydney for a holiday.

I confess I wasn't too keen on their cohabiting, but it was clear to me and my wife that they were exceptionally happy in each other's company.'

The next to give evidence was Police Inspector Paul White, in charge of the Ramsey Division of the Isle of Man Constabulary.

'My divisional sergeant received a phone call on Wednesday, 12th May 2004, at 1135 hours from a public phone box in the village of Bride. The caller, Mr Thomas Williams, described how two cars were parked on the east side of the road less than a quarter of a mile from the Point of Ayre lighthouse. Both cars had their keys left in the ignition. Intrigued, the caller had walked towards the sea and found some discarded clothes and shoes. He told us that a fleece had been folded neatly and had a large stone on top of it. There was also a woman's shoe that appeared as if it could have been discarded in a hurry.

'We asked the caller to wait by the cars until we arrived. My sergeant and I arrived at the scene at 1200 hours. In the car, which we now know belonged to Mr Moore, there was a letter addressed to *Officer i/c Ramsey Police*. Shall I read the letter?'

'Yes, please do,' answered the coroner.

'It reads:

In the event of my car being found abandoned at the Point of Ayre and your inquiries find that I have disappeared, please inform the manager of Lloyds Bank, Ramsey to open a letter that I have left in a deposit box at his branch.

'The letter is signed by Mr Moore.'

'And what did the further letter contain?'

'It was his will, sir.'

'Did you find anything else at the scene?'

'The abandoned clothes were saturated with rain-water; not surprising as it had rained heavily the previous night. Their state was not due to the sea as they were at least five yards from the high water-mark. We made enquiries and took statements from several people who saw the pair on Tuesday, 11th May.'

'The previous day?'

'Yes. Mrs Cookson's neighbour, Mrs Joan Connell, who lived opposite and was in the garden, had seen her early that afternoon. She described how Mrs Cookson had waved to her and asked if she wanted anything as she was going to the supermarket in Ramsey. She had seen Mr Moore leave Mrs Cookson's property about forty minutes previously.

'Another relevant statement was given by the priest of the Church of Our Lady in Ramsey, Father Bernard Tyson. He saw Mr Moore in the church between 1415 and 1430 hours. During this time Mr Moore had knelt in prayer, lit some candles and left.

'A further statement is that of the concierge, Mr William Gale, of the apartment block where Mr Moore lived. He described seeing Mr Moore entering the block shortly before two o'clock, leaving twenty minutes later and going across the road to the Catholic church. He stayed there for about quarter of an hour before driving away. Mr Gale said that he thought Mr Moore was, and I quote, "in a distraught state". Five minutes after he drove away, Mrs Cookson arrived. She asked for Mr Moore and then left in what Mr Gale described as, "a bloody hurry".

'As a result of driving the respective distances ourselves, I believe Mr Moore entered the sea at approximately 1500 hours that Tuesday. Mrs Cookson arrived a few minutes later, saw her partner struggling in the water, and rushed to try and save him. They drowned together when her partner grabbed her waist.'

'Thank you, you may stand down.'

The pathologist from the West Cumberland Hospital, Dr Hillary Timms, then gave evidence. She explained that the sea temperature for the four months the bodies had been in the water had been 6°C plus or minus 1°C and that the bloating of the bodies was due to their immersion in water for longer than eight weeks. The process is called saponification, she explained, and is the transformation of the body's fat into a soap-like substance called adipocere. She pointed out that Mr Moore must have been alive when he put his arms around Mrs Cookson's waist. Therefore, the obvious conclusion was that they drowned moments later. However, rigor mortis takes up to two hours to set in and, therefore, could not account for their bodies being locked together. She added the rigor would eventually have dissipated and the bodies would have become flaccid. However, because of the temperature of the water this was probably halted.

'So how do you explain the locked bodies?' asked the coroner.

'The post-mortem revealed a surprise,' she replied. 'Mr Moore died of a massive and sudden stroke that was brought about by the cold. Heat is taken from a body twenty-five times quicker by water than by air at the same temperature. Mr Moore had been in the sea perhaps two minutes longer than Mrs Cookson. In that time his blood pressure would have shot through the roof.'

'So what you're saying,' queried the coroner, 'is that he died as he grabbed Mrs Cookson's waist while simultaneously having a massive stroke?'

'Yes.'

'Surely, she would have been able to get free from his grip and save herself?'

'The grip of his two hands locked around her waist coupled with his dead weight would have pulled her down.'

'Why are his facial features damaged?'

'A drowned body always lies on its front with the head facing down. As the two bodies were washed ashore, Mr Moore's face would be underneath and, therefore, would be scraped on the seabed. The injuries are consistent with my hypothesis, and had been made after the process of saponification had occurred.'

'Before giving my verdict, I would like to see Mr Moore and Mr Cookson in my office privately. I will resume the inquest in half an hour.' The coroner stood.

'Court rise,' shouted the clerk.

'I am reluctant to give a verdict of suicide in the case of Mr Moore,' began the coroner. 'However, I thought I should get both of you together to hear my theory of what occurred. Is that OK?'

The two half-brothers nodded.

'There is no doubt that Mr Moore intended to take his own life when he entered the sea. However, something changed his mind when Mrs Cookson swam to rescue him. Have either of you any idea what that could be? I suspect I know the answer having read Mrs Cookson's letter, but I would rather one of you tell me.'

The two men looked at each other. Matthew Moore looked at his elder half-brother to explain.

'When he entered the water, my father was unaware that he had two sons. I believe my mother, in desperation to get him to come back, may have shouted that I was his son. For the entire time they had been together, she had allowed him to believe that my father was Phil Cookson. Until this tragedy occurred and I returned to the Isle of Man to sort out my mother's will, I didn't know either. For my entire life, I had always believed Phil was my biological father.'

The coroner nodded. 'For a man struggling in the sea with his blood pressure many times higher than normal, this sudden news could have been the trigger for his stroke. At that critical point in time Mr Moore must have desperately wanted to survive. Instantly, he grabbed Mrs Cookson for help, but died. I am going to return a verdict of death by misadventure on both Mr Moore and Mrs Cookson. I can only commiserate with you both on your losses.'

'Thank you, sir. Your decision will make it easier for us to arrange a Catholic burial service for our father,' said the elder brother.

Three weeks after the inquest in Whitehaven, a Requiem Mass was held in the Roman Catholic church in Ramsey. Afterwards Mia and Mike were transferred to a double coffin and placed in a small boat in the nearby harbour. There, the two Matthews placed the specially designed, lead-weighted coffin on a ramp. The coffin was then taken to a point a mile from the Point of Ayre Lighthouse and allowed to slide slowly into the Irish Sea. An inscription on a metal plate attached to the coffin read:

Mia and Mike were separated in life, but united in death.

Chapter 39

January 2005

The two brothers were waiting at Ronaldsway Airport for their respective flights, having buried Mia and Mike the previous day. Matt Cookson was on his way to Manchester Airport from where he planned to catch a QANTAS flight to Sydney via Dubai. Matthew Moore was returning to London City Airport and his boring job in the financial sector.

'What was our father like?' asked Matt Cookson.

'In what way? You met him twice.'

'Yes, but I didn't know he was my father. On the first occasion in Waterstones, I felt antagonistic because he and my mother showed such enthusiasm for each other. They chatted for half an hour, but couldn't take their eyes off each other. When we drove back from Douglas, I could tell she was excited that she was going out with him the following evening. Meeting Mike had taken twenty years off her. I was embarrassed and, frankly annoyed.'

'I can understand that. When they went out to Sydney for the New Year, what were they like?'

'It was even worse. By then they were co-habiting. I wanted to have words with Mum. But how could I? It was obvious they were in love – like a pair of teenagers. It was uncomfortable because people were looking at them. They didn't seem to notice, or if they did, they didn't care. I saw Mike as having usurped my father's memory. I couldn't understand what Mum was thinking by getting involved with a retired teacher. Little did I know, of course, that he was my real father. So, what was he really like? He must have taught you at school.'

'He was a good schoolmaster. He was popular because he was

excellent at his job. He made maths interesting and easy. In all those years teaching he never had anyone fail at "A" Level. So being his son at school was trouble-free. No one ever ribbed me. Perhaps if he had been useless like some of the other members of staff, it would have been different. In class he treated me like the others. I got my "A" Level, but he never coached me or anything like that. He was quite happy for me to study economics at LSE. As a father he was OK too. When we were younger, my sister and I used to sit at the top of the stairs and listen to him and Mum arguing – they would leave their quarrelling until after we had gone to bed. We both decided we would go and live with Dad when they split up. But they never did; at least not until he rediscovered Mia and by then, of course, we had both left home. We watched him slowly change over the years as he got older. Mum ground him down. He wasn't spineless, but I guess his personality was like a piece of elastic.'

'Elastic?'

'She slowly stretched his patience further and further. He would give way to her; their arguing gradually lessened as they grew older. But finally the elastic must have snapped. There were rumours at school that he was fond of the lab technician and was having a bit of nooky on the side. I don't know. I guess I didn't want to know. When he took retirement that would have stopped. At that point he probably began thinking the easy way out might be to commit suicide.'

'It takes a lot of courage to take your own life.'

'Looking back now, I can see the signs that he was something of a depressive. He would go into a shell, sometimes for days.

'I would say, "What's up, Dad?"

'He would smile and reply, "It's only me getting old, son."

'He would use any excuse to get out of the house and be away from Mum. You didn't know Joyce. It's rather apt, but I understood he never got on too well with his own mother either. Sis and I watched him and Joyce drift apart. They became two people living in the same house with no common interests and hardly ever speaking to each other. Frankly, I was glad when I went to university. It looks to me that the only woman he was compatible with was Mia. What was she like?'

'Mum was beautiful; she never aged. My recollection of her, when I was at junior school in Sunningdale, was how young she looked compared to the other mothers. When I was at Wellington College I could see my friends in the sixth form eyeing her up. They fancied my Mum! When Dad died I was over thirty and Mum came back to

Australia with me for about four months. My pals there thought I'd brought back a dolly bird. Imagine… playing golf with your mother in a mixed four-ball competition and everyone thinking she was my bit-on-the-side.'

'How did she get on with Phil?'

'Fine, as far as I could see. Dad was a successful businessman as well as a gifted architect. He was shrewd when it came to investing. He bought properties all over the place, putting them in either my name or Mum's. As a couple they had a lot of friends and were forever going to dinner parties – that sort of thing. If you're asking me whether they loved each other, I think they did. Now I've read that letter and seen what happened, however, there are some doubts in my mind about her death.'

'What are you trying to say?' asked the younger brother.

'Did it not puzzle you… why is it that my mother only took one shoe off when she went into the sea to save our father? And why did she not take her skirt off before diving in to rescue him?'

'Maybe one of the shoes was washed away. Maybe she didn't have time to remove her skirt.'

'The shoe that was found was above the high-tide mark. It would have only taken a few seconds to drop her skirt.'

The city accountant didn't reply. He had no answer.

'I think the coroner's explanation for their death at the inquest was wrong.'

'Go on,' replied Matthew.

'For some reason, that we'll never know, Mike was furious with Mia. Perhaps they'd had a row about Phil. I don't know. It could have been anything. Mike decided to show her who was boss and lured her to the Point of Ayre. When she arrived, he surprised her and grabbed her. She struggled and one of her shoes fell off. As they fought, he dragged her into the sea. By the time she'd told him I was his son, they were out of their depth and the strong current whipped them away from land.'

'What you're saying is Mike murdered Mia, but tried to make it look as if Mia was rescuing him from suicide.'

'Yes. I think it's possible,' said Matt thoughtfully.

'Mm… I'm not so sure. It seems a bit implausible to me.'

'In France it would have been seen as a crime of passion.'

'That would still be manslaughter,' said the younger man.

'Whatever you call it, my father killed my mother. Deliberately or accidentally – we'll never know.'

The two young men fell silent; their sombre mood reflecting the dismal rain streaking across the windows of the departure lounge. When Matthew Moore's flight was called for London, the two brothers shook hands. They promised to keep in touch, but they would never see each other again.

Epilogue

May 2004

A man can experience love many times, but he can only love once.

(Persian proverb)

He saw her speeding up the road toward the lighthouse and knew she would see his car. He knew she would screech to a halt beside his vehicle and run towards the sea. He positioned himself behind a small sand dune, having already placed his fleece and shoes in an obvious place where she couldn't fail to notice them. True to expectations, she ran to his pile of clothes and stopped. She looked at the sea.

'Hello, Mia.'

She swung around, her face registering surprise.

'Are you shocked at seeing me?' he asked.

'I thought you had committed suicide.'

'That's what I wanted you to think,' he replied.

He walked up to her. He roughly put his arms around her waist and lifted her off the ground. She looked into his eyes and stretched upwards, expecting him to kiss her.

Instead, he turned and ran towards the sea.

'You're coming with me, you bitch. I'll show you who was the better man, me or your bloody Phil. You're going to die with my arms locked around your waist.'

She started screaming and kicking, but to no avail. She felt one of her shoes falling off. She fought him, wriggling this way and that, but his grip remained locked tight. He was so much stronger than her. She bit him on his nose. He shook her and cursed, 'Your God can't help you now.'

They were soon in the water. Mike was a strong swimmer. As a young man he'd swam in the Douglas Bay Races. He had even thought of training for the English Channel. Swimming singlehandedly was no problem and they were soon out of their depth.

Mia was protesting, 'I only ever loved you, Mike. What I said about Phil wasn't true. Matt is your son. You did get me pregnant.'

But it was too late.

Now eight yards out from the shore and in the fierce current that rapidly races northward, the waves had become unpredictable. They rose to a height as great as five or more feet. Mia's struggling was causing her to choke as she swallowed large amounts of sea water. They were being carried, out of control, towards the maelstrom. The waves were crashing over them, but Mike's grip around Mia's slim waist remained locked like a bank vault. Gradually, her kicking lessened and her body began to go limp. She was freezing cold. She looked at him. He was already dead.

Her fight to release his grip failed. His arms remained locked around her waist. She couldn't undo them. His deadweight was dragging her under.

She remembered Mike once telling her, 'We are no longer who we are, but who we were.'

Her last thought was, *Mike, when we're together, the world is empty.*